To Survive the Earth

To Survive the Earth

William Stroock

Copyright © 2016 William Stroock

All rights reserved.

ISBN-13: 9781532876721
ISBN-10: 1532876726

INTRODUCTION

I had originally planned to title this book *To Liberate Mars and Other Stories of the Jai Invasion*, but the more I wrote, the more I saw the Battle for Mars as a stand-alone book. So here are six more stories about the Jai invasion of Earth, the 'other stories' as it were.

To Defend the Earth dealt mostly with, well, defending the Earth.

I have found myself fascinated lately by smaller stories; people enduring a massive battle fought in the sky, or trying to make it through the first winter in the invasion's aftermath. Forget what happens to fighter pilots and ship captains. Just what does one do in the middle of an alien invasion when you're a middle-aged suburbanite schlub?

A lot of what I wrote was inspired by my experience in Super Storm Sandy, when for four days my family and I hunkered down in our home without power- with a newborn mind you. Looking under the deck for things to burn to keep warm and sitting around at 9 PM wondering how to pass the time gave me a new appreciation for modern life.

A lot of the characters here have to deal with the same thing.

To *Liberate Mars* is coming (2017, we think). This too will be a series of short stories, each advancing the story of humanity's attack on a Jai occupied Mars. There will be others. I suspect this is a universe I will play around with for some time.

William Stroock

In the meantime, please enjoy To *Survive the Earth*.

The cover photo comes courtesy of 3000ad, 123RF.com.

Thanks always to my editorial team, Lee and Sharon Moyer, and of course Editor Extraordinaire Mrs. Stefanie Attia, who deserves a medal and comes with my recommendation.

William Stroock
Great Barrington, Massachusetts

PROLOGUE

CONNECTICUT

As he drove his navy issue electric car, Commander Tony Rodden pined for his old Porsche. It didn't matter, he knew. The car had been destroyed during the war, and even if it had survived the virtual destruction of California, he didn't have enough gas rations to drive it anyway. So instead he putted along at a steady 35 miles an hour down the rebuilt Interstate 95. He got off at an exit for one of the old fishing towns, took a back road to a row of old cottages, and pulled into the driveway of a beat up cottage. The paint was peeling, roof shingles were coming off, but it had heat, light and a view of Long Island Sound.

Rodden got out of his car, walked up to the small stoop, and knocked on the door. When his friend opened the door he reached into his pocket and took out a green government medical card. Commander Cosgrove reached into his pocket and took out his own government medical card; also green. Like Rodden's, it had been punched eight times and read: 'The bearer is entitled to one yearly thyroid exam.' On the back was information for the appropriate government offices to contact for reimbursement.

'Hey I guess the bet is still on!' said Commander Peter Cosgrove.

Rodden smiled, 'No cancer for another year. We won't be able to go to the Officer's Club and tell cancer sob stories.'

'Yeah, but at least I have these radiation burns on the side of my face,' Cosgrove turned his head to show a series of deep scars on the right side of his face. He rubbed them appreciatively. 'No one questions you when you have these kind of battle scars,' he boasted. 'Come in, come in.'

Cosgrove opened the door and let his friend inside his small cottage. The two men hugged.

'Good to see you pal,' Cosgrove said.

'You too,' replied Rodden.

'C'mon, it's a nice day, let's go out back.'

Cosgrove and Rodden walked through the small house and into the backyard. They sat in a couple of pre-war Adirondack chairs and gazed out at Long Island Sound.

'How are things over at Atomic Boat?' Cosgrove asked.

Instead of answering, Rodden reached into the pocket of his uniform blazer and took out a small bottle of Scotch.

Cosgrove's eyes lit up. 'Where'd you get that?'

'I was just across the pond, consulting with the Brits about their spaceship program,' Rodden said. 'We need glasses…and ice.'

Cosgrove turned back to the house, 'Melody!' he shouted. A female face poked out of the kitchen window. 'Glasses and ice, when you have a chance, please.'

A girl far too young for Cosgrove came out and put a pair of glasses on the small table between the two chairs.

'Thanks, sweetie,' said Cosgrove. He slapped her ass as she walked away.

'Damn,' Rodden said. 'How'd you manage to get a girl like that?'

'Easy,' said Cosgrove as he poured himself a scotch. 'I have a home, electricity and food.'

'Jesus,' Rodden said.

'I have a commodity. She has a commodity.'

'I didn't see a ring.'

'Nor will you,' replied Cosgrove.

Cosgrove took a sip of Scotch. 'They just haven't been able to get this stuff right since the war,' he said.

'Well, the Jai did annihilate half of Scotland,' replied Rodden.

Cosgrove reached into the pocket of his blazer, took out a cigar and held it out to his colleague.

'Please,' Rodden took out another cigar.

Cosgrove took out his Zippo, leaned forward and lit Rodden's cigar. He then did the same for his own. 'Where did you get these?'

'Got a friend in Reconstruction Command down in Cuba.'

'Ah,' said Rodden. 'I hear that's good duty.'

'Sure, if you don't mind Cuban insurgents.' Cosgrove sipped the Scotch again and winced slightly.

'C'mon, Pete, things are not that bad.'

'Things are not that good, either.' He drew on his cigar.

The two naval officers smoked their cigars and gazed out across Long Island Sound. A pair of navy cruisers drifted in the distance, and across the Sound were massive missile batteries and the great antenna arrays of the nuclear powered fission guns; all to protect the nearby Atomic Boat Works.

'Think there's any point to those ships out there?' Rodden asked.

'Not really.'

'Their time has passed,' said Rodden. 'I think Captain Masters proved that.'

'Yes he did.'

There was silence.

'So, you think Masters mutinied?' Cosgrove asked.

'Yeah, I read that book,' Rodden said.

Cosgrove pressed, 'Well, do you?'

Commander Rodden didn't hesitate. 'No way, Cosgrove, no way.'

'That's been the rumor.'

Rodden shook his head. 'Not Steve Masters.'

'He never did like being told no.'

Rodden glared.

'That's OK, Pete, I don't feel the alleged mutiny is the relevant question here.'

'Yeah?' Rodden chomped on his cigar. 'Then what is the relevant question?'

'Do you think Masters got lucky?'

'Never heard it put that way before.'

'What, you think he was good?'

'He accounted for a dozen Jai carrier-ships and destroyed their presence on the Moon, all without losing either one of his battleships.'

Cosgrove took a drag from his cigar. 'The Jai were stupid.'

'Stupid. How so?'

'Think about it. They flung their carrier ships at Masters in bits. It was like feeding a meat grinder. Four at a time. The first four I understand, but after that they should have held back.'

'And stuck by the Moon?'

'Yes, by their supporting missile and laser batteries. There they could have gathered their strength and fought with the support of their moon bases.'

'Hmmm,' said Rodden, 'ten carrier ships left after the first round.'

'Exactly.'

'You think Masters could have fought ten ships?'

'I don't know. We know he could fight four at a time.'

'They underestimated us.'

Cosgrove sipped his Scotch, 'Yes, again.'

'That's what our report on the war says.'

Cosgrove laughed. 'That's a secret. If the official history ever got out...'

Rodden smirked, 'Could you imagine what would happen if the flag-wavers ever saw the official history?'

'When the president saw, it gave him great pause.'

'Probably why he was always reluctant to launch the attack to begin with.' Said Rodden. 'I never got that. We always had to get the Jai off the Moon.'

'You sound like one of those flag-wavers.'

'You disagree?' asked Rodden.

'Let's just say I'm not as eager to pick a fight as some of the magazine editors.'

'They always were, weren't they?'

'Yep.'

'Hey,' offered Rodden, 'we won.'

'Barely. If Zetroc Nanreh had been a better commander...'

'We'd all be working for him now.'

'Or his cronies.'

'I'm not sure you're giving us enough credit.'

'He kicked our asses in the Aleutians,' Cosgrove pointed out.

'Yeah,' said Rodden. 'The Jai gathered their strength and bombarded our island bases one by one. Kiska, Attu, Adak, Kodiak…They knocked our air cover out of the sky and pounded the ground defenses.'

'How many carrier ships did they lose?'

'Two,' said Rodden.

'What about their fighters?'

'We turned the Aleutians into a Jai fighter graveyard,' Rodden said with pride.

'And then they landed ground troops.'

'The Marines made them pay, at least.'

There was silence for a few moments, until Cosgrove said, 'And they kicked our asses in the Battle of Japan.'

'The Chinese bailed out at the last minute.' Rodden shrugged, 'That's all.'

'The Chinese left the *Washington* Carrier Battlegroup wide open on the north flank.'

'And knocked the Japanese and South Koreans right out of the war.'

'Well, they did get one carrier ship at least.'

'After the battle was already lost,' said Cosgrove.

'We beat him on Antarctica,' Rodden offered.

'We got lucky.'

'You think so?' Rodden asked.

'Zetroc Nanreh fell for our gambit.'

'True, but do you think it was luck?'

'Look, we and the Russians sent wave after wave of jets, B-1s, F-35s, everything we could throw at the North Pole Ship, right?'

'Right.'

'Air, land, and sea launched cruise missiles.'

'Right.'

'We engaged them with every weapon at hand and forced Zetroc Nanreh to divert ships from Antarctica.'

'Yeah, they came over North America and hit our bases in New England and in Canada. I ought to know, I was on a Tico in Hudson Bay.'

'Exactly, and only when they stripped the Southern Hemisphere defenses were we able to hit the Antarctica Pole Ship. Even down there we took heavy losses.'

Rodden nodded in thought. 'True…'

'You suppose we could have punched through their Antarctic defenses if those carrier ships were down there?'

'I doubt it.'

The pair drank and smoked in silence. Then they talked of trivial things for a while. Eventually Cosgrove stubbed out his cigar and said, 'So what are the design geniuses working on up there?' as he nodded north, toward the big Atomic Boat Base at Groton.

'It's coming along.'

'What does that mean?'

'Sorry, security.'

'Aw come on, Tony. Give me something.'

Rodden cleared his throat. 'Let's just say we've come a long way since *United States Space Ships Wasp* and *Hornet*.'

Cosgrove smiled 'How so?'

'Hmmmm,' Rodden thought about how to avoid violating security. 'Better weapons.'

'More advanced?'

'Absolutely.'

'Like what?'

Rodden smirked. 'Sorry old pal, can't say.'

'How about a hint?'

Cosgrove glared.

'I can tell you about artificial gravity.'

'Artificial gravity?'

'Sure, you create a gravitational field and…'

Cosgrove waved his hands, 'Never mind.'

'*The Big Bang Theory* types think it will lead to all sorts of technological marvels.'

'So that 24.5% national sales tax I'm paying is going for something.'

'Yes.'

'Brits working on the same stuff?'

'And the Canadians, the Aussies and the Indians.'

'High tech, huh?'

'Yeah,' Rodden leaned back in his chair, 'But we still feel our program is behind the Russians and Chinese.'

'They're planning something.'

'Yeah.'

'I think they're going to beat us.'

'What do you mean?'

'Whatever they're planning, they'll be able to do it first.'

'Well, Peter let me ask you this. What is our target?'

'I honestly don't know.'

'Well, let's see. The Jai have that big base on Mars.'

'And a pair of smaller ones on Phoebus,' Rodden added.

'They have those space stations in the asteroid belt.'

'A lot of mining operations. I know some Intel guys who are convinced Zetroc Nanreh's headquarters is on Ceres.'

'Makes sense.'

'They have those two orbiting pole stations on Venus. And those bases on the moons of Jupiter.'

'Hmmmm,' said Rodden. He sipped his Scotch. 'Which would you hit first?'

'You know me, Tony. Go for the jugular. Hit Mars!' Cosgrove looked to the kitchen window, where Melody waved.

'That's her signal that she's starting dinner. Gonna stay?'

Rodden shifted in his chair, 'Gee…I dunno.'

'C'mon, stay for dinner.' Cosgrove patted his friend on the back. 'Melody has friends, you know.'

Rodden smiled.

CHAPTER 1

ARRIVAL

I took a selfie and posted it to my Twitter account. #KingoftheBurbs. Abby slapped my shoulder, and not playfully.

'Put that thing away, would you?'

I slipped my phone back into my pocket and turned to the TV. Abby made a face at me and went back to the kitchen where she and the other wives were drinking wine.

Next to me, Keith resumed the conversation. 'Where was I?' he asked.

Seeing there was no escape, I said, 'You were explaining how to light off your Roman candle gun.'

'Roman candle mini-gun,' Keith corrected. 'I thought I'd just use a Zippo, then Viv was watching one of those cooking shows, and there was this chef using a propane torch and voila! I had it.'

Keith had spent the last five minutes describing his latest home built toy, a dozen Roman candles duct-taped to an aluminum cylinder. He liked to tinker with stuff like that and then tell the rest of us about it. More than once he had run afoul of the town and its over officious busybody bureaucrats.

'C'mon,' I said, 'Let's go see what the news is saying.'

We walked over to the TV and stood next to Jim our host.

'Ooooooo....' I said as ironically as possible.

Jim swigged his beer and said, 'C'mon, man. This is history.'

'Whatever.'

Jim and Carroll had invited us over, and also Keith and Viv and their four kids. Why not? The kids would remember it the rest of their lives. Besides all these overworked IT and Pharma professionals looked for any excuse to throw a party. It was a Wednesday, but the president had declared the next two days national holidays, so everyone was staying home and staying up late. Not that it mattered much to us. Abby and I were a good 10 years younger than they were and we didn't have any kids. But this is the kind of life Abby wanted and she insisted on going. Me, I wanted to head into Boston and join one of the Arrival parties. However, this little suburbanite party was important to Abby so I agreed.

Jim's massive 60 inch TV was tuned into the Fox News broadcast of the alien's arrival. In the bottom left corner, a clock ran down to their expected arrival over the North and South Poles. They had the ships, on a split screen, the blonde anchor droning on with pointless speculation, and just to be annoying, the right split in two as well, with the northern-bound ship on the top screen and the southern bound ship on the bottom.

I swigged my beer and smirked. 'Just to be a prick, I'd reverse the shot.'

Jim was annoyed. He was a major nerd, I mean you could have slipped him onto the set of *The Big Bang Theory* and no one would have noticed. All he wanted was a good glimpse of those two alien ships.

He grumbled, 'C'mon,' he said. 'I mean, here is human history splitting in two and the news network was showing this blonde's head.'

He had a point. Who thought the world wanted to see this dumb blonde? She thought so, no doubt.

'Why don't you change it to CNN?' I asked.

'Na.'

'They may be boring but they're not dumb,' I offered. 'They won't have this chattering caterwaul.'

Chattering Caterwaul turned to her panel, a popular physicist and a celebrity rabbi. All day, Fox had been convening these panels at the top and bottom of every hour.

'What do you suppose the president is thinking right now?' Chattering Caterwaul asked.

Celebrity Rabbi said, 'I hope she is consulting her maker.'

Popular Physicist said, 'Silly.'

'Why?' asked Celebrity Rabbi, 'Don't you think a little guidance from God is in order?'

Popular Physicist smugly replied, 'Really, Rabbi?'

'Why not?'

'Don't you think beings as advanced as these visitors long ago cast aside these superstitions?'

Before the panel broke down Chattering Caterwaul interjected, 'That's a good question, gentlemen, in fact why don't we go to our Rome correspondent, 'Cindi?'

The TV screen flashed to another scene, this time to a brunette reporter in Vatican Square. Behind her were tens of thousands of people. Even through the TV you could see the air was festive. The gatherers flew dozens of banners, many with Bible quotes, a bunch just said 'Welcome Aliens' and things like that. Many formed prayer circles and the like. I could see one such circle, but people were not praying. In the center was a trio of musicians, and around them people were dancing.

'I'm here at the Vatican where the faithful are waiting for the alien's Arrival.'

'Cindi, what is the mood there?'

'I would say people are joyful and optimistic. The Vatican issued a statement yesterday declaring that the Pope believes beings as advanced as these must be near to God.'

In studio, Popular Physicist snorted while Celebrity Rabbi nodded approvingly.

'Rabbi,' began Chattering Caterwaul, 'You have to admit, we're religious and still stuck here on Earth. And look at the problems religion is causing right now.'

As Celebrity Rabbi responded, the TV showed footage of people rioting before the Wailing Wall in Jerusalem; a bubbling cauldron of flaying Keffaya clad Palestinians and black hat wearing Haredi Jews.

I yawned at the religious discussion. Nothing was happening, and I had become convinced that nothing was going to happen.

Chattering Caterwaul held her earpiece close and nodded. 'Ok, Ok, we are going now to Houston, where our special correspondent has an update from NASA's Alien Tracking Desk. Chase?'

The screen flashed once more.

'Hi, yes,' said a middle-aged man trying hard to look like he was in his early thirties by wearing a tight shirt with the top two buttons opened. 'The Tracking Desk is showing that the two alien ships have slowed nearly to a stop.'

Behind him was a projection map of the globe, which indicated the exact position of each alien ship. In each corner of the projection was a live feed from satellites positioned over the poles for that purpose. Dozens of NASA technicians and analysts sat at various computer monitors.

'Is that so, Chase?'

'Yes. In fact, the director here anticipates the Aliens will fire their engines one last time as they approach the poles.'

'I see.'

'I have here now with me the director of the Tracking Desk.' Chase pulled a man on camera. He wore a dark blue polo shirt emblazoned with the NASA logo. 'This is Dr. Kamath, director of the NASA Tracking Desk. What can you tell us?'

'Well, the Aliens are acting as we anticipated. They have entered Earth's orbit and are now almost directly above the Poles.

'I see.'

I remarked, 'Well duh.'

'Shhh!' Jim said.

Back at the studio, Chattering Caterwaul said, 'Hold on there, Chase. My producer is saying the president will speak soon, maybe even in a few minutes.'

'What's she gonna say?' I asked sarcastically.

Jim offered, 'How about WELCOME?' He turned to the kitchen, 'Hey everyone! The president is about to speak!'

The image on the TV screen changed to the Oval office. The president sat behind her desk, hands folded before her. Her face seemed serious but non-menacing.

This is Kelly Alford, President of the United States of America with a message for the approaching space ships. Let me be the first to welcome you on behalf of the people of the United Sates and all humankind. We are excited about your impending arrival and look forward to meeting you and have no doubt that our relations will be pleasant and mutually beneficial...

She went on for a few minutes before signing off.

'Well that was profound,' Keith said. 'That's all she has to tell them?'

I looked over at Keith, wondering if he was going to say anything else. He didn't. Instead he sipped his beer.

I walked over to Keith and slapped his broad back. 'What did you want the pres. to do?' I asked, a little more jocularly than I had intended. I was on my fourth beer myself. 'Tell the aliens to stay away or she'd nuke 'em?'

Keith looked at me, 'Yeah.'

For the first time I could see in his eyes, he was actually a little scared.

I found this unnerving. Keith was a big man, kind of quiet and perpetually busy. A do-it-yourself kind of man, he was always working on his car, or yard or roof. Aside from home projects, Keith worked his job as an IT consultant and was utterly devoted to his wife and sons, who were always assisting him. The year before, during the big blizzard that dumped two feet of snow on us, he went around the neighborhood with his snow blower clearing everyone's driveway. That's the kind of guy he was. He helped me out a lot in our first year.

Abby and I are new homeowners. We just celebrated our first anniversary here, actually. I don't think I'd have made it without guys like Keith. I'm an IT guy myself. The difference is Keith comes from a working class background, his old man was and is a UPS truck driver. My father is an insurance salesman and all thumbs. I never got the home improvement bug. When I needed to replace some screws in a closet door I went to the local Home Depot, it was the first time I'd ever been in one. After that I resolved to leave things to the pros. But after Keith saw a contractor's pickup parked in front of my house; I'd called him to install a new faucet, Keith came over and insisted on helping me. Ever since he's been showing me the ropes. He helped me, or I should say, I helped him replace a window, showed me lawn mowing basics after I mentioned I was going to hire a guy (I'm a Boston guy), and helped me paint the spare bedroom. We have 1800 square feet, three bedrooms. One of the spares is Abby's office. We turned the other into a nursery.

And then Abby miscarried.

I looked at the TV, where they now had moved on. Fox was showing stock footage of F-22 fighters, air-craft carriers and ICBMs. 'There you go, Keith.'

Chattering Caterwaul narrated, 'Even as the president welcomes the aliens, the armed forces of the United States are on full alert. All reserve and guard units have been called up. The entire United States Navy is at sea, much of it off the Atlantic and Pacific coasts, with carrier battle groups deployed in strategic locations throughout the globe.' She introduced a pompous defense analyst.

Jim made a point of turning down the volume with an app on his phone, 'Yeah, yeah…'

Keith said, 'Don't do that, I want to hear what we have waiting for them.'

'Like it matters,' said Jim.

Ever since the presidential announcement three months before, Jim had insisted that anyone who could travel across the stars would laugh at our weapons. He spent a lot of time on this almost laughing at the folks who had left Boston, heading for the hills, so to speak. There was even a program in our town to take in kids whose parents sent them to the countryside. There hadn't been a lot of takers, and now a few dozen kids were housed at a hotel at the town's expense.

'Jim,' said Carroll, 'Let Keith listen please.'

'Oh, okay.'

Pompous Defense Analyst spoke at length: '…I don't necessarily think that at all. But the simple fact is that two massive alien star ships are about to take up orbit over the Earth's magnetic poles. The military implications are obvious.'

'What, then, could we do?' Asked Chattering Caterwaul.

'Ballistic Nuclear Submarines,' Pompous Defense Analyst said. 'If I were the president, I'd station these under the North Pole…if necessary that is.'

Chattering Caterwaul interrupted. 'My producer tells me now that we've received some really sharp images of the alien ships. I'm seeing for the first time like all of you folks. Hold onto your hats. Here they are.'

The screen changed showing a swath of black, a bit of blue and white in the bottom left corner and in the center a long, thin looking cylinder, only a few inches on the screen, but said to be nearly eight miles in length.

'Hey kids!' Jim shouted. 'Aliens on the TV!'

Children came from all corners of the house and swarmed to the television screen. They seemed disappointed. *Probably expecting Star Wars*, I thought.

Carroll suggested the kids all go outside to greet the aliens. She gleefully took them to the backyard where they stood shouting, 'Hi Aliens! Hi Aliens!' The dads were indifferent while the Moms went about sipping their wine. I noticed Abby was opening another bottle.

For a long time the TV just showed the alien ship while Chattering Caterwaul engaged in pointless chatter with "experts". *Who the hell's an expert on aliens?* I wondered.

A correspondent came on, this one in front of the White House, 'Sources are telling me that multiple attempts to contact the aliens have been made. So far, no response.'

Chattering Caterwaul asked her panel of experts, 'What could that mean?'

Pointless speculation ensued until one of the pundits said, 'Can your producers zoom in on the spacecraft?'

'No, it's an image beamed from a NASA satellite.'

'From here it seems like objects are detaching from that ship.'

'Where?'

'You can see little gray dots, right there.'

Another pundit chimed in, 'Oh yeah...'

'This is beginning to look like Independence Day,' said Keith.

'A bit,' I admitted. I swigged my beer. I looked back and saw Abby pouring everyone more wine.

Carroll said, 'Don't you think the kids are making too much noise outside?'

Jim dismissed the comment with a wave. 'Ah, let them play.'

'It's getting late...'

I turned back to the TV which had flashed back to the White House correspondent.

Chattering Caterwaul asked, 'What new information do you have for us?'

The correspondent replied, 'Well, my contacts have suddenly gone dark and…'

Pompous Defense Analyst interrupted, 'Why are all those people running behind you?'

'Wa?' the correspondent turned around.

All of a sudden I heard this screeching sound from the TV. I turned and saw that the Chattering Caterwaul was gone and replaced with an image of the Oval Office. The president was just sitting down at her desk when the TV went blank.

'Hey what the heck?' Keith said. 'Jim is your satellite out? I can go up there and take a look.'

'Na, its fine. I..'

The TV flashed, popped, and the words EMERGENCY ALERT came on the screen. A voice said, 'We interrupt this broadcast at the request of the White House. We interrupt…'

The TV went blank again.

Jim looked down at his phone. I took mine out as well.

'My alerts are exploding,' I said.

'Mine too,' said Jim, 'Everyone is wondering what the heck just happened to satellite TV.'

I went to Twitter. Needless to say #Aliens was trending as was #Arrival.

'Let's see,' Jim said. 'Uh oh…'

'What?' Keith asked. 'Where are you, what do you see?'

'@Whitehouse says the Emergency Alert System is activated.'

'Jim, get the radio,' Carroll said.

'Hold on…I'm on BBC, unconfirmed reports…explosions? Lost contact…'

'Jim!' said Carroll, 'Get that transistor radio you bought last week.'

'OK.'

I kept scrolling twitter. '@RT says they've lost contact with the International Space Station.'

Keith stood by the satellite receiver, futzing with it in an attempt to get the signal back. 'If we switch to antenna…' he looked back, 'Carroll you have an old fashioned TV antenna?'

The lights flickered for a second, then went dark, then came back on again.

'What was that? Carroll asked.'

Keith said, 'Someone was probably re-routing power.'

Jim emerged from the basement. 'Got it!' He said, triumphantly holding the radio high.

'What does it say?' Keith asked.

'Lemme turn it up.'

We all stood around Jim and his radio, waiting for the message to begin again.

> The Emergency Alert System has been activated. Repeat, the Emergency Alert System has been activated. People are advised to remain indoors and await further instructions from local officials. This station will broadcast further updates as events warrant....

There was a pause and then beeping as the message began anew.

'I wonder what's happening,' said Abby.

Viv said, 'I think we better get the kids inside.'

Carroll said, 'I think you're right.'

The two went outside and began corralling kids. When they were all indoors, Viv said, 'Keith I think we better get home.'

'Yeah, you're right,' agreed Keith.

The TV came back on. The satellite company ran a message crawl across the bottom of the screen: WE ARE ON EMERGENCY BACKUP TRANSMISSON AND CANNOT GUARANTEE CONTINUOUS BROADCAST...

Above that Chattering Caterwaul spoke, more to her producer than to the audience '...definitely at this point...' she held her earpiece close to her ear and said, 'My producer tells me we have confirmed reports of some sort of...the term that was just used was alien action, yes some sort of alien action over the South Pole. We have footage from the South Pole Base and are working to get that on air...yes...here it is.'

The screen changed to a view of a dim, cold looking sky. The old South Pole Dome was visible in the foreground, and beyond that, several dots seemed to be making their way down to Antarctica. Beyond those was a long, gray cylinder.

William Stroock

'As you can see…' said the somewhat flustered anchor. The screen flashed and then the camera image went black. With no news to deliver the Chattering Caterwaul said, 'Gentlemen, what do you make of this?'

The pundits chattered.

Keith said, 'I think we better go.'

'Alright,' Viv said.

'Well,' Jim said, 'thanks for stopping by.'

Keith looked up. 'I guess we'll be sleeping in the basement tonight.'

'Right,' Jim said.

'I got it all set up, you know.'

'Yes, you told me.'

'Well, we better go.'

'Night.'

Abby began cleaning up for Carroll. She had been almost compulsively helpful since she miscarried. Especially with Carroll, who had lost her mother recently. Abby had tried to fill that void. Carrol was upstairs getting the kids ready. Jim and I were out on his back porch drinking beer. He looked up at the sky in astonishment.

'I just can't believe this is happening.'

I nodded sympathetically.

'You know what I really can't believe?'

'What.'

'That right now, aliens are up there attacking us. It's actually happening. *War of the Worlds. Independence Day*. It's actually happening.'

'It is,' I said. 'Nothing we can do.'

'You know what else is funny?'

I shook my head.

'It doesn't seem like the end of the world.'

I looked around.

'The lights are on. The TV is still babbling.' He took his phone out of his pocket and held it up. He tapped a few buttons. 'My twitter feed is still updating.'

'What's trending?' I asked.

'Hashtag Alien Invasion.'

'Makes sense, I…'

'Tyler.'

It was Abby.

'Time to go.'

I slapped Jim's back. 'See you tomorrow.'

He grunted.

Abby and I walked across the street to our house.

'You seem calm,' I said.

'Why be excited?'

Abby grabbed my hand as if she was pulling a child along. 'So you think it's smart to stand outside gawking at the sky? C'mon.'

'Yes, mommy,' I said. The moment it was out of my mouth I cringed, but if Abby was hurt, she didn't show it.

I thought of Keith and wondered if we should be taking any precautions. 'Want to sleep in the basement?' I asked.

'No,' Abby said.

That ended that. We went upstairs to bed.

I turned on the television, where the news anchors kept saying the same thing over and over again. After a few minutes Abby said, 'Are you going to turn that thing off?'

I turned off the TV.

I put the remote on my nightstand and held up my arm, an invitation for Abby to come lay her head on my chest, but she just turned her back to me.

'Abby, what did I do now?'

'Nothing…'

Suddenly I awoke I reached for my phone and looked for the time, it said just after five am. The alarm clock blinked. We'd lost power again, not that I noticed. I had slept through, nearly six hours. For a few moments I wondered if I had dreamed the previous night but quickly realized I hadn't.

Abby was already downstairs and I heard the TV on Fox. It was the only damned thing she watched anymore. I guess that made sense now. The voices were talking about aliens. I went downstairs, Abby was on the couch in her pajamas, mug of coffee held in both hands. She looked like she had been crying.

I sat next to her and said, 'Look, I'm sure we'll win this thing.'

'I'm not crying about that.'

'Oh.'

I got myself a cup of coffee and sat on the love seat across from Abby.

A tired looking news anchor talked. Not Chattering Caterwaul from the night before. A different one, but also blonde. We were watching Fox, after all. It was the only network Abby would watch. She hated the others. I've always been indifferent myself. While New Blonde talked, the producers ran B-roll footage of various scenes across the globe. It included; a seaborne view of Boston aflame, grainy cell phone footage of explosions over Edinburgh, gun-camera video from a Canadian fighter jet, and an unidentified shot showing yellow streaks of light shooting up into the sky.

'Jesus,' I said.

A small box in the corner showed the Earth with two flying saucer icons above each Pole.

Abby sniffled. I wondered how she could be upset about the whole kid thing when the Earth was under attack.

'Any news?' I asked.

She pointed to the TV. 'It's a war,' she said.

'I know. I mean...'

'The aliens are attacking us all over. We've already used nukes. The Feds are saying to stay indoors.'

'Nukes? Jesus.'

I got up and looked out the window. The sun hadn't come up. The sky looked perfectly normal.

'I don't see anything.'

Abby got up and poured herself more coffee.

Abby's cell phone rang. She went to the counter and picked it up.

'Hi, Mom,' she said. 'You just heard? Just now? Well, I know you and dad have to be in bed by ten but...no. No, we're ok. Nothing has happened mom.'

Abby rolled her eyes and made a face at me.

'Mom, I really don't think...well...right now? Mom. Mom. Stop, Mom. I am not...what do you mean?'

I got up and held out my hand for Abby to give me the phone. I knew where this conversation was heading, as the conversation always did when Mother called.

'C'mon,' I said. 'Give me the phone.'

Abby shook her head.

'She wants to do this right now?'

Abby turned from me and walked out of the TV room. 'Because this is where the government IT jobs are, Mom, that's why…why can't…No, don't get Daddy.'

I threw up my hands, and went down to the basement. This is where I kept my 'electronic toys' as Abby liked to call them, remote control cars which I had outfitted with GoPro cameras. You could have a lot of fun with those. For my birthday, Abby bought me a drone, which she now regretted as I got a big kick out of hovering outside her office window when she was working. I sat at my drafting table, another gift from Abby, I should note, and went back to work on my latest project. This was a 4x4 off road remote control car. The tires were twice as high as the body of the car and it could go just about anywhere. I'd been trying to fit a GoPro onto the chasse without upsetting the car's equilibrium.

While I tinkered, upstairs Abby fought with her parents. "Mother", as I condescendingly liked to refer to Abby's mom, never wanted us to move to Springfield. She blames me for that. Which I suppose is right, since we moved here so I could take an IT job here. She blames me for Abby miscarrying too. You see, in Mother's mind, if Abby and I had stayed with them back in South Carolina where she could stuff Abby full of pre-natal vitamins and hermetically seal her in a germ free room…I have tried to be understanding. Abby is their only child. But still, we've been married two years and they still haven't figured out they need to give us some space, and Abby won't tell them. Maybe it's me. I'm the youngest of five. My folks aren't even entirely sure where I live right now.

After getting off the phone Abby spent the next few hours glued to the TV. I don't know why, the "news" seemed to be on a continuous feedback loop. The same thing was happening over and over again. About noon the power went out.

'Damn it,' Abby said.

I tried the light switch but nothing happened.

'Ok,' Abby said, 'I'm going to take a shower while we still have a little hot water.'

'Wait.'

I picked up my phone. It showed a very weak signal and when I tried to go onto my Instagram account I couldn't get there. I tossed it back onto the table and looked at Abby.

I put my hand on her knee.

'What are you doing?'

'Nothing else to do. You just want to sit here?' I kissed her neck, which wasn't really fair, it had always been Abbey's vulnerable point. She pushed me away.

We napped most of the rest of the afternoon.

The power came back on about 5:30 PM.

We watched TV for a while, Abby insisted on Fox again. I went back outside and saw Keith carrying a bunch of pillows and blankets over to Jim's.

Jim was hauling a bunch of firewood into the house.

'Seems like a good idea,' he said.

'Yeah,' I agreed.

I saw Viv and her boys coming up Jim's driveway. Keith said, 'We're all ready?'

'What's going on?' I asked.

'Well, we thought if everyone is going to be sleeping in the basement we'd turn it into something fun.'

'Yeah,' Keith said. 'Basement campout sleep over.' He turned to the children, 'Right kids?!'

The kids cheered.

'Sounds fun.' I said.

They all walked into Jim's house. I waved and went home.

Abby and I got all of our pillows and blankets from our bedroom and from the guest bedroom and went down to the basement. It was finished so it was comfortable enough. Under a fluorescent camping light we played cards. Later I read a book while she listened to the radio. Finally, about nine we heard jets, and distant explosions and the Emergency Alert over the radio. Even though it didn't make much sense we both decided to turn off the camp light.

Abby and I got on a bed of pillows and pulled the large down comforter over ourselves.

The battle drew closer, the jets and explosions louder until, despite ourselves we pulled the blanket over our heads.

'I hope all the kids at Jim and Carroll's are asleep,' I said.

They were probably all awake. Pillow and blanket forts, games of hide and seek, tricking the adults into thinking they were asleep when they were really playing video games under the covers. I bet they were having a great time. I looked over to Abby, with a few ideas for a great time of my own, there was nothing else to do, but I saw she was crying.

'What's the...ohhhhh.' I said.

I cursed myself. Talking about the kids like that. I knew Abby was thinking about the slumber party too.

Abby turned her back to me again. I tried to put my arm around her but she flinched away. I watched lights flickering off the window until I fell asleep. The fighting lasted till late morning.

I went outside after lunch. You could smell something strange in the air, almost as if a house had burned down, but subtler and not as strong. There was haze in the sky above. Jim was in his driveway, holding up the phone to the sky. Keith was doing the same.

I wandered over, 'Watcha doing?'

'Trying to use my phone as a Geiger counter.'

'Anything?'

'No,' said Jim. 'I think all the smoke and haze is messing with the sensor.'

Keith said, 'I'm trying to track that ship's movements.'

'What ship?' I asked.

'It'll come.'

'You know those weird sounds in the sky?' Keith asked.

'Yeah.'

'That's a Jai ship. Jim and me were standing out here looking for it. He says he saw it before.'

'I did see it before.'

'Well,' I said. 'That explains the binoculars.'

'It'll come back,' Jim said.

'How'd you guys do last night?'

'What the sleepover?' Keith asked. 'It was fun, right Jim? Why we…'

'Here it comes!' Jim shouted. He pointed to the north. 'Look at that thing!'

I looked to where he was pointing.

There it was, moving lazily across the sky; a stubby gray thing with wings and a tail. Keith watched it through his binoculars.

'How big is that thing?'

'Hard to tell, isn't it,' Jim said. He tried to grab the binoculars from Keith, who elbowed him away.

'Knock it off,' Keith said. 'It looks like maybe the size of an airliner.'

'Yeah, but what kind?' asked Jim. 'A 787, Eurostar, what?'

'I don't know.'

'Well, how high is it?'

'How the hell should I know?'

Jim squinted. 'It's pretty high up.'

From the doorway Carroll shouted, 'Would you guys stop gawking at that thing and come in?'

'Why?' asked Jim.

'It's dangerous!'

'What does that thing want with us?' Jim retorted.

We stood there gawking until the ship disappeared to the north.

'She's right you know,' Keith said. 'No point in just standing here.'

'I guess,' I said. 'Nothing else to do though.

'Be nice if we could do something,' Keith said.

'Like what?' I asked. 'Do you even have a gun?'

Both Keith and Jim shook their heads. 'I never thought it was a good idea with a lot of kids around the house.'

'Ok, so what should we do then?' I asked.

'Well,' Jim said, 'We can report this thing.' He pointed up to the sky.

'To whom?' I asked.

'I don't know, the cops?'

Keith said. 'Now that's not a bad idea.' He took out his phone.

'What are you doing?' I asked.

'I'm calling the cops.'

'I'm heading in,' I said.

I left Keith and Jim to gawk at the alien ship. But before I got to my driveway Keith said, 'hey look at that!' He pointed to the sky, where the alien ship now hovered high up, maybe a few miles away from us.

I walked back over to Keith and Jim.

'Wonder why?'

We watched as the Jai ship flew overhead and then settled in the sky, hovering a couple thousand feet in the air.

Jim came out with beer.

'Look,' said Keith, 'all I'm saying is we're sitting around here doing nothing, right?'

Jim smirked. On his third beer he admitted, 'Well, Carrol and I haven't been doing *nothing*.'

I looked at Jim with distain. How was this middle-aged guy with three kids getting more tail than me?

Keith didn't laugh. Right now, he didn't have a sense of humor about anything.

'C'mon, Jim.'

'Alright,' Jim asked, 'what do you want to do?'

Keith pointed to the sky.

'What? That ship?'

'Yeah.'

'What do you want to do about that ship?'

'Shoot it down.'

Jim laughed and patted Keith on the back. Then he took a deep swig from his beer and looked at it. 'These microbrews, who knows what they put in them, because I swear I just heard you say you want to shoot down the alien ship.'

'Why not? It's hovering right over there.'

'How the hell do you plan on doing that?'

I chimed in, 'Have you been building a missile in your garage?'

'Just listen for a second. Ok?'

'Alright,' Jim said as he polished off his beer. 'I'll listen, because I want to hear this.'

Keith looked at me, 'Well, you're the key to the whole thing.'

'Me?'

'Yeah. I need your drone.'

'What are you going to do with my drone?'

'Here's the way I see it. That ship up there has a couple of engines just like a fighter jet right?'

'Okay,' said Jim. He popped open another beer.

'What if we flew your drone right into one of the engines?'

'It would probably just burn up,' I said.

'Ahhh…' Keith held up a finger. 'What if we strapped a gas can to it?'

'Well, I suppose it could…'

'Tyler could fly it right into the engine and…boom!'

'Could it even carry a gallon?' asked Jim.

Not yet realizing that Jim was starting to take this scheme seriously I shrugged and said, 'Yeah. In fact, it's checked out for twenty plus pounds.'

'Twenty plus!' exclaimed Jim, 'Why a propane tank is 18.'

'Could you get the drone up there?' asked Keith.

I looked up at the ship. 'What do you think? It's maybe… 5,000 feet?'

Keith held up his phone, 'This says four thousand.'

'We could do it.'

Jim swigged his beer, 'Oh hell, why not. I'll get my propane tank.'

Jim and Keith stood up. I asked, 'We're doing this?'

'What the hell,' said Jim.

'Go get your drone.'

I shrugged. 'Ok.'

Still not really taking the whole scheme seriously, I went to my garage and took out my drone.

'That thing is impressive,' Jim said.

'Where would we put the propane tank?'

I pointed to the undercarriage clamps and platforms.

'Ok,' said Jim. 'Let's say you get that thing up to the ship, which I doubt, since they'll probably just shoot it down. What makes you think a twenty pound propane tank will do any damage?'

Keith replied. 'Like I said, get it up by the engine and blow up one of the exhausts.'

'But it will just make a lot of fire.'

'Ah, but if the tank explodes it will make a lot of shrapnel,' countered Keith. 'And you know what, we could duct-tape a lot of nails to the tank, make even more of a mess.'

'Now hold on,' I said. 'This thing ain't cheap you know.'

'Well,' Jim said, 'Let me play devil's advocate here.'

'Screw that,' said Keith. 'We're at war.'

'Ok, I get that, but this thing costs thousands of dollars. Abby used her Christmas bonus to buy it for me.'

'So let me get this straight,' said Keith. 'You're not going to defend your country because wifey might get mad?'

'It's not...' I thought for a second, and thought about all the grief Abby had been giving me. I felt bad for thinking that way. But then I thought about Mother, and I didn't feel bad anymore.

'Fuck it,' I said.

Keith slapped my back. 'That's the spirit.'

Now determined, I attached the propane tank to the drone. Jim duct taped dozens of nails to it. I turned on the engine and tested the drone. It wobbled a bit but stabilized and easily took the tank 50 feet into the air. Carefully I landed the drone.

'Well, what are we waiting for?' Keith asked.

'Hold on,' I said. 'Let me get my laptop. It's linked to the GoPro on the drone.'

I went inside and got my computer. 'What are you doing?' Abby asked.

'Nothing,' I said.

When I got back outside, Jim handed me a beer. 'Thought you'd like this.'

I took the beer and swigged. 'Thanks.'

'Is that everything?' Keith asked.

I shrugged. 'I guess.'

'Well,' Keith said, 'Let's do this.'

He swigged his beer.

'Now?'

'Why not?'

'Now?' I repeated.

'You got something better to do?'

I looked back at the house.

'Fuck it.'

'That's the spirit,' said Jim.

I activated the drone and took it into the air above my house and pointed the camera down toward us.

'Jim,' I said, 'monitor the computer. You'll navigate, ok?'

'Sure,' Jim leaned down and swigged his beer. 'There we are.'

'Come up behind the ship,' Keith said. 'Take out those engines.'

'I know,' I said as I brought the drone up higher.

'Wow, we're getting smaller and smaller,' said Jim, swigging his beer.

'I'm pointing the camera toward the ship, now.'

Jim swigged his beer. 'Probably won't matter.'

'Huh?'

'They'll just blow your drone out of the sky long before that.'

'Hey, what the heck?' I said.

'You don't really think…wow there's the ship on the screen.'

'Hey, you're getting close.'

'Wow,' said Jim. 'You're getting really close.'

'Can you speed up?' Keith asked, 'You know before…'

The engines loomed as I piloted my precious drone toward the alien ship, not really believing my eyes as it was getting closer and closer. All of the sudden the camera cut out. I looked up to see a puff of fire besides the ship. Then I heard a small booming sound.

'Holy crap!' Keith shouted. He pointed.

'I agree,' said Jim. 'Holy crap!' He swigged his beer.

I looked up and saw a line of smoke coming from the ship, thin, wispy, almost like the engine had backfired or something. The ship wobbled a bit and then started losing altitude. It was at that point that I heard something like a rattle, almost like when loose change gets rolled around a clothes drier. The ship moved, wobbling to our east and losing even more altitude. You could really hear the rattling now. We watched it for a few more seconds and then there was a small burst of fire from the engine and then we heard the explosion.

'Whoa!' Jim shouted. 'I think we got it.'

'That thing is coming down,' said Keith. 'Right over at that field across the street.'

We heard a crash, like a big rig slamming into a guardrail, tipping on its side and screeching to a halt.

'Well,' I said ruefully, 'That's nine thousand bucks pissed away.'

'Hey, in defense of America,' Jim said.

'Get me a beer, will you?'

'Sure.'

Jim grabbed a beer from the cooler and undid the cap for me. We toasted. 'To nine thousand bucks!'

I chugged about half the beer.

'Let's go check it out,' said Jim. I had drunk just enough beer for this to seem like a good idea. 'Bring the beer cooler.'

We headed out of the neighborhood. There was an empty field across the street, formerly the site of a mini mall. Jim said a developer bought the acreage and leveled the mini mall, for a new housing development, but could never get things worked out with the town, and the field to this day was undeveloped and overgrown.

'Wait a minute,' I said. 'We're just going to waltz over there and demand the aliens surrender.'

Keith laughed, 'My Roman Candle Cannon!'

'Be serious,' I said.

'I am. We set it off and scare the crap out of them.'

Jim said, 'You remember the premier of Deep Space Nine?'

'No.'

'The Federation convinced the Cardassians that the station was armed to the teeth, when they really only had one launcher and six photon torpedoes.'

'If you say so.'

'Could work,' said Jim. 'But we still need a gun.'

'Karl has a gun,' Jim said.

Karl was the old guy down the street. He and his wife were the block's designated old married couple. They were really nice to the kids.

Jim and I walked down the street to Karl's house while Keith got his Roman Candle Mini-gun.

Jim pounded on the door until Karl opened. 'Hey fellas,' he said.

Karl was always happy to see Keith and Jim, and even me. I think it made him feel young again.

'We need your rifle,' Keith said.

'Yeah,' added Jim.

'Huh?'

'Did you hear that crash?'

'Uh huh.'

'We did that. It was the alien ship.'

'Oh come now.'

'Look,' Jim said, 'We need your rifle.'

Karl shook his head. 'Alright.' He disappeared into his basement and came back with his rifle. 'I'm coming with you.'

'Great!' Jim said.

'What's Ginni going to do?' I asked Karl in reference to his wife.

'She's napping.'

'Smart.'

'What are we waiting for?' Keith asked.

We walked out of the neighborhood and to the field across the street. There we saw the alien ship. We all stood there, dumbfounded for a minute. It had landed toward the far edge of the field, knocking over a couple of trees and churning up some earth. It was slightly bigger than a 727 and standing outside were two aliens; the Jai as the news called them.

'Oh wow,' Jim said.

'That's all you can say?' I asked, not taking my eyes off the aliens. 'Wow? You're the sci-fi fan.'

'They look about like us, don't they?' said Jim.

In fact, they did. Two arms, two legs, one head. I don't know what I was expecting. Tentacles maybe.

A pair of boxes were at their feet and a couple of panels on the ship were open on the engine. It looked like they were trying to fix something.

Keith walked forward several yards. He took the propane lighter out of his pocket and handed it to Jim. 'Light me up,' he said.

'Ok.' Jim opened the lighter, producing a cone of blue flame. 'Hold on. They haven't seen us. Let's get closer.'

They walked forward until they were about sixty yards from the alien ship. At that point the Jai heard us and turned around. One pointed at us.

'Karl get over here with your rifle and fire.'

'What? There's no ammo.'

'What do you mean no ammo?'

'I haven't even cleaned this thing in years.'

The aliens waved in our direction and shouted something. It looked like they were telling us to go away.

'Oh hell,' Keith said. 'Jim light me up!'

'Fuck it,' said Jim.

He stepped forward and lit each bundle of Roman Candles.

'Get behind...'

Before Keith could finish, his mini-gun exploded in a stream of sparks and fireballs and whistles. Keith pointed his mini-gun at the ship, sending a stream of whistling fire into the air. The two aliens standing outside, saw and heard the fireballs coming toward them and ran. Keith followed them, sending a shower of fireballs after the Jai. Then he turned back to the ship, dozens of fireballs bounced off the hull and fell to the ground. Luckily, I suppose, the field was dry and the Roman Candles ignited the grass, beginning a small fire beneath the ship. Gradually the Roman Candles expired until just a few flittered across the space between us and the ship.

'Karl,' Keith said, 'step forward with your rifle and look threatening.'

'Gee…'

'C'mon, before those aliens figure us out.'

Karl rather reluctantly walked forward, rifle at the hip and pointed in the general direction that the aliens ran off to.

'You guys come out and surrender!' Keith shouted. 'Or I'll turn my death ray on you!'

'Death ray?' Jim asked

'I doubt they speak even English,' I offered. I pointed to the mini-gun. 'And you're empty.'

Flames still came out of the hot tubes, setting the cardboard containers alight. To be honest, despite being blackened and charred, the thing still looked pretty scary.

'You two! Keith repeated. 'Come out or…'

Before Keith finished, the alien ship exploded. The blast had been enough force to knock us all over. Bits of charred metal, grass and turf fell all around us. I looked up and saw the alien ship had snapped in half and aflame. Beside it the two Jai lay, also aflame. They didn't move at all.

'Wow!' Karl said.

'Uhhh,' I added, 'I think we got it.'

'What now?' Jim asked.

'Take pics,' said Keith.

It hadn't even occurred to me. I took my phone out and shot a minute or so of video.

'Hey,' Karl said, 'Police cars.'

I looked down the road, three cruisers were coming our way, lights blaring. They skid to a halt, Starsky and Hutch style. Three cops got out of each cruiser, all wearing military style helmets and body armor. To my surprise they leveled their rifles at us.

'Freeze!' one shouted.

He didn't have to tell us twice.

Three cops, automatic rifles at the ready, trotted over to us, while three more made their way to the alien ship.

With two cops covering, one searched each of us and made us sit on the ground cross-legged.

'Just what are you four doing here?' one cop asked.

Keith pointed to the flaming wreckage. 'We shot down that ship and blew it up.'

'How the hell did you do that?'

'Can we get up please?' Karl asked, 'My hip is killing me.'

'Yeah, alright.'

We stood up.

'You guys weren't supposed to do that.'

'What were we supposed to do?' Jim asked.

'Let the authorities handle things,' the cop replied. 'Just how did you guys bring that thing down.'

Keith explained.

'That's a felony what you guys did, you know that, right?'

'That's bullshit,' said Keith.

'Now hold on, let me finish. I'm going to cite you for the fireworks, but that's it.'

'Phew,' Karl said.

'To be honest, what are we going to cite you for, shooting down an enemy ship? There would be an uproar. Besides, you're going to get it from your wives anyway.'

'Oh boy,' Karl said, 'Ginny is going to kill me.'

More sirens, 'That's the fire department.'

The cop looked at the four of us, looking chastened and slightly disheveled, 'Ahh, hell with it. Get out of here.'

'Thank you, officer,' Karl said.

Viv and Carrol were hollering when we got back to our street. I actually saw Viv slap Keith about the head several times, like he was one of their boys. I guess, really he was. The whole scene was comical really. Across the street Carroll admonished Jim and wanted to know what he was thinking drinking so much in the afternoon like that.

I went inside. Abby was on the couch. Fox News ran as always. She held her phone in her hand, reading intently.

'Hey.'

'Hey,' she replied.

'You mad?'

Abby shook her head. 'It's your life.'

'That's all you have to say?'

'What am I supposed to say?'

'You could at least be pissed.'

'You want me to be pissed?'

'Carroll and Viv are pissed.'

'You want me to be like them?'

'Why not? You do.'

'I don't want to fight.'

'You never do. You never want to do anything.'

Abby held up her phone, 'Look.'

'What is this?'

I took Abby's phone. 'The town needs volunteer foster parents?'

'Yes.'

'And you want to do this?'

'It says a lot of people from Boston sent their kids out of the city.'

I pursed my lips. 'And these aliens blew up Boston. So there are a lot of orphans.'

'And now they need parents,' Abby said. 'Can we?'

I looked into Abby's eyes, they gleamed with hope. I nodded.

For the first time in weeks Abby smiled. She got up and threw herself in my arms. 'Thank you, Tyler,' she said I felt her hands squeezing me to her and for the first time in weeks, I smiled.

CHAPTER 2

FEDERAL PREPPER

The fish hatchery lay on over a hundred acres of pristine forest. To access it one had to drive up a long road for nearly a quarter of a mile, past evergreens that closed in on the road. The road ended in a small clearing. There was an old house, a couple of long buildings that used to be stables but now served as offices, and several circular enclosures. The hatchery had underground electrical and phone lines, making it an even more ideal location for Yi's plan.

The curator of the hatchery spoke on, 'We have about six hundred fish,' he pointed to one of the enclosed pools. 'As you can see, these here are near two feet long, some three. These are breeder fish. All are at least six years old. Many are ten, a few are nearing twenty years.'

Lara Yi looked around and asked, 'I'm a bit unclear on something.'

'Sure, ma'am,' the ever polite curator said, 'what can I clear up for you?'

'You're sitting on all this land, but you only have six of these pools, and they're not even that big.'

The curator inhaled deeply and said, 'Well, that's all we've been budgeted for. We're on a hundred and seventy acres here. Honestly, a good part of that is just for a forest reserve. Land preservation and the like.'

'Sure,' Yi said. She looked at her phone. 'Now, I have here a copy of the hatchery's deed and charter.'

'Wow,' said Luke. 'In my line of work I don't use that stuff much. You got the deed on your phone?'

'I do,' said Lara. 'Now, there's nothing in these documents keeping you from expanding, is there?'

'No, ma'am,' Luke said ever so cordially.

'Would you like to?'

'Like to what?'

'Expand?'

Luke shrugged. 'Well, we never really thought about it. I mean, we have six pools.'

'That's right,' said Lara. 'And with those six pools you stock the entire Great Lakes.'

'I see, you need us to produce more fish in case the aliens start a fight and wipe out the fish population in the Great Lakes.'

'No,' Lara replied. 'I want you to farm and stock fish to feed people.'

'Feed people?'

'Yes. In case of war, millions of refugees will be coming north from NYC and west from Boston.'

'This is serious then,' said Luke. His normally pleasant face becoming grim.

'I'm afraid it is,' said Yi. 'Now, what would you have to do to expand?'

Luke thought for a moment. 'Well, more pools, the domes of course. More power, but that's no problem, and the pools are just a concrete base.'

'What about fish? More fish.'

'We can massage the eggs out of the females and the sperm out of the males. Then we just mix 'em together.'

'So it can be done.'

'Oh, absolutely. But we aren't budgeted for that. Besides, you're talking about months to grow the fish.'

'This is a long term project,' Yi said. She looked behind her to the eager young aide. He was dressed in khakis and a polo shirt. His hair was immaculate. 'Preston!'

The young man walked forward.

Lara looked at Luke and asked. 'How much do you need?'

'Well I…'

'How much do you need? Would a hundred thousand dollars do?'

'A hundred thousand? Be serious.'

'I am,' Lara replied. 'Preston?'

Preston handed Lara a checkbook and went back to the car.

'Federal Marshall,' she said. 'FEMA figures I should have some muscle with me, strictly for protection. I figured I might as well get some use out of him. She held the check book open to Luke and said, 'See that? It says Federal Emergency Management Agency. This is a government check drawn on the United States Treasury. Where does the fishery bank?'

'Uhhh, Berkshire.'

'The one in town?'

'Yeah.'

'You can take this check and deposit it, you'll have a hundred thousand dollars at the end of the day.'

'Wow.'

'Can you make this work?'

'Absolutely.'

'Preston...'

Preston came back and wrote out the amount payable. Yi signed it and handed it to Luke. 'We'll be staying at the Holiday Inn Express in town. Get me a plan tonight.'

'OK.'

Later as Preston drove down the hill and back toward Great Barrington, he said, 'You sure you should be giving them a hundred thousand bucks like that?'

'What's the problem?' Yi asked without looking up from her iPhone.

'He could take off with it.'

Yi thumbed back toward the hatchery. 'That guy? He's perfectly honest and I think all he cares about is his fish.'

'If you say so.'

'I was a practicing attorney for twenty years and a politico to boot.'

'Yeah, you were on her campaign staff. I know.'

'It's my business to read people. And I say so.'

'You're the boss.'

I am, Yi thought.

They drove out of the mountains and down into town.

'Let's go through town.'

'What for?'

'See what we can see,' Yi said. 'That's part of my job.'

Down in town they saw a great flatbed truck backing into the lot of the local hardware store. A quartet of Latin day laborers waited to unload stacks of lumber. As they drove past the store, they saw the front festooned with signs reading 'ALL OUT OF TOOLS AND LUMBER.' And next to it 'MORE ON THE WAY' and 'SEE ED INSIDE TO RESERVE YOURS.'

Preston asked. 'Think that will do any good?'

'What?'

'Boarding up windows. Against aliens, I mean.'

'Can't hurt, can it?'

'I suppose.'

'And besides, it gives people something to do.'

'You mean instead of worrying about the aliens.'

'Yes.'

'Is that what the president told you?'

Yi laughed. 'That's what she and I decided.'

Yi noticed Preston's eyes wandering over her.

'The hotel is right over there.'

'Oh crap,' Preston said as they drove past the Holiday Inn Express.

'You know what, let's just keep going.'

'Ok.'

'This road leads into Pittsfield, and I'd like to see what's happening there.' She looked down at her phone. 'There's some sort of weapons plant there…ah yes, General Dynamics…'

'Why do we have to go?

'So we can give the president a report on what's happening there.'

'In Pittsfield?'

'She wants on the ground reports.'

'On Pittsfield.'

'As much hard field data as possible. That means someone she trusts getting on the ground and relating what she sees. That means me.'

They drove on in silence through the picturesque New England landscape. When they stopped at a light in Stockbridge, Yi noticed they were next to a large hotel.

'The Red Lion,' she read.

Yi tapped the name into her phone. 'Look at all the rooms…there must be a capacity for hundreds of people here.'

'I bet,' said Preston.

They drove on into Pittsfield.

The streets were thronged with people, most shopping or going to work. The vast majority of these were dressed in jeans, flannel shirts, and carrying hardhats. Preston took the car past several people standing on street corners handing out pamphlets and one protest at the main traffic circle. Here a few dozen people had gathered below a large banner calling the president a fascist. Several carried homemade signs decrying the president's new security measures and plans to prepare the country in case of war. Most people ignored them.

'I thought Pittsfield was supposed to be some sort of burned out factory town,' said Preston.

'Well, they still have the General Dynamics weapons plant, let's go take a look.'

They drove to the factory on the north end of town. Hundreds of workers were leaving, the emergency night shift having ended. On the far end of the factory a train loaded large crates, none marked, but Lara knew what was inside.

'Railguns,' she said.

'Wow.'

'Remember the Raytheon plant over in Waltham? Same kind of stuff. They're cranking out dozens of missiles a day. Over there.'

'Wow.'

'Here they must have hired hundreds of new employees.'

'Wow.'

'Is that all you can say?'

'Sorry.'

'Let's get out of here.'

Back at the hotel Yi changed into her U-Penn Law sweats and got to work. She spent the evening making notes and filing reports with the Preparatory Coordinating Office. She had the TV on in the background, mostly for white noise, a study habit she picked up in college. When she finished with the reports she turned the TV to one of the political shows. She watched two know-nothing-pundits argue about the president. She knew one of them a bit, they'd worked on the president's campaign together. She had taken her current gig to forget the campaign. Yi turned off the TV.

There was a knock on the door. It was Preston.

'The check has been cashed.'

'Good, we'll run up there tomorrow before we head out.'

'Ok.'

Yi walked back to her table. Preston lingered.

'Something else, Preston?'

He smirked and sat down on the corner of the bed.

Yi looked down her glasses at him. 'Really?'

'Really.'

'Preston, I'd break you in half. Get out.'

Preston's face turned bright red.

'Let's go. I have work to do.'

He skulked out of the room.

Idiot kid, Yi thought.

Then she laughed. Good looking though, *probably not used to hearing no*. For a moment, Yi felt bad for humiliating him. But for only a moment. She'd been rejecting over confident, smirking jerks like him her entire career.

Yi shook her head and dashed off a quick report of what she'd seen and sent it to the Oval Office email. She spent an hour looking over potential sites in New York State, making notes on which locations to see in person before turning in.

In the morning Yi did a quick five miles on the hotel treadmill.

She met Preston for breakfast. Lara had fruit and the first of many cups of coffee.

She touched her phone to his.

'What's that?'

'A list of public works and utility people I want you to contact this morning.'

Preston scrolled through the list. 'Ok. What's this address?'

'It's over in Orange County, New York. We'll head over there tomorrow.'

'What for?'

'That old Red Lion Inn gave me an idea.'

'OK.'

At the Red Lion Lara presented herself to the front desk and asked for the manager.

'My name is Lara Yi, I'm the president's special advisor for Arrival preparation.'

'Yes, Ms. Yi, I remember you from the Iowa Caucus controversy. How can I help you?'

'Could we have a quick meeting, Mr...?'

'Murphy.'

'Mr. Murphy.'

'Yes, please come to my office.'

Inside the office Lara said, 'I will come right to the point, Mr. Murphy. What is the capacity of the Red Lion Inn?'

'We have one hundred and twenty-five rooms.'

'So, say five hundred persons then?'

'I would say so.'

'But more in an emergency.'

'I know where this is heading, Ms. Yi. I knew the moment I saw you.'

'So then you know I am designating you as a refugee settlement site.'

'Yes.'

You don't seem too upset.'

'Do I have a choice?'

'I suppose you could fight it in court.'

'After what FEMA did to that hotel in Nyack?'

Yi said nothing. She was the one who had the local health department shutdown a hotel whose owner refused to cooperate. Playing hardball was an old habit from her campaign days.

Murphy shrugged, 'We'll do our bit. Now as to capacity, I am assuming one family per room. But to answer your question. Yes, we could squeeze more people here. The lobby, the dining area.'

'Of course.'

'So then can I plan for a thousand?'

'I do not have many spare cots.'

'Make a list of what you need. I will make sure you have it within the week.'

'From the Federal Government? A week? Please.'

'Mr. Murphy,' Lara began matter-of-factly 'I am special assistant to the president. You see this phone?' Yi held up her phone. 'This red button here, it gets me directly to the oval office. So if you need something, you'll get it from me, and fast.'

'Ok.'

Lara reached into her briefcase and took out a packet. 'This is an information packet of everything FEMA would like you to have.'

Murphy took the packet, put on his reading glasses and flipped through it. 'Very well, Ms. Yi. You will have our complete cooperation.'

Lara raised an eyebrow.

'Surprised?'

'Usually there is some complaining.'

'What is the point? The aliens will be here in three weeks.'

'Three weeks and two days, actually.'

'If I have to cancel some reservations because of an alien invasion, it won't really matter will it?'

'That's my thinking, Mr. Murphy.'

'Now, as to the matter of payment…'

'You will be sent a voucher book in which you will note all of your expenses.'

'Oh, well then…'

'Also, I am prepared today to cut you a check to defray your upfront costs in the amount of…' she made a show of thinking about it for a moment 'one hundred thousand dollars.'

'It's a start.'

'Very good, Mr. Murphy.'

Before leaving Yi wrote out the check. As she and Murphy shook hands, Lara handed him a card and said, 'If you have any trouble you call or text me, right away.'

'Any trouble?'

'Call me. I *will* take care of it.'

Back in the car Preston said, 'Look, about last night...'

'Oh shut the hell up about it would you?'

'I just...'

'Preston, you think you're the first jerk to make a pass at me on a business trip?'

'Where are we headed?' Preston asked, hand ready to punch the destination into the car's GPS.

'East Fallsburg, New York.'

Preston was quiet. He turned on the AM radio, but Lara was so absorbed in the morning batch of emails that she didn't notice for several minutes.

'The president thinks she can control everything,' said the host. 'Well she can't control the laws of supply and demand and that is exactly what she is trying do with the freeze plan she just announced. It makes no sense and if she persists the president will bankrupt the country before the aliens even arrive and we will need that money for the military so we can defend ourselves...'

Yi looked up from her phone.

'Turn that crap off, would you?'

Preston switched off the radio. 'Sorry, I just wanted something to listen to.'

'Try something else.'

Yi cursed at her email as Preston switched the dial to another station. This host was in high dudgeon as well, only over sports. In a thick New York accent, the host proclaimed. 'You know, I think it is important to maintain the air of normalcy, that's really important I think, so I think the NFL is right to keep the season going just for the aspect of normalcy... Your calls after this...'

'Plan for the coming attack!' A great disembodied voice proclaimed. 'When the aliens arrive, you don't want to be stuck in or near a high value target. Get out now, to our beautiful spa forty-five minutes west of NYC...'

Another commercial came on, this one for power generators and solar cells. Preston said, 'That's a business I wouldn't mind being in.'

The radio host came on and read an advertisement, 'Our basement finishing system converts your basement into a safe, secure bomb shelter...'

Lara overheard that and laughed.

'It gives people peace of mind,' Preston said.

'It gives people a rip-off. Why I hope the AG...'

Yi couldn't finish the sentence because her phone rang.

'Ah...good,' she said. 'Mr. Lele, so glad you called.'

'How can we help you?' Lele asked.

'As you know, I'm the president's special advisor for Arrival preparation, and I am going to be in your part of New Jersey and my office would like to do a walkthrough of your facility.'

'Sure, we can do that,' said Lele.

'Now, your company has a large campus, several buildings, and if I understand correctly a large underground facility.'

'Yes, yes. That's right,' said Lele. 'When will you be dropping by?'

'Honestly, I am not sure yet. In a few days, I think. Right now my team and I are in Upstate New York.'

'I see, well, just let me know and we can set something up.'

'Thank you, Mr. Lele, will do, goodbye.'

Preston asked, 'Your team?'

'Sounds more impressive. Makes him think there are scores of us swarming up here.'

They reached the Hamilton Fish Bridge. It was a large span, overshadowed by the more impressive Tappan Zee and George Washington bridges down the river. It was the main means of crossing the river in the Central Hudson Valley between Peekskill and Poughkeepsie and the main link between the Mid-Atlantic and New England. Already the National Guard was digging revetments on the heights above. A Coast Guard cutter patrolled the waters below.

'Never thought I'd see the military out and about like this,' said Preston.

'Meh,' Yi replied. 'I worked in Manhattan on September 11th. A few days after the attack, I looked out my office window and saw a Blackhawk Helicopter hovering outside.'

'Wow.'

She spent most of the car ride researching the resort they were heading for.

'It says here that this place was part of the Borscht Belt.'

'Borscht Belt?' Preston asked.

'Haven't you ever seen *Dirty Dancing*?'

'No.'

Yi laughed, Preston was too young to care about or to even have seen the movie. Lara had been 13 when she saw *Dirty Dancing*....

'The Borscht Belt was a great ring of Catskill Mountain resorts.'

'If you say so.'

When they came to the resort, they saw a collection of old abandoned buildings. One facility had even burned down. The grounds were overgrown with vegetation. It had been decades since the place was in use.

'There's a couple of cars over there at the gate. One says it's from the Public Works. The other from the power company.'

'Well, take us over to the gate.'

Preston pulled up to the cars and stopped. Yi got out and waved.

'Hello there,' she said.

A burly man got out of the power-company truck. Another burly man got out of the Public Works truck. 'Good morning,' said the burly Public Works man, 'Don Jackie, South Fallsburg Public Works.'

The power company man said, 'Bill Walker.'

They shook hands, 'How do you do?'

'Ma'am,' began Jackie, 'You're that specialist from FEMA.'

'Yes, sir. I asked you here because I'd like to talk about the feasibility of getting this facility up and running.'

Jackie, his eyebrows raised said, 'This joint? It hasn't been operational in a longtime.'

'Well, Mr. Walker, could you get the power turned on?'

'If we had to, yes,' Walker replied.

'What about you, Mr. Jackie? Can your office get this facility cleaned up? Get the water turned back on?'

He made a face and said, 'Sure.'

'When can you get started? Today?'

Jackie laughed. 'We have a schedule.'

'Schedule?'

'We have projects to complete. Job categories to maintain.'

Yi held up a finger, 'Alright, hold on,' she turned to Walker. 'What would it take to get the power back on here?'

Walker pursed his lips in thought. 'I'd have to get into our file on this place. Look around, see what needs repairing, see how much line we'd have to string....'

'I should add that the Feds will underwrite this. I can write a check to you today.'

Walker smiled, 'I never saw the Feds act that quickly.'

'You never saw me.'

Walker said, 'Now, I suppose you want to turn this into some kind of refugee center.'

Jackie spoke, 'I'm not sure the town is going to like that.'

Yi replied, 'We are approaching a national emergency.'

Walker said, 'Ms. Yi, I'm going to head to my office and make some calls. I'll have some information for you today, ok?'

'Thank you, Mr. Walker. What about the public works, Mr. Jackie?'

'Ahh… geee… I dunno…I better talk to the mayor. I'll be in touch too, ok?'

'Soon, please.'

Walker waved as he headed back toward his public works truck.

'He doesn't seem too cooperative,' said Preston.

'No,' Lara replied as she watched him drive off.

'What now?'

'Find a hotel, we'll stay here, tonight.'

'Ok.'

'Well take a drive around. See what else we can find.' Lara looked at her phone. 'In fact…wait a minute. Let's head west.'

'OK.'

Yi punched the destination into the car's navigation system and let the driving directions app lead the way.

By the time she was finished they pulled up to a vast field. On one side was an old dairy farm. In the center, an open-air stage and to the left, a parking lot. A crowd of several hundred people were in the field.

Yi looked at the parking lot and laughed.

'What's funny?'

'They actually put up a parking lot!'
'Huh?'
'Oh you wouldn't get it.'
'What is this place?'
'Oh come on, you really don't know where you are?'
Preston shook his head.
'What did you study in college?'
'Criminal justice.'
Lara laughed again. 'This is Woodstock.'
'Ohhhhh…the concert?'
'Yep. I was here.'
'You were here?'
'Yes, in 1994, sophomore year.'
'Wow.'
'Wanna know a secret?'
'Ummm, I guess.'
'So was the president.'
'The president?'
'Uh huh.'
'She and I drove here in her beat up Celica. We slept in the car.'
'Oh wow. I knew you two went way back…'
'Yeah, we roomed together at Columbia. When we heard Melissa Etheridge was playing, we came right up.'
'Melissa Etheridge?'
'The president and I were big fans.'
Yi winked, but it was way above Preston's head.
'The other acts were good too. Aerosmith…Cheryl Crow, Spin Doctors…. Anyway.'
'Who are all those people?'
Preston pointed to the gathering of people in the field. They heard some distant acoustic guitar and rhythmic clapping.
'Let's go over,' Lara said, allowing a sense of nostalgia to get the better of her.

'Do you remember the exact spot you were?'

'Nope.'

'How come?'

Yi looked askance at Preston.

As they got closer Preston said, 'Wow, that's an impressive audio set.' He pointed to a stack of speakers, antenna and computers. 'I used to DJ in high school and college.'

'And look at that. It's all wired to a satellite dish.'

Preston walked up to the electronics array. Sitting before a large mixing board was a clean cut technician wearing headphones.

'That is some serious equipment,' Preston said.

'Yeah,' replied the technician. 'Hope they're listening. I ain't cheap.'

'Who?'

'The aliens. This is all going right to them.'

'Oh wow.'

Lara and Preston walked up to the assembly. They listened as an older, bearded gentleman spoke into a microphone, preaching to the hundred or so assembled people. Looking closely, Lara saw the man's collar. He spoke at length about Martin Luther. Lara was impressed with the man's sincerity. After a bit the preacher saw Lara and Preston and turned his attention directly to them. Lara held up her hand and waved. The preacher smiled and waved back. When he was finished he handed the microphone to an old hippy lady who talked about telekinetic positive energy.

'This lady is useless,' Lara said, 'Let's go.'

As they went back to the car Preston asked, 'What makes that priest more useful?'

Lara shrugged. 'His faith is real.'

'And that hippy lady's isn't?'

'I have no idea what telekinetic energy is supposed to be.'

They drove back to the resort, Jackie was waiting there and he did not have good news.

'Look, Lara, I've spoken to the mayor, and he agrees, we can't just go up-ending our work schedule for this place. And he's not so sure about bringing a bunch of refugees into town.'

'Mr. Jackie,' Yi said, putting on her negotiating voice, 'We have the prospect of millions of displaced persons coming north from New York City. They have to go somewhere.'

'I'm sorry, Lara, but the mayor's answer is no.'

Yi stared at Jackie for a long second and decided further arguing was pointless. 'Very well, Mr. Jackie.'

Yi and Preston got back in the car. 'Move on?' Preston asked.

'Not on your life,' said Yi. 'Let's go into Monticello, I want to check out the racetrack and casino.'

'I didn't know you were a gambler.'

'I'm not, idiot.'

'Oh.'

'Drive.'

On the way over, Lara phoned a colleague in the U.S. Attorney's Office for Southern New York. Preston heard only Lara's end of the conversation.

'Yeah, the Pines. The town has ownership of the place…yeah that's right. Complete non-cooperation. No, the utility guys are cooperative and are working on the problem…you can…this afternoon? Great. I gotta go.'

They pulled into the casino parking lot. It was jammed, Preston was only able to find a spot at the back near the gate.

'Jesus,' he said. 'This place is packed.'

'Lot's of people going out with a bang.'

Indeed. In several spots the parking lot was filled with revelers, people tailgating beside open grills and coolers, several just sitting in their cars and drinking. A few were obscured in thick smoke. Of course, a couple of cars rocked back on their shocks. Fortunately, people were too busy with their revelry to notice Yi and Preston. Once in the casino the scene repeated itself but on a vaster scale. They were met by a cacophony of shouts, screams, laughs, crashes, fist fights all to the beat of slot machines. If people inside the casino had guns, they'd be firing them into the air.

'Uhhhhhh…' Preston said.

'Exactly.'

'Who's in charge here?'

'Nobody,' said Yi.

They made their way through the crowd. Preston remained alert and prepared to defend Lara, but everyone was far too concerned with their own fun to bother with them.

'Look at those three…err four people,' he said.

'Prude.'

By then they were lost in a sea of reveling people.

'I think we're stuck!' Preston shouted.

Lara looked around for a way out of the scrum. A large man in a red blazer grabbed her wrist and said, 'Come with me, folks.'

Lara in turn grabbed Preston's wrist as the red blazered man lead them off to the side.

'You two alright?'

'How did you know we needed help?' Lara asked.

'Look around,' the man said. 'You two don't look like you're here for a good time. No offense ma'am, you're wearing too many clothes for that.'

'I see,' Lara replied. There was no arguing with that logic. 'Can I see the manager?'

'Sure, who are you?'

'Lara Yi, FEMA.'

He raised an eyebrow. 'FEMA? OK, sure. Come with me.'

The man unlocked a door and led them into long corridor to a small office.

It was nondescript with a battered desk, undecorated walls and a pair of florescent lights. Behind the desk sat a prim looking woman more or less Yi's age. A placard read 'Stern'. Yi took note of Stern's business suit attire, gray suit, blue blouse, and well-tailored. Her hair and makeup were perfect. Yi liked her right away.

Stern looked up from her desk and said, 'You're Lara Yi.'

Yi held out her hand, 'How do you do?'

'Fine,' Stern said as she shook Yi's hand. 'I remember you very well from the campaign. Interesting shenanigans you pulled, no?'

'Yes, well…' Yi said. Preston was surprised to see his boss look uncomfortable for once.

'I don't suppose you're here to gamble.'

'This is your office?' Lara asked looking around at the sparse accommodations.

'This is more of a ready room,' Stern said, 'I have an ornate office upstairs. But I like to work down here. Close to the action.'

'You have a lot of action. This is quite an operation you have here, Ms. Stern.'

'People are blowing off steam.'

'Is that what this is? A public service?'

'No, we are a money making operation and making money we are. The marketing department began a three-day two-night campaign.' Stern positioned her hands as if showing a gleaming sign '*Go Out with a Bang!*'

'Ah.'

'It's always like this. I have to close the casino from two to six, but otherwise, it's always jammed.'

'Speaking of closing the casino…'

'Oh no.'

Yi held out her hands. 'Now hold on…not yet, not any time soon.'

Stern sighed. 'I suppose you want me to convert this place into a refugee center.'

'I do.'

'You're looking at our floor and thinking you can house a couple thousand people here.'

'At least.'

'When I inform the board of your visit, they'll freak out.'

'Am I going to get trouble from you?'

Stern thought for a moment, 'I suppose it makes sense to bow to the inevitable.'

'Look, Ms. Stern. It's Ms. Right?'

'Do I look like I have time for a family?'

'No one is saying you have to shut down. You just have to be prepared to take in refugees. Probably nothing will happen. You're a gambler, right?'

'Na,' said Stern. 'I know the odds. My training is in finance.'

'But you know being prepared is a good bet.'

'It's not a bad one,' Stern said. 'We can clear out the slots, make room for cots, sleeping bags and the like.'

'So glad to hear.'

'A thousand people.'

'Probably more.'

'Ok, two thousand?'

Yi nodded.

'Shouldn't put stress on the wash facilities.' She looked at Yi. 'I assume you're going to provide us with provisions?'

'MREs to start. We are making other arrangements as well.'

'Security?'

'I'm afraid that's up to you.'

'Well, we can always hire more people…'

'Can you have a plan for me this evening?'

'Sure,' Stern said as her mind was already lost in the solving the problem at hand.

'Wonderful. I can see you're busy. We'll find our own way out.'

In the car Yi said, 'Smart woman, I like her.'

'Sure you do,' replied Preston. 'She's just like you.'

'Let's head over to the resort.'

Preston listened to sports radio on the way over. After the bloviating host cut to commercial, a government PSA came on.

'Remember,' a great disembodied female voice said, 'Towns should stock two weeks' worth of non-perishable food items, equip a refugee space for fifty persons, and plan for extended periods of isolation…'

'You know what's not in that Public Service Announcement?' Yi asked.

'Uh…no.'

'They're telling towns to stock up on weapons and ammunition.'

'Really?'

'If needed.'

'People are going to fight the aliens? What is this, *Red Dawn*?'

'The FBI is already establishing teams throughout the country to coordinate resistance.'

'Jesus.'

At the resort entrance, Walker and Jackie were waiting, as was a car from the county sheriff. When Jackie saw them pull up, he got out of the cab of his truck and angrily walked toward Yi.

'You Bitch!' he shouted. He stomped toward Yi, his fists clenched in anger. Then they were raised in anger. Yi stepped back in anticipation of Jackie's fist. Instead Preston stepped forward and blocked the punch and then another. Preston pushed Jackie away and got down in a stance, his fists raised. The burly Jackie was surprised and didn't move. By then Walker had run up behind him with the Sheriff.

'Easy there, Bill,' Walker said.

'You know what this cunt did?'

'Yeah.'

Jackie held up a federal writ. 'She has a court order transferring operation of this property to the federal government.'

Yi smiled. 'If you had shown any willingness to cooperate, Mr. Jackie I wouldn't have gotten the order.'

Jackie stepped forward. So did Preston, who said, 'You try that again I'll drop you.'

Walker put a hand on Jackie's shoulder. 'C'mon Bill. You've already lost. You try anything else she'll have the sheriff bring you in. You want that? The woman just got a federal judge to do what she wants. What do you suppose she could do to you?'

Jackie actually growled. 'Fine! You want this place? It's all yours. Have fun, sweetheart.'

Jackie walked back to his truck and drove off.

'Thank you, Mr. Walker,' Lara said.

'No problem.'

She looked at Preston, 'And you.,,'

'I've been taking karate since I was ten.'

'You could really have hurt him.'

'First time I ever had to use the stuff.'

Walker said, 'You'll have power in a few days. I don't know what you'll do with this place. The town won't be helping you, that's for sure.'

'Well,' said Lara 'thanks again.' She turned to Preston. 'Let's go in and see what we have.'

The sheriff opened the gate.

The courtyard was completely overgrown. The hotel was divided into several buildings, some were rooms for accommodations, one for staff, and a pair that had been recreational. Piles of chipped concrete lay before the buildings. The portico of one building had collapsed. All the windows were broken, some simply via the passage of time, many with round holes in them had clearly been shot out by vandals.

'C'mon let's see the inside.'

'In there?'

'What are you worried about?'

The door to one of the buildings hung on its hinge.

'Whoa.'

Inside the floor was covered entirely in moss, soft and wet as they walked down the corridor. The walls were water stained and in many places pock marked with paint ball splotches. All the rooms were open, most still had 1960's era furniture in them, with cheap modular pieces and water stained mattresses. In one room they found several shriveled up condoms.

'What kind of girl would have sex in a room like that?' Preston asked.

'One without self-worth.'

Yi walked into another room. She punched the wall, it held up to her fist, and jumped on the floor. It was dirty but solid. She repeated the same experiment in a few other rooms.

'Down and dirty but still habitable.'

'Seriously?'

They continued deeper into the resort to an hourglass shaped pool. An arch connected the two halves. Yi walked over it and stood in the middle. She looked around.

'I bet we could house thousands of people here if we had to.'

'Seriously.'

'Why not?'

'How are we going to get this place fixed up?'

'Hmmmmm…' She thought for a moment and then started searching on her phone. 'That's it.'

'What?'

'To Home Depot.'

'Home Depot?'

'There's one just a few miles away.'

Like other hardware stores Home Depot was packed. A constant stream of people walked in, or walked out with a large cart. Many were filled with lumber. Yi saw one with a generator on it and another packed with power tools. A line of pickup trucks waited at the contractor pickup zone. These too were loaded with building materials. In what had previously been the garden center, the staff had built a great fortress of plywood and lumber, a massive gathering that rivaled photos of World War I era ammo dumps. Several people walked atop the great assemblage of wood. The lawyer in Yi winced at the liability exposure. Off to the side, a dozen or so Hispanic men milled about.

Yi walked over to them.

'You sure you should be going over there?'

'What, you think they're Mexican narco-terrorist kidnappers?'

'I…'

'Shut up.'

'Ok.'

She turned to the laborers. 'Aye Muchachos!'

One man stood up. 'Si?'

'¿Quién quiere trabajar?'

'Aye,' said the man. 'Caballers!'

'Dinero en efectivo. Diario!'

'Si! Si!'

'¿Tienes transporte?'

The man pointed to a pair of pickups parked by the side.

Yi gave them the address. The man punched it into his phone and nodded.

'See. You. There.' He said in broken English.

'Traer palas!'

'Aye! Muchachos. Palas!'

Back in the car, Preston asked, 'You speak Spanish?'

'No, dipshit I was temporarily possessed.' Yi rolled her eyes. 'I did a lot of immigration law.'

'Oh,' said Preston. 'You sure you should be hiring illegals?'

'I want to get The Pines habitable. I couldn't care less how. Those guys want to work.'

'Yeah.'

'And there's plenty of other hotels to fix up.'

'Really think we'll need them?'

'Honestly? I have no idea.'

'I thought you were an expert at reading people.'

She raised an eyebrow at that. 'Well, if you must know what I think, it doesn't make much sense to fly trillions of miles just to conquer a planet.'

'I'm terrified.'

'There is no point in speculating. We'll know in three weeks and one day.'

'I guess.'

'Now, we're going to head to Jersey tomorrow. I'll send the destination to your phone.'

Preston looked and said, 'Peapack? Where the hell is that?'

'About forty minutes west of the Lincoln Tunnel. A few months ago we had a meeting there with Pfizer about pharmaceutical production, they have a big campus there. It could house a lot of people…'

Arrival + Ten Days

The sky flashed.

'What was that?' Preston asked.

'No idea,' Yi replied without looking up from her phone.

'Could you take a look, at least? That was a big one.'

'They finally got the network back up, I need to send some messages. Don't know how long it will stay running.'

The sky flashed again. 'Jeez look at that.'

'Mmm.'

'I bet that was a nuke.'

'Uh huh.'

'Look, up there. Alien ships!'

'Sure....' Yi still didn't look up from her phone. 'Just drive.'

'But the aliens,' Preston mockingly pleaded.

'They can wait till we get to the Pfizer campus.'

'Well here's the turn off.'

Yi finally looked up.

Preston drove down a long access ramp. Approaching the facilities' front gate they saw several security guards and a pair of policemen. One of the security guards stepped forward and held up his hand. Yi handed her identification to Preston who gave it to the guard. He gave the ID a quick look over and handed it back.

'OK, park in the garage over there.'

There was a low rumble and high up in the night sky an expanding explosion of blue fire.

'Damn,' said the guard. 'Somebody got something.'

Several ambulances were parked in the garage. EMT crews did maintenance on their vehicles or simply lounged in anticipation of the next call. Several slept on gurneys. One looked up from a defibrillator he was servicing and saw Preston and Yi.

'Feds?' he asked.

Yi ignored him.

'Hey! I'm talking to you!'

'Keep walking,' said Yi.

'I know,' Preston replied.

The EMT followed them, 'When you gonna get off your asses and get us some supplies?!'

The EMT caught up to them. Preston turned around and said, 'back off.'

'You gonna make me?' He reached out for Yi.

Preston grabbed the EMT's wrist and twisted, forcing the man around and to the ground. He cast the man's arm away, 'Leave us alone.'

Another EMT stood but Preston stared him down. Preston looked mad, and his three day's growth gave him a vaguely menacing feel. He looked down at his knuckles, still sore from a confrontation at a rest area the day before. He had to punch a raving man in the face and then sweep his legs out from under him.

Preston and Yi walked in through the garage entrance. This put them at the beginning of a vast underground tunnel which linked the Pfizer Campus' half dozen buildings. Once inside they were blasted by heavy air pungent with the smell of body odor.

'Wow,' Preston said.

'We don't smell so good either.'

'Five days on the road.'

On the left side of the corridor was row after row of bunks and to the right, folding chairs leaving enough room for a person with a cart to walk through. Each and every bunk and chair was occupied. Only every third fluorescent light was on.

Yi looked at Preston. 'You wearing anything that can ID you as a Fed?'

'No.'

'Let's go.'

They had learned the hard way that walking through a refugee center with Federal markings meant being swarmed by desperate people. Mostly, the thousands of people in the tunnel looked bored. Many slept or sat about reading books or chatting. Ever present was the sound of hand held video games played by children. Now that the power was back, dozens and dozens of power cords were plugged into the wall or snaked up to the ceiling. Every hundred yards or so was a small atrium originally meant for impromptu meetings and contemplation. Each had a shaft leading up to ground level, capped off with a glass dome. These had been painted black against nuclear blasts. No one in the tunnel had gotten any sun in several days.

Near the end of the tunnel Mr. Lele waited.

'Good of you to come, Ms. Yi,' he said.

'That's my job. Can we talk in your office?'

'Yes, this way.'

He lead them up a stairway to the ground floor.

They were in the Pfizer cafeteria. As planned this had been turned into an infirmary. Hundreds of people were here on guerneys and cots or cafeteria tables. At the head of each impromptu bed was a bucket, hundreds of them, which made for a strong stench. Everyone wore masks. Hundreds of other people milled out, some stood, others leaned against the walls, some lay down and slept. Yi held her hand against her nose. Preston ran to the corner, found a garbage can and threw up.

'What the hell is this?' Yi asked through grinding teeth.

'Well, the plumbing comes and goes and people are afraid to go outside to empty the buckets.'

'You idiot you have a Geiger counter. We just came from outside and everything is fine.'

'I...'

'Shut up. You're fired.'

'What?'

'You're fired. Go get me your subordinate.'

'You can't....'

Yi held out her phone. 'Press the button. It will put you right in touch with the president. Try me.'

Lele didn't take the phone.

'Now go get your assistant and have him...or her meet me in your office. Where is it?'

Lele pointed to a door by the kitchen.

'Move.' She turned to Preston. 'You done hurling, sweetie? C'mon.'

She went to Lele's office and sat at his desk. To her surprise it was organized and she easily found his files, kept by hand. She nodded in approval. Everything was to be computerized and hard-copied in case of blackout. Yi flipped through the roster. More than five thousand people had signed into the Pfizer facility. Over a thousand of these reported some kind of injury. Lists of food stocks showed these were depleted but still adequate for several more days. Eighteen people had died at Peapack, eleven from wounds, two suicides and the rest heart attacks.

A middle-aged woman came into the office.

'I am Sally Reardon, Mr. Lele's assistant.'

'You're in charge here, Ms. Reardon.'

'Uhhhh…'

'If you don't like it we can call the president and she can explain it to you.'

'Ok.'

'Now,' Yi began, 'The infirmary above is a disgrace. I wouldn't be surprised if Lele has started a dysentery epidemic. What the hell happened here?'

'Well the electricity and the plumbing…'

Yi angrily slammed her closed fist on the desk. 'The Raritan River is less than a quarter mile from here. Send some people to wash out the buckets and bring fresh water.'

'Ok.'

'Make it happen. Now. Or I'll come back here and fire you.'

'OK.' Reardon said, 'We can use the golf carts…'

Disgusted, Yi left the office, 'C'mon Preston, let's get out of here.'

As they drove out of the complex Preston said, 'How many times are you going to use that fist pounding the desk trick?'

'As many times as I need to.'

'Won't it only work once?'

'So I will use it once. Once at each location.'

Yi's phone buzzed, actually startling her.

'Haven't heard that for a while.'

'Yeah nice to have the phone back up and running.'

'Shh,' Yi replied. 'This is from Washington.'

'Wash…'

Yi held up her hand for quiet.

'Yes, chief,' Yi said. 'Yes. Yes we can do that. Right away. She wants us up there, we will go up there and check things out, okay, I…right.'

'So what's up?'

'We're heading to New York City.'

'Is it smart to go there?'

'The president wants a report, she gets a report.'

'Why can't she call the mayor?'

'You'll learn, kid.'

'What?'

'She trusts me. Let's go.'

They took it slow up the New Jersey Turnpike, even though the northbound spur was almost empty. Nobody was heading to NYC. The south bound spur was filled with cars and became more choked as they drove north. At the split for the Lincoln Tunnel and the George Washington Bridge, the State Troopers had closed off the far left lane, leaving it for 'official' traffic. State Troopers also blocked off the entrance ramp for the Lincoln Tunnel; why would anyone want to get in? Yi showed them her ID and a car escorted them toward the entrance.

They drove through darkened Weehawken; the road wound down toward the tunnel. The exit was jammed with cars moving at ten miles an hour. From there they could see Manhattan, which was also blacked out. The great buildings and skyscrapers' dark shadows silhouetted against the night. Tiny lights flickered across the island, small lamps, candles, even barrel fires.

'Wow,' said Preston, 'I never saw Manhattan like this.'

'Meh,' said Yi. 'I was there during the blackout of 2003.'

'Oh.'

The State Trooper led them through the tolls, (all but one was closed) and then pulled over. He rolled down the window. 'Ok, folks. NYPD is on the other side and has been told to expect you.'

'Thank you!'

The tunnel was dark.

'I halfway expect to run into aliens.'

'They haven't landed here.'

'I mean like from the movie.'

'Shut up.'

A line of NYPD cruisers waited on the other side. An officer walked forward to the driver's side. He leaned down and spoke, 'OK, Ms. Yi remember, wherever you go just keep your lights on and the doors locked.'

'Oh honestly, officer,' said Yi, 'I was here in the 2003 blackout, the streets were fine. 1977 won't happen again.'

'So was I, Ms. Yi. You've seen New York during a blackout, but you haven't seen it during an alien invasion. People are scared.'

'On 9/11 I lived in Soho. I've seen scared New Yorkers.'

William Stroock

'Just be careful.'

'Will do. Thank you officer.'

They drove up 42nd Street and through Times Square; it was dark and empty.

'It was like this the night of 9/11.'

'Where did all the people go? Remember seeing that footage the night the aliens got here? It was jammed.'

Yi vividly recalled Times Square filled with thousands of people. Many had gathered to watch Arrival on the big TV only to be horrified when the aliens started shooting. All kinds of people were in the square that night; peace activists holding hands and singing Kum Ba Ya, conspiracy theorists claiming the aliens were a Jewish plot, Seventh Day Adventists saying the aliens were the return of Christ, Muslims praying for the aliens to annihilate Israel, Tea Party types demanding the nation's liberal president unleash nuclear Armageddon on the aliens, race hustlers who insisted that so technologically advanced aliens had to be black, and on and on. It was Woodstock, the Haj to Mecca and the Hindu pilgrimage all rolled into one, right up until the moment one group of protestors started a fight with another group. The authorities never had been able to determine who started it. A riot ensued. With an alien invasion unfolding above, the NYPD had no choice but to let the riot run out on its own. Dozens were killed. The Times Square Riot was the worst violence the city had seen since the Civil War.

'I guess people decided the smart thing was to stay home,' said Preston.

'That and the police decided for them, here's a road block.'

Indeed all exits to the square were blocked off by barriers. Yi talked her way through one of the points.

They proceeded across Midtown. Here and there people shuffled down the streets, flashlights in hand. Groups of people also gathered around barrel fires, hands held out to the flames, shifting from one foot to the other against the cold autumn air. People looked askance at Preston and Yi as they drove past. At one intersection, several men walked out into the street to try to block them.

'Keep going.'

'But...'

'I said keep going. In fact, floor it.'

Preston did as he was told. All of the men except one got out of the way, he jumped onto the hood and plastered his face against the front windshield. He wasn't threatening, not really. He was college age and was laughing manically.

'Slam on the brakes!' Yi shouted.

Preston duly applied the brake; the kid went flying back, and got onto his hands and knees and scrambled toward the sidewalk.

Preston drove on.

Ahead someone else stepped into the road and threw a brick that bounced off the trunk of the car.

'Hey!'

'Just keep going,' said Yi.

'What is wrong with all these people?'

'Just freaking out, I guess,' Yi said.

At another intersection a crowd of people were holding hands and dancing in a circle.

Yi laughed. 'Hear that?'

'What are they singing?'

'I feel fine. I feel fine, over and over again.'

'Huh?'

'As in -...*it's the end of the world as we know it, I feel fine.*'

'Never heard of it.'

'What's your cultural reference point, Preston? Jesus.'

They passed this group unmolested.

Coming up on Park they saw several police cars, fire trucks and ambulances.

'What's this?'

'I don't know.'

A pair of officers stepped forward and motioned for Preston to stop. He rolled down the window and handed them Yi's ID.

'OK, go on through.'

Preston took back the ID and asked, 'What's going on?'

'We keep getting jumpers on the Met Life Building.'

'Oh.'

Yi leaned over and said, 'You know, there's a bunch of people standing out in the street back there. Throwing bricks and blocking traffic.'

The officer replied, 'Lady, right now there are thousands of them. Move along.'

'Ok,' Yi said. 'Let's go.'

They turned north onto the West Side Highway. Here the road was lined with army trucks and even tanks.

'Wow! Look at that!' Preston said, pointing to the blasted out hulk of the *Intrepid*.

'The Aliens blew up the *Intrepid?* It's a museum.'

'Just looks like a carrier to them.'

Yi nodded. 'Makes sense.'

Here the traffic thickened as people made their way north out of the city. They slowed to ten miles per hour in the stop and go traffic.

There was a flash to the west, and then another to the north, up the river beyond the George Washington Bridge. Suddenly, across the river, the Palisades lit up. Preston slammed the brakes hard enough to jolt Yi forward.

'What the hell?'

'Traffic has stopped, look.'

He pointed across the river to the Palisades. The great plateau was alive with light as missile after missile streaked into the air.

'Wow.'

Another volley let loose, and then another. They left contrails trailing up into the northern sky and in the distance, Yi and Preston saw tiny dots of light.

Preston opened the driver's side door and got out.

'What are you doing?!' Yi shouted.

'We're not going anywhere. Might as well watch the action.'

They saw a series of great ground level explosions to the north. As fire billowed into the sky the sound of explosions reached the West Side Highway and distantly rumbled almost like a car going over rumble strips.

'Whoa.'

'At least that's different than wow,' she mocked.

Preston turned around and opened his mouth, but before he could say anything there was a flash of light over the Palisades that slammed him to the ground. That was the last thing Yi remembered seeing…

Arrival + 15 Days

'We weren't prepared for this,' said Yi.

'No,' replied the National Guard colonel. She hadn't bothered learning his name and she couldn't see his tag in the fading light. He was a large African American man. His face weary and unshaven. He looked like he hadn't slept in days.

'Colonel, I don't know what I can get you.'

'We need help, Ms. Yi.'

'We are working on it.'

'Working on it?' the National Guard colonel asked. 'Just what the hell does that mean?'

'It means I will get you the help I can, when I can.'

'Is that right?'

'It is.'

Behind the National Guard colonel, the road was packed with refugees streaming away from the coast and into the Imperial Valley. They were a disheveled and sad looking lot. People who had gotten away from the coast after the Jai practically annihilated most of the state.

'You see those people?'

'I do.

'Tomorrow I'll have a special unit drive down the road just to pick up bodies. There will be hundreds.'

Yi nodded.

'Last night a brawl broke out on this road. My troops shot and killed two people to stop it.'

The National Guard colonel held out his Tablet. It showed a map of California. 'You see this mushroom cloud here? This is San Diego. You see the one?'

'Yes I know L.A. The Jai didn't use nukes though.'
'Does it matter? Millions of people are coming here. Don't you get that?'
'Isn't this the agricultural hub of Southern California.'
'Not for millions and millions of people.'
'Colonel, for the time being you will just have to make do.'
'That's impossible.'
'Let me explain something to you, Colonel. I just flew out here from the North East. In the mountains of New York are hundreds of thousands of people out of the city wondering how they are going to survive the winter. You know what a New York winter can be like? Now you don't have food but you have water and the weather. When we get New York situated help will come.'
'I don't…'
'Right now, people are desperate in New York. They come first. Then you.'
The National Guard Colonel threw up his hands in disgust and walked away.
Yi thought about following the National Guard colonel but went back to her car instead. Beneath the light she looked at her face.
'Time to change the dressing.'
Slowly she peeled the bandages from her face, revealing dozens of tiny pock marks made by bits of Preston's shattered skull. Yi winced as she ran a baby wipe across the side of her face.
'You need a hand?' asked Kayvon, her new U.S. Marshall escort.
'Na, I got it.'
'We received first aid training in the navy you know.'
'I got it.'
When Yi was satisfied she cleaned the wounds out and looked at her pock marked and scarred face. 'Guess I'll never get married now.'
'You're not…'
'Shut up.'
Yi placed a fresh bandage across her face.
'I didn't do it, ma'am.'
'Get us out of here.'
'Alright,' Kayvon said. 'Where to?'
'Get us back to the airport.'

'Ok.'

Kayvon did a U-turn around several National Guard vehicles and took them back toward Palm Springs International. As they traveled east, the highway foot traffic thinned out, but there were still large groups of people camped or simply milling about on the side of the road. Several cars were behind and in front of them, all civilian. The westbound spur traffic was entirely military, a seemingly unending column of trucks and Humvees making their way toward the battle area on the coast.

'Man I hope my folks are ok,' Kayvon said.

'Where are they?' Yi asked.

'Sacramento.'

Yi checked her phone. 'According to this update it wasn't hit.'

'Can I call them?'

'What about your phone?'

'It is not one of those fancy government phones like what you have.'

'Sure.'

Kayvon pulled over, a car angrily honked as it drove past.

'What are you doing?'

Kayvon held out his hand for the phone. 'Now.'

'Right now?'

'You don't know how long that thing is going to work.'

'Alright.'

Kayvon took the phone and dialed.

'It's me, mom.'

Yi heard Kayvon's mom on the other end.

'Yeah, Mom. No, Mom. I'm working. I'm a Federal marshal, you know. Yes I know the power is out there. It's out everywhere right now. Look, Mom… no, I can't call someone…' He looked over at Yi, 'Look, Mom, you have plenty of food? Water? Okay….Okay…Mom I don't know where Deshawn is…I'm a little busy…I…'

Yi got out of the car and stretched. The night air was cool. To the west the horizon glowed yellow and orange, faint but constant. Yi saw a few blue lights high up in the sky, almost indistinguishable from the stars except they were moving across the sky toward the Pacific. The night was actually quite beautiful. Yi smiled but winced at the pain in her face.

'Hey...'

Yi turned around. Half a dozen people were standing in the desert scrub. She couldn't tell anything more about them in the lightless night.

'Ummm, hey.'

'Got any food?'

Two of them stepped forward.

'Sorry I don't have anything.'

'How about money?'

The two men kept coming forward.

'Listen you guys, you better back off?'

'Why you some sort of Japanese ninja?'

One of those men then reached out and grabbed Yi's wrist and pulled. She felt a bolt of pain up her arm and fell to the ground with a shout. Another man was standing over her. Then she heard two gun shots and a then a third. The man before her was gone, and the other lying on the ground. Behind them two women screamed.

'You shot my husband! You shot him!'

'Well he was attacking my boss!' Kayvon shouted. 'Step back now!'

The two women kept screaming, and then they heard children crying.

'Oh my God,' Yi said.

'I said get back!' Kayvon shouted.

Yi picked herself up. She couldn't feel her right arm and cradled it in her left. She winced in pain.

'Get on the ground!' Kayvon shouted.

'You shot him!'

'Now!'

The two women and the kids behind them got down on the ground. Kayvon grabbed Yi by the scruff and pulled her over to the car.

'Ouch! Crap! What are you doing?!'

'We are getting out of here!'

'We have to...'

'Shut up! Look around at all these people! We're about to get lynched!' Kayvon shouted, 'Everyone get the fuck back. Now!'

He opened the passenger door and shoved Yi inside and then got in over her, roughly jostling Yi and sending a shot of white-hot pain up her arm. He locked the doors and looked at Yi's phone.

'What are you doing?'

'I'm trying to call for some help…no signal.'

He held the screen to Yi. She took it and tapped the number in. 'It was working a second ago right?'

Someone jumped onto the hood of the car.

'Oh crap!' Kayvon shouted.

'We better…'

Kayvon was cut off by a series of loud booms from the sky. The people gathering around the car looked up and then ran away in all directions. The booms stopped, then came again, louder than before and then louder still. Kayvon and Yi looked up through the windshield, dumbfounded until yet another boom, so close and loud that it cracked the windshield and rocked the car back on its shocks.

'Oh crap! Get out!' Kayvon said.

'Isn't it safer…'

'No! We have a gas tank!'

The angry mob had dispersed, leaving Yi and Kayvon alone beside the car. Now they could see what was making the booms, wave after wave of U.S. Air Force jets heading west, low and at supersonic speed. Off to the west were pinpricks of light in the night sky, and long green lasers stabbing out at seemingly invisible targets. They saw an orange ball of fire, then another, then a whole series of tiny yellow pinpricks of light.

'What's that sound?' Yi asked as a different droning sound vibrated through the air.

'I don't know…oh wait, I recognize that from my navy time. Those are missiles.'

They heard more jet engine sounds and looked up. These were much higher. In the air, at least 10,000 feet up were a quartet of blue dots. Blue lasers emanated from them, stabbing out through the sky west toward the pacific. Gradually the aerial duel migrated west and the noise of battle above subsided, like a thunderstorm gradually receding.

'Come on,' Kayvon said.

'Let's get out of here before those people come back.

'Alright.'

After a few minutes on the road, Yi was crying.

Kayvon looked over and said, 'I could have let those people kill you, you know.'

'You just made a widow and a bunch of orphans.' She winced at the pain in her elbow. 'Ah, Jesus this hurts.' She ground her teeth against the pain and then laughed.

'What the hell is so funny?'

'I always thought the Iowa Caucus would be the worst thing I ever did.'

'What the hell are you talking about?' Kayvon asked.

'I hope it was worth it, Kelly…'

'Huh?'

'Winning is everything right?'

Kayvon listened as Yi babbled. It made no sense to him, something about rumors, and vans and tires, until finally she said 'Two more people dead because of me…'

Now Kayvon got mad. 'Maybe they shouldn't have attacked a federal agent,' Kayvon said. 'Maybe they should have thought of that before they tried to mug you.'

'Yeah, I know.'

'What about all the people who didn't attack you?'

Yi said nothing.

'You got any answers for them?'

Yi cried.

'And what the hell you crying for anyway?' he demanded. 'I'm the one with blood on my hands. You see me crying? No. You know why? Because when I signed up to be a federal marshal after the navy, I knew I might have to shoot somebody.'

'You ever shoot anyone?' asked Yi. 'Before this, I mean?'

'No.'

Yi's phone came back on just as they were approaching the Palm Springs turn off. The exit ramp was blocked by several police cars.

She seemed to snap out of her stupor. 'God damn it,' said Yi. 'They're not supposed to do that.'

Kayvon pulled the car up. He flashed the lights and rolled the window down.

'Federal agents,' he said to the police officer as he handed him their IDs.

Yi said, 'You have to allow traffic you know.'

'Yes, ma'am,' the cop said without looking at the IDs.

'You can't have this road block.'

'Take it up with the mayor.'

'I will.'

The cop handed the ID's back to Kayvon. He waved them through.

'I'll take it up with the president!'

As they drove into Palm Springs Kayvon said, 'Can you still get through to her?'

'Barely.'

They went right to the airport.

Since arriving in southern California, Yi had operated out of the airport, renting out the airport manager's facilities, working and sleeping out of his plush office. The airport itself was ringed with National Guard troops. One cargo aircraft was lined up on the tarmac, as was a small four seater aircraft that was pressed into service for information gathering and message delivery. Next to the airport, the Palm Springs Golf Course was dotted by large tarps, beneath which were millions of rations. Yi looked out on the assemblage with pride. Seventy-two hours before, none of it had been there. Kayvon parked the car and they headed to the office.

'Hey look at that,' Kayvon said, pointing to the western sky.

Yi looked and saw a bunch of blue lights.

'Uh oh. I think those...'

Before Yi finished the airport sirens blared.

The mountains around the airport glowed with tiny flashes of light and the sky filled with tracer fire and small explosions. Suddenly there was a great orange flash in the sky and then another. Something on the airport tarmac exploded.

'Down!' Kayvon shouted.

He tackled Yi and shoved her to the ground. She screamed in pain as her already throbbing arm slammed against the asphalt. They heard more explosions; one was close enough to rock the car back on its shocks, and then the scream of engines. There was a fire and small secondary pops and the blare of the air raid sirens, but the jet engines receded. Kayvon pulled Yi out from under the car and helped her up. The cargo plane burned and so did the four-seater.

'Let's get out of here,' Kayvon said.

Yi knelt over as white-hot pain shot up her arm.

'Sorry.'

'Ugh...' Yi said. She gritted her teeth against the pain.

Kayvon took Yi by the shoulders and knelt against the car.

'I'm going to get you a gurney.'

'I don't need...' she tried to stand but winced in pain again 'OK.'

Kayvon came back with a wheelchair. He reached down to pick Yi up but she slapped him away.

'Stop treating me like your elderly grandmother.'

Yi stood and then plopped herself down in the chair.

'Can I do that now?' he asked angrily.

'Go.'

The air raid took the power offline. Inside, the terminal was illuminated by emergency lights. Dozens of airport employees had taken shelter inside.

Kayvon wheeled her to the emergency triage. Yi had organized a transit hospital in the Sonny Bono Concourse. There gas generators kept the two operating theaters operational. They had a hundred cots, each individually screened off. Most had patients. The entire facility smelled of bleach. Yi found this comforting, a sign her organizational efforts were working. An admin nurse pointed them to a waiting area of army cots and folding chairs. Several people sat or lay down. One man on a cot slowly shifted from side to side, groaning with each move. Next to him, a man with a bandaged head and broken arm appeared to be sleeping.

Kayvon saw a triage nurse and waved to her. Clipboard in hand she came over. 'Need to get this facial wound re-dressed?'

'My elbow,' Yi said.

'Ah, ok,' the triage nurse wrote. 'Can I have some ID?'

Yi took her federal ID out of her pocket, she didn't have a driver's license. As the nurse took down her particulars, Yi looked her over. She seemed tired, with bags under her eyes and short black hair in a ponytail. Yi saw a star tattoo behind the triage nurse's ear. Her hospital scrubs were clean, though. She asked. 'How are things here?'

'Fine,' said the nurse without looking up from her clipboard.

'I mean, do you have everything you need?'

Now she looked up. 'What's it to you?' She looked down at the federal ID. 'Oh, I've heard of you…sure!' the nurse said enthusiastically. 'Lot's of people coming in and out.'

'Any shortages?'

The triage nurse shook her head. 'We had a flight come in this morning.'

'Good.'

'One minute.'

The nurse went over and spoke to the admin, turned around and waved for Yi to come over. Kayvon wheeled her over.

'C'mon back,' said the admin nurse.

Yi said, 'You don't need to bump me to the front of the line because of who I am.'

'Sure I do,' the admin nurse said. 'We need to get you on your feet and running things.'

'Oh.'

'Dr. Chandra will see you shortly.' She pointed to a screened in cot. 'Over there.'

Inside Kayvon said, 'Alright. A little preferential treatment.'

'Shut up.'

An Indian man in a white coat said, 'I'm Dr. Chandra Ms. Yi. What seems to be the problem?'

Yi pointed to her arm.

'OK, let's take a quick look.'

Chandra knelt down beside Yi. She asked. 'You have everything you need?'

He looked up, 'Huh? Oh, you're that special presidential aide. I was wondering why they called me over here.'

'Lara Yi, yes.'

We are doing well enough.' He pointed back to the facility. 'You arranged all this?'

'I did.'

'Impressive. Your elbow is dislocated,' said the doctor.

'Well I, ARGHHHH!'

He quickly popped it back into place.

'Jesus!' Yi shouted.

'I'm Janist, actually.'

'Could you have warned me?'

'No. I don't have time for that. There are people here who need my help.'

Kayvon asked, 'You want something for the pain?'

'She can't have it. We'll need all the drugs we have for when refugees arrive.'

They heard fire engines in the distance. Dr. Chandra looked out the window. 'Now why did they do that?'

'What?' Yi asked.

'The Jai. They took out the Aviation Museum.'

'Why on earth would they do that?' asked Yi.

'They had a vintage P-51 Mustang out front.' Chandra shook his head. 'Damn.'

Kayvon laughed. 'That's it!' he laughed more. 'They saw all these old air planes there and just figured they were a threat.'

'You know, they do have an F-18 Hornet out front by the gate' said Chandra. 'The Jai must have assumed…'

'You know, it is pretty funny,' offered Yi. 'A few days ago we were in NYC when they blew up the *Intrepid*.'

Kayvon said, 'There's something about Earth they just don't get.'

Dr. Chandra shrugged.

'Maybe,' Kayvon said. 'They're getting jittery. I mean look at all that hardware we're throwing at them right now.'

'Hmmm.'

'Hear that?'

They heard far off explosions.

'That's not the Jai. That's the United States of America, giving it good.'

'And nukes,' said Dr. Chandra.

Yi shook her head. 'The president must hate that.'

'What?'

'The nukes.'

'That's what it takes,' offered Kayvon.

'She hates it.'

'You know what the president is thinking?'

'I know.' Yi looked at Dr. Chandra. 'Am I ok to go?'

'Yes, ma'am.'

Kayvon helped Yi up.

'Where to?'

'Back to the office.'

'Alright.'

When they got there a stack of papers was waiting for Yi.

'No way,' Kayvon said.

'Sorry?'

Kayvon pointed to the couch. 'Sleep!'

'Excuse me?'

'I said sleep. Get some rest.'

'First off, there is far too much work to do,' Yi began, 'second, who the hell do you think you are?'

'A federal marshal with an assignment, that's who. I'm supposed to keep you safe. You were delirious before, you know that?'

'No.'

'You don't remember, do you? You kept talking about Iowa and vans. You made no sense. You didn't snap out of it till we got to the Palm Springs road block.'

Yi thought for a moment. 'You know, I don't remember...'

'Yeah, exactly. Even when you're not behind a desk you're on the phone talking. You are burnt out.' He pointed at the couch. 'It's my job to protect you. So get some sleep.'

'But...'

'If the phone rings I'll take a message. Believe it or not, the world can get by without you. Capice?'

An hour later Kayvon nudged her awake.

'C'mon,' he said.

'What?' Yi asked groggily.

'We've been ordered to the airport?'

'Airport?'

Yi tried to sit up but winced in pain from her elbow and shoulder. She slumped back down on the couch.

'Ughhhh...' she said.

'C'mon,' Kayvon said. He took Yi's hand and tried to pull her off the couch, but all she felt was red hot pain shoot up her arm.

'We don't have time for this,' he said.

Yi groaned and closed her eyes. In seconds she was snoring.

He reached under Yi and tried to scoop her up in his arms. Yi's eyes opened wide and she yelped in pain. Kayvon dropped her back down on the couch eliciting more cries.

Yi drifted off and didn't see Kayvon leave or come back with Dr. Chandra. She vaguely heard snippets of conversation.

'What do you want me to do?...'

'I have to get her to the airport...'

'Well medically...'

'Doctor, this comes from the White House...'

Someone put pills in Yi's mouth and made her chew them up...

'Wake up.'

'Huh?'

'Wake up,' Kayvon said.

Yi sat up, this time she was on a plane.

'Holy crap, where the hell are we?'
'We're at the airport.'
'How the hell did we get here?'
'The doctor gave you some oxy so I could get you on the plane.'
'My arm doesn't hurt anymore.'
'It shouldn't. Not with all the pills Chandra gave you.'
'You had him dope me up?'
'Hey,' Kayvon said. 'We were ordered to the fly out by the White House.'
'Where to?'
'They didn't tell me. The pilot told me that we were headed for Sacramento for a meeting with the president.'

Yi looked out the window. They were flying low, about five thousand feet. To the west she saw a haze punctuated occasionally by smoke plumes rising in the sky.

'The Jai really nailed the coast, didn't they?'
'Why don't you get some more sleep?'
'You're meeting the president.'
'I just woke up.'
'You're all medicated, go back to sleep.'

Yi relented and closed her eyes.

When she opened them again they were on the ground and taxiing down a runway. The copilot opened the door and lowered the gangway. Yi and Kayvon walked down to a National Guard Humvee. The driver took them across the tarmac, past radar dishes, missile launchers and sandbag emplacements. They went into a garage where the driver turned off the ignition.

'We switch,' he said.

Yi shrugged. 'Ok.'

The driver took them over to a sedan marked 'Military Police.'

Two men in suits waited.

'Ms. Yi?' one asked.
'Yes.'
'Agent Harris, Secret Service. We'll take you to the meeting place.'
'You mean with the president?'

'Shhh...'

'Huh?'

'We think the Jai might be able to listen in on individual conversations.'

Yi shrugged. 'Very well.'

They got in the car and waited. The Humvee left first, only then did they drive out of the garage and out of the airport.

'Isn't this all a little melodramatic?' asked Yi. 'I mean, distant airports? Late night car transfers?'

Harris turned to face Yi. 'I'll tell you this, Ms. Yi, because of who you are. We've had a lot of security issues.'

'Security issues?'

'This is absolute top secret, ok?'

Yi nodded.

'Three days ago the Jai took a shot at the President of the United States.'

Yi raised her eye brows.

'They tracked Air Force One and then launched a suicidal attack on her motorcade. We think we badly underestimated their surveillance ability. Frankly, we don't know exactly what they can do. So we're taking some pretty severe precautions.'

'Let me guess, you guys want to put her in some bunker and she refuses.'

'Uh huh.'

'I know my old college roommate,' said Yi. 'I think she's really tough. One of the mistakes the Secret Service made on 9/11 was carrying the president all over the country. It made him look scared. He needed to look like he was in charge.'

'Well, we're worried about keeping her alive.'

The agents took them to a small Holiday Inn about five miles west of the airport and told them to wait in the lobby.

'God, my head is killing me.'

'Guess that's my fault.'

'I guess.'

'You were delusional again, you know.'

Yi looked askance at Kayvon.

'You were so gone you were talking about Iowa again.'

'Oh.'

'What's that about?'

She looked at Kayvon. 'You really don't know?'

'I've never followed politics.'

'Well, if you must know, I was on the president's campaign.'

'I knew that already.'

'I was head of the president's special committee.'

'Special committee?'

'That's what we called it. It was the dirty tricks squad.'

'Ohhhhhh.'

'We went into the Iowa Caucus in a dead heat with the other guy. The day of the caucus there was a snowstorm. We knew we were weak in certain sections of Des Moines, so with the snow coming down I sent some people to slash the tires of a bunch of plows. Keep people from coming out.'

'That's shitty.'

'It gets worse. A lot of people went out anyway. One van from a retirement home got in a wreck trying to get out in the snow. Four people were killed.'

'You suck,' said Kayvon.

'I certainly do.'

'They ever pin it on you?'

'Na, I'm too good at covering my tracks. I've been pulling dirty tricks for the president since her student council days.'

'That doesn't make it right.'

'No, it doesn't.'

'Wait a minute. You were some bigwig in her campaign, right?'

'Yeah.'

'Why didn't you get a job in the White House?'

Yi shook her head. 'After Iowa I was sick with myself.'

'You should have been.'

'After the announcement the president offered me a "dirty tricks" position.'

'Why not?'

'I wanted to make amends. Do something to help people.'

'Makes sense.'

'What about…'

Yi waved her hand. 'Enough.'

They drove on in silence till they came to a Days Inn. The Secret Service agent took them inside and asked them to sit in front of the hotel's small conference room.

The door opened, out stepped an assistant clad in jeans and boots. 'Ms. Yi,' she waved.

Yi gingerly sat up. 'Coming.'

She walked into the conference room. It was a small meeting room really, with a table, a couple of computers and a dozen chairs. The president sat at the end of the table. She stood up and smiled.

'It is good to see you, Lara,' she said.

The president looked thin and frail, like she had lost a few pounds.

'Thank you, Madam President.' Yi walked forward and extended her hand. The two shook. Then the president hugged Yi. 'Good to have you here, old friend.'

Yi backed up.

'What's wrong?'

Yi looked at the Secret Service agent, pointed to the president and said, 'That's not the president.'

'What do you mean? C'mon, Lara.'

Yi stepped back several feet. 'The president never called me Lara, never, ever. Whoever you are.'

Yi looked closer. The woman before her bore a strong resemblance to the president but there were subtle differences which up close became pronounced.

'Ok, it worked,' said the woman pretending to be the president.

'What is this?' Yi asked.

'I'm an actor,' the impersonator said.

'An actor?'

'Yes. An actor hired because I look a lot like the president. I did a lot of bit parts on TV, Lifetime movies and the like.'

'Oh.'

Agent Harris came into the room. 'We arranged this to see if we could fool a close confidant into thinking Ms. Yeager here,' he pointed to the impersonator 'was the president. Obviously it worked.'

Ms. Yeager said, 'Thank you.' She turned and left them.

Another woman came in, this one also looking like the president. 'Hello, Yi,' she said.

'I'm not falling for that again.'

'You don't think it's me?'

Yi smirked. 'Ok, if you're really the president answer me this.'

'Shoot.'

'In the summer of '94, what was our song.'

She smiled. '*Come to my Window*, Melissa Etheridge.'

'That was a dirty trick you just played.'

'We had to be sure,' said the president. 'And now I need you.'

'For what?'

'I want you to run another "dirty tricks" operation for me.'

Yi held out her hands and shook her head. 'No way. I swore that off after Iowa.'

'I know,' said the president. 'And look you're doing a great job here.'

'Thank you.'

'But I need my dirty tricks specialist back.'

'After Iowa, even? You fired me.'

'I'm hiring you back.'

'I don't know.'

'You and me, just like it always was. Only this time, you'd be running dirty tricks against the Jai. Deal?'

This time Yi smiled.

CHAPTER 3

SARAH JANE WAYNE

The windows rattled with the sound of jets engines overhead. In the distance there was a bang, and then another explosion. Mr. Dennison stayed down on his living room floor expecting another flash of light. When none came, he dared a peek out the living room bay window. There were no new explosions, but the mushroom cloud about Seattle continued to spread. He heard a slow rumble, and the windows rattled again. This time there was a booming sound followed by another and then another. The boom dissipated to the east.

The doorbell rang.

'Jesus Christ,' Mr. Dennison said.

He crawled across the floor to the entryway. Cautiously he stood up and looked through the peephole. It was Miss Sarah.

'One minute!' he shouted.

'Make it quick!' she shouted back.

Mr. Dennison got down on the floor and crawled to the basement door. He opened it up and shouted down, 'Madison!'

Delicate feet crept up the basement stairs. Madison Dennison walked up to her father. She wore blue jeans, a sweatshirt, boots and a windbreaker. She had a pack on her shoulders and a small backpack in her left hand. Mrs. Dennison came up behind her, sobbing quietly.

'I'm ready to go, Daddy,' said the 16 year old.

There was an insistent knock on the door. 'Mr. Dennison, we don't have a lot of time!'

'I know!' he shouted back. 'Let's go.'

To Survive the Earth

The trio walked to the front door. Mr. Dennison opened it. Miss Sarah stood on the front stoop in combat boots, camouflage pants and a denim work shirt. A pistol was on her hip. Behind her was a blue Lincoln Navigator and a white pickup with a snowplow attached. Miss Sarah was all smiles as she adjusted her glasses. 'You all ready, Madison?'

Madison nodded.

'Let's go through the check list, honey.'

'OK.'

Two pairs of denim jeans?'

'Yes,' said Madison.

'Two pairs, long underwear and four changes underwear?'

'Yes.'

'Nothing fancy now.'

Mrs. Dennison spoke up. 'Plain and gray. I bought a four pack at Walmart before the invasion.'

'Good. Four T-shirts?'

'Yes.'

'Two sweatshirts, two sweaters?'

'Yes.'

'Heavy coat and windbreaker?'

Madison nodded.

'Boots, sneakers?'

'Yes

'Multi-tool?'

Madison patted the leather tool affixed to her belt.

'Oh, and your Girl Scout Troop vest?'

Madison nodded again.

'Paper work?'

Mr. Dennison took a fold of papers out of his pocket and handed them to Sarah.

'Alright, then dear, say your goodbyes.'

Mrs. Dennison sobbed more loudly. Mr. Dennison was stoic but clearly heartbroken. When they were finished Miss Sarah said, 'Off you go, sugar.'

Madison said one last goodbye to her folks and then walked out to the Navigator. Seven of her fellow troop members were already in the back.

Jet engines roared overhead and disappeared to the east.

'Well it looks like the Battle of Seattle is over and we lost,' said Sarah. 'We better go.'

They shook hands.

Sarah trotted to the driver's side of the pickup. She stood on the running board. Sarah looked over to the young woman behind the wheel of the Navigator. 'Is that the last one, Jamie?' she asked.

Jamie looked at a small concave clipboard on her forearm. 'Yep, Ms. Sarah.'

Sarah looked back at the Navigator, driven by her daughter, and twirled her finger. The two-vehicle convoy started up and went down the street at fifteen miles per hour.

Mr. Dennison watched the Navigator. His eyes fixed on the two bumper stickers, an American flag crossed with a Gadsden Flag on one side, and a green decal with the Girl Scout Troop's number, 4232 on the other. 'Miss Sarah is not your typical Girl Scout leader, is she?'

'No,' said Mrs. Dennison through her tears. 'Letting that woman take our baby away during this…'

'Where would you rather have her?' Mr. Dennison said, more to himself than to his wife, 'In suburban Seattle or out in the mountains?'

'With us…'

'You agreed to this too,' said Mr. Dennison.

'I know!' sobbed Mrs. Dennison.

'Why are you crying? Miss Sarah isn't some woman we just met, she's a certified Girl Scout leader. We've trusted Madison with her for years.'

'That horrible woman with the legal trouble!'

The clouds opened up, filling the air around them with soft, cool drizzly rain. The wet road reflected the pickup's headlights, and the streetlights, which were still on. The entire street seemed to be sheathed in white light. Sarah drove out of the housing development onto the main road. With alien destruction raining down on the West Coast, most people stayed indoors, though a few people were out, heading east like they were. Miss Sarah drove past dozens of car wrecks; people who crashed as the blast hit Seattle. Beside an overturned SUV, a man waved frantically. Sarah ignored him. After about half an hour Sarah could see strings of tall power lines crossing the road. This was her first landmark and she pulled over. A string of several cars passed as she got out of the pickup. She walked over to the back.

'Well, Jamie, what do you think?'

'Traffic is picking up.'

'Yeah.'

'Looks like people are getting the hell out of here.'

'I would say so.'

'It's only going to get worse.'

'Yep.'

Sarah pointed to the power lines and the dirt road running beneath them. Jamie flipped opened her clipboard and took out a small map she had stuffed inside. She pointed. 'We can take it thirty miles north, practically to the foot of the Cascade Range.'

Sarah wiped rainwater from her forehead. 'I think you're right.'

'No one is going to drive the utility access road, not in this rain.'

'Alright then.' She said. 'You drive the Navigator, send Maggie up here to ride shotgun with me.'

'Yes, Miss Sarah.'

Jamie slung her M-4 Rifle, trotted over to the Navigator, and motioned for Maggie to get out. The 17 year old walked forward to the pickup and got in. Like her mother, Maggie wore camouflage pants tucked into combat boots and a flannel shirt.

'Everything OK back there?' Sarah asked.

'Some of the girls are a bit weepy,' said an annoyed Maggie.

'Well, not everyone is prepared for this, honey.'

'McKenzie is sitting in the back seat sobbing about her boyfriend.'

'She's in love,' said Sarah.

Behind them, Jamie honked and flashed her lights.

'Well, I guess she's ready to go,' Sarah said.

Maggie said, 'She doesn't want to listen to Mackenzie crying anymore than I do.'

Sarah pulled onto the access road. It ran straight for miles. In the dark and rain, visibility was limited, so Sarah kept her speed at 15 mph.

'Turn on the radio, Maggie,' she said. 'Let's see if we can find out what's happening.

Maggie switched on the radio and heard nothing.

'Stations out of Seattle have been destroyed,' said Sarah.

She hit the scan button. The radio stopped after several seconds. They heard the drone of the Emergency Broadcasting System. 'Seattle is under imminent attack,' proclaimed an oddly serene recording.

'Kind of behind the times,' said Sarah. She shook her head, 'Government. Keep scanning, Maggie. The scanner finally settled on a smaller station out of Spokane.

'Isn't that one of your rap stations?' Sarah asked.

Maggie smiled. 'Yep!'

'K-R-A-P?'

'Yep!'

They listened to the DJ. 'This is DJ Tin-dog yo! The Jai have completely smacked Seattle, Yo!' he reported.

'I knew that already,' said Sarah.

Tin-dog went on. 'And get this. They got mad weapons, see, and they hit all of the West Coast. Not just Seattle, but San Diego, San Francisco, the whole state, ya'll.'

He babbled on like that for a while.

'I've heard enough,' Sarah said. She turned off the radio.

'Mother, why not just try the phone?' said Maggie.

Sarah snapped her fingers, and laughed. 'Thanks for reminding your Luddite mother.'

Maggie took out her phone and looked at the screen. 'No bars,' she said.

'Suppose the Jai finally took out the cell network?'

'How would I know, Mother?'

They drove on through the drizzle. Sarah looked at her daughter, knowing she would resent what she was about to tell her. She put off speaking for a while, girding herself to say what she thought she needed to say. Maggie wrapped her coat around her and looked out the window, saying nothing.

Finally, 'Now Maggie' Sarah began.

'Oh no,' Maggie said, recognizing the way her mother began lectures.

'Now, I'm going to need you.'

'I know, Mother.'

'I know you think I'm strange. I know you've never liked to tell people about my disaster preparations…'

'Mother…'

'Let me finish, please.'

'Ok.'

'But you know more about what's ahead than these other girls. And I'm going to need you to set an example.'

'I knooowwww.'

'Do you?'

'Yes, Mother.'

'Their parents have put their trust in me. And I'm putting my trust in you. Ok?'

'Ok.'

They went over a small rise in the access road. When they topped it, they could see a trio of utility trucks parked a few hundred meters away. Sarah slowed down and approached at five miles an hour. When they got close to the trucks two men, clad in yellow jackets walked forward. One held out his hand for them to stop. Sarah stopped and rolled down the window.

One of the workers walked up to the driver's side and said, 'Excuse me, what do you think you're doing?'

'Good evening,' Sarah said as politely as possible. 'We're headed for the mountains.'

'Not on this road,' said the utility worker. 'It's restricted. You have to get off right away.'

Sarah adjusted her glasses. 'And where are we supposed to go?'

'If you head up there a little bit,' he pointed behind him, 'The road links to the main road. Take that to a state refugee camp. They're already taking people there.'

'We most definitely are not refugees,' Sarah said.

'Look, lady, I ain't gonna argue with you. You gotta get off this road. We need to keep it clear.'

'Then let us proceed and we'll get out of your way.'

'You need to get out of here now.'

'Now you listen here, Mister. I'm not taking orders from some government pole jockey.'

'Lady, what are you gonna do?'

Sarah pointed to the plow at the front of her pickup. 'You move those trucks out of my way or I'll go right through them.'

The utility worker laughed.

'Think I'm kidding?' Sarah leaned out the window. 'Jamie!' she shouted. 'We have trouble.'

Jamie got out of the Navigator, M-4 rifle in hand. 'Problem, Miss Sarah?'

The utility worker stepper back and held up his hands. 'Easy.'

'I'm not easy. Get out of our way.'

The other worker shouted back to the trucks, 'Jimmy, call the cops.'

Sarah laughed. 'I think they have more important things to worry about.' She reached down to her holster and motioned to her Beretta. 'You going to let us through?'

'Fine,' said the utility worker, 'but it's your ass.'

'I've been taking care of my own ass for 44 years. I don't need you or any man to look out for it.'

'Alright.' He shouted down to the trucks. 'Move out of the way! Annie Oakley here has got everything under control!'

Jamie got back in the Navigator. They drove slowly past the utility trucks and continued down the road.

When they were safely past, Sarah said, 'Ha! Annie Oakley.'

'Mother...'

They drove down the access road without further incident. When they got to Route-31 Sarah pulled over for a bathroom break. Jamie came over to talk to Sarah, M-4 rifle slung over her shoulder.

As the girls relieved themselves, Jamie and Sarah watched the traffic.

'Looks like it's picking up, Miss Sarah.'

'We better not waste much time.'

'Right.'

'We'll take Route 31 to 7, then cut north.'

'Ok.'

'From there it should be clear all the way to the cabin road, Lord willing.'

'Ok, you know…'

Jamie was interrupted by the scream of jet engines. A pair flew low overhead and was followed by another pair, the engine sounds dissipated to the east.

'Those air force guys keep flying in the wrong direction,' Sarah said.

'Uh huh.'

'Let's get going.'

They drove down the single lane roads until they came to a state highway. Here they saw dozens of cars pulled off the road. Plenty of people were holed up inside their vehicles, and plenty more camping on the side of the road. Here and there Sarah saw people changing flat tires or peering under an open hood.

After an hour, Sarah slowed and led the two-truck convoy onto a dirt road. The track was bumpy and almost totally enclosed overhead by tall trees. After half a mile, the layout of the ground began to gradually slope upwards. They drove for several hundred yards until the road became little more than a trail so narrow that pine branches brushed against the pickup.

Finally the road opened into a clearing. The pickup's headlights shined on an idyllic looking two-story cabin. Two small flagpoles adorned the doorframe. On the left flew the Stars and Stripes. The yellow Gadsden Flag was on the right. Sarah parked the pickup on the side of the cabin. Jamie parked the Navigator behind her. Sarah got out and clapped her hands.

'Everyone out!' Sarah shouted. 'We're here! Everyone out!'

The girls tiredly got out of the Navigator, rubbing eyes, scratching heads, and looking around at their surroundings. They couldn't see much in the dark, wet night. A dog barked inside the cabin.

Jamie popped the back hatch and took out their packs.

'Ok, girls line up!' Sarah shouted.

When they were all in a ragged line she got out her checklist and read off names, 'Hailey and Bailey, Madison, Sami, Mackenzie, Taylor, Piper, and ...'

'All here, Miss Sarah,' Jamie said.

'Everyone grab their gear and get inside,' said Sarah. 'Let's go, let's move, girls.'

'Alright. Jamie, pop the back trunk.'

'Yes, Miss Sarah.'

'Girls get your things. We'll head inside and go through them.'

The cabin door opened, a younger, slightly trimmer version of Sarah stepped out. 'Hey, Mom. 'Bout time you got here.'

'Watch the sarcasm, Reagan,' Sarah said to her eldest daughter.

A Golden Retriever shot out from the door and galloped to Sarah. The dog jumped up at her and nearly knocked her over.

'Good Girl!' Sarah said as she knelt down and petted the dog, 'Good girl.'

'She misses, mama,' Reagan said.

'Where are the cats?' Sarah asked.

'Inside by the fire, where else?'

'Is the firewood piled in the back?'

'Big mess, Mom.'

'Ok, good. Jamie, take the Navigator and pull it around back, and shine the headlights on the wood pile.'

'Ok.

'C'mon,' Sarah said to the dog. 'Let's go in.'

Sarah walked inside and shouted up to the loft. 'Jamie, when everything is set up bring the girls down here! Make sure they have their boots and work gloves.'

'Yes, Miss Sarah.'

Sarah went back out to the porch and looked at her watch. It was just past four AM.

The girls made their way to the first floor and lined up in front of Sarah. She looked them over. All were properly attired in jeans, boots, sweatshirts and windbreakers. To Sarah they looked tired, confused and scared. She couldn't blame them for that.

Reagan held the door open for the girls as they filed in. The cabin had a small kitchen on the right and a communal room on the left. A big fireplace was on the far wall. The room was lit by several kerosene lamps. It was furnished with a large table capable of seating twelve, a cushy chair, sofa and love seat. Stairs led to the loft above. Next to the kitchen was a tall locker, with a sign stenciled across the top reading FIRE ARMS. Next to it was another locker with stenciling that read AMMO.

'Ok girls, take your things upstairs. Bunks a plenty. Everybody pick a bunk and come back down here. Two minutes,' Sarah clapped her hands. 'Jamie, head up there and make sure everything is stowed away and set up right.'

'Yes, Miss Sarah.'

Sarah turned to Reagan and asked 'Pantry stocked?'

'Plenty of food. Oh, and plenty of game on the mountain.'

The girls wearily filed downstairs. 'Line 'em up, Jamie,' said Sarah.

The girls formed a ragged line.

'Ok, girls,' Sarah began. 'I bet you're all wondering where we are. Well we're a hundred miles east of Seattle in the Cascades. This cabin is mine, it's been in my family for four generations. We own all the land around here, 160 acres in all. This mountain here is ours. Don't you forget that. We've all been out in the woods before. But this is going to be different. There's a war on, and we're going to be out here for a long time. You listen to me and Miss Jamie here, we'll get you through this, and we'll get you home.

'Now, I know you're all tried, but we have a lot of work to do today.'

The girls groaned.

'Settle down, girls. We've all been camping before. You know the drill. We'll all have daily chores.'

There was more groaning.

'First off, there's a huge pile of firewood out back. It needs to be stacked and put under a tarp. Jamie and Reagan, would you please get them started?'

'Ok! You heard Miss Sarah!' Jamie shouted. 'Let's go, move it! Move it!'

'Oh!' said Sarah. 'Paper work.'

Jamie reached into her back pocket and took out a sheath of papers. 'Already collected it.'

Jamie took the girls outside and started them stacking the firewood. Sarah sat down at the head of the table and went through the paperwork, making sure each girl had a medical release, temporary power of attorney and a legal waiver allowing them to handle firearms. The dog lay at her feet.

Jamie came back inside.

'You sure all of that's necessary, Miss Sarah. This might be the end of civilization, don't you think?'

Sarah rifled through the papers, 'Well, until civilization does end, we'll live by its rules.'

'Yes, Miss Sarah. I better go back out.'

'Jamie?'

'Yes, Miss Sarah.'

'The girls aren't your marines; go a little easier on them please.'

'Yes, Miss Sarah.'

It took the girls about an hour to get the firewood stacked on the side of the cabin. When they were finished, Jamie and Reagan gave them a lesson in splitting wood. Each girl got a turn taking whacks at a tree stump. By then the sun was up. Sarah led the girls in the Pledge of Allegiance. After that was breakfast and a hike around the mountain. Jamie wanted to bring a gun but Sarah said no. 'There might be trouble,' Jamie said. 'Then run away.' Sarah replied. The hike took the rest of the morning. They had Ramen noodles for lunch. After sundown they lit several oil lamps and started a three-log fire which bathed the cabin in orange and yellow light.

Sarah looked at her watch. 'Alright girls. It's just after eight now. I'm thinking upstairs at nine. Lights out at ten.'

There were tired nods.

Reagan took out her guitar and started playing folk songs, Jamie got out a deck of playing cards and a deck of UNO cards and started some games.

'Can we turn on the radio?' asked Madison.

'Sure, see if you can get some news. And after that some music.' Sarah looked over to the couch, where one of the girls was already asleep. She smiled.

With the girls occupied Sarah stepped out onto the front porch and sat in one of the rockers. The night was cool and wet, there was a faint orange glow on the distant horizon. Sarah reached into her pocket, took out a cigar, and lit it. She inhaled deeply, exhaled and smiled to herself.

She had smoked a quarter of it when Margaret opened the front door. 'Got some news over the radio, Mom. Seattle has been destroyed, and there is lots of fighting out at sea. The governor is urging everyone to remain calm.'

'Good for him,' Sarah said skeptically. 'Could you ask Jamie to come out here when she has a chance?'

'Sure.'

Jamie came out a minute later. 'Have a seat, Jamie.'

Jamie sat down.

'Give the girls a chance to be alone without you and me around.'

'Sure thing, Miss Sarah. The girls are exhausted.'

'That's my plan. Too busy to worry, too tired to do anything but sleep.'

'You sure you want Reagan playing all that hippy music for them?'

'They're just songs.'

'Hippy songs.'

'It's her way.'

There was silence except for Reagan's guitar.

'Keep a small fire going in the loft.'

'What for?'

'If any of the girls wake up firelight will be comforting.'

Jamie spat. 'When I was their age I'd already ran away from home.'

'Well they haven't.'

'Yes, Miss Sarah.'

'For the time being,' said Sarah, 'someone should be on guard at all times at night, out here.'

'I'll go first.'

'No I'll take it.'

'You have to sleep sometime, too. Miss Sarah.'
'I will. Come get me at three.'
The two women looked out at the horizon. The West Coast burned.

The next afternoon Sarah sipped her tea and smiled at herself as the girls busily went about their chores. The redhead twins, Hailey and Bailey chopped firewood while Madison dutifully, though unhappily pulled the buckets from the outhouse. Two other girls built a fire while Jamie skinned a pair of rabbits that Maggie had found in the traps that morning.

Jamie came into the clearing with three girls in tow
'How was the hike?' Sarah asked.
'The patrol was fine. Saw signs of deer but couldn't catch up to them,' Jamie said as she unslung her rifle.
'Any sign of people?'
'Saw a couple of trucks out on the highway, heading toward LA.'
'Government?'
'Who else would head there? Saw some folks heading east too.'
'Driving?'
'Driving, riding bikes, walking.'
'How many?'
'Not too many.' Jamie set her rifle against the wall.
'How were the girls?'
'Fine,' replied Jamie. 'Except for Mackenzie. She took to crying a lot over her stupid boyfriend so I gave her a talkin' to and told her to knock it off.'
Sarah sipped her tea and looked inquisitively at Jamie. 'Weren't you ever in love?'
Jamie glowered. 'No.'
Reagan came out onto the porch with a big bowl. 'Dinner! she shouted. She walked over to the picnic table and put the bowl in the middle. She went back inside and got small wooden bowls for the girls to eat out of. The girls sat at the table. Sarah sat down on a stool at the head. 'Join hands,' she said. 'Lord, Jesus, thank you for this meal, and for our company here. Please watch over us, and our families, and most of all, America. Amen.'

'Amen,' the girls repeated.

Sarah looked over at Sami, who simply bowed her head but said nothing. 'I'm sorry, Sami, would you like to say a prayer too?'

'Um…sure, Ms. Sarah. Can I go get my Koran?'

'Of course.'

Sami excused herself and went into the cabin.

'I didn't spend two tours in Afghanistan to hear a lot of crap about Mohammed,' Jamie said.

Sarah glared at the marine. 'Knock it off.'

'Yes, Ms. Sarah.'

The girls looked ravenously at the wooden bowl, which was filled with noodles. Sarah looked at the hunger in their eyes. 'I hope you see now, girls, the value of a good meal. I hope you see that all that dieting you girls think you have to do is wrong.'

'C'mon, Mom,' Maggie said.

Reagan put a hand on her mother's knee in the hopes of restraining her. Before Sarah could give Maggie a talking to Sami returned. She read a quick passage from the Koran. When Sami was finished Sarah passed the bowl around the table. Sarah got hers only after each girl took several scoops. There were some scraps left.

'Slowly, slowly,' Sarah said as the girls woofed down their noodles.

'Sami, would you be willing to teach us about Islam?'

'I guess,' she replied.

'I learned plenty about it on the sharp end.'

'Jamie…'

'Anything in there about suicide bombers?'

'Jamie, why don't you go to the well and check the water level?'

'Fine, good.'

Jamie finished what was left of her noodles and got up from the table. One of the other girls, Mackenzie tried to follow her, Sarah motioned for her to stay seated.

'Sorry about that, Sami,' Sarah said.

'It's alright,' Sami replied.

'No it isn't,' said Sarah. 'I'll have a talk with her.'

'You don't have to. I know how some people feel. Especially after the Pakistani nukes.'

'Are you Pakistani?' one of the girls asked.

'No, my parents were from Egypt. They left in the 80s.'

As the sun went down the girls started a small bonfire. Reagan played guitar and led half the girls in a sing along. Inside, illuminated by the fireplace, Maggie and Madison played Uno. In the corner, Hailey and Bailey played chess.

As Reagan began the cords to *John Brown's Body*, Sarah walked around the cabin. She found Jamie in the back by the trail entrance. She had her AR-15 slung over her shoulder while she smoked a Marlboro. Sarah walked up next to her and stared down the trail. There was nothing to see in the darkness. In the background, she heard Reagan play *Over the Hills and Far Away*.

'I was wrong to say that to Sami,' Jamie said without prompting.

'I know you didn't mean it.'

Jamie threw her cigarette to the ground and viciously stomped it. 'I did mean it.'

There was silence for a few moments.

'It's just…you didn't see them do to girls what I saw them do in Afghanistan. Acid in their faces, clitorectamies.'

'They're not all like that.'

'All the one's I saw were.'

'But Sami isn't from Afghanistan.'

'I know. I won't do it again.'

Sarah patted Jamie on the back. 'I know you won't,' she said. She headed toward the door but stopped and turned around, 'We'll start teaching the girls to shoot tomorrow.'

Jamie smiled.

Behind the cabin, next to the outhouse, Sarah and her daughters had long ago constructed a makeshift firing range. The firing line was marked by a long log, Sarah fondly remembered felling the tree with Reagan and Maggie and dragging it back to the cabin. Twenty yards, paces really, to the front was a trio of posts, each with a pair of bull's-eyes affixed to them. The girls all stood along the firing line, Jamie stood in front of them. She wore a belt on her hip and a holster.

'Now, you all know what it's like to be afraid,' she began. 'You all know what it's like to be home alone and hear something moving outside, or walking down the street at night and hear footsteps behind you. For your entire life, you haven't been able to do shit about it. You had to rely on your daddies. Shit, I never had a daddy. You had to rely on your boyfriend, hell I never had much use for one of them anyway, 'cept for maybe a trophy now and again.'

Behind the girls, Sarah cleared her throat, 'Ahem.'

'Right, Miss Sarah. I was like that once, but I'm not anymore.' Jamie smiled and un-holstered her pistol and held it out for the girls to see. 'This is a Beretta 9 mm and it will make you safe.' Jamie grinned from ear to ear. 'Even better than safe, it'll make you dangerous.'

Jamie gave the girls a quick course in gun safety and then let each of them empty a magazine into the targets. Sarah enjoyed watching the girls as one by one, a light turned on in their heads: *I have power*. When they were finished shooting, Jamie issued each of the girls a Berretta and taught them how to clean and care for it.

'Now, you'll all wear that on your belt without ammo. Once we see you can be responsible with your weapon, we'll issue ammo to each of you. Since none of you are boys, I don't guess that'll be a problem.' The girls laughed. Each had a brother or boyfriend who'd crashed a car, nearly blown a hand off, or otherwise hurt themselves via some stupid, testosterone fueled prank. Sarah saw that Mackenzie didn't take her eyes off Jamie the whole time, they seemed to glow as Jamie talked of firearms.

Around three, Jamie went out on a hike with Maggie and the twins. She got back around five, just as Reagan was tuning her guitar by the freshly started campfire.

Sarah undid her boots and put them on the mat by the stairs. As she did every night, she craned her neck and listened. All was quiet upstairs. She crept up the stairs and peeked inside the loft. To her surprise, Sarah saw a few of the bunks were empty. Several of the girls were sharing beds. Sarah went back downstairs

89

and out to the porch. Jamie sat in the chair, rifle on her lap. She was wrapped in her poncho.

She looked up at Sarah. 'What are you doing back here?' she asked.

'Can I ask you about something?'

Jamie nodded.

'I saw some of the girls sleeping in the same bunk.'

Jamie seemed unimpressed. 'Yeah.'

'Well, I saw some of the girls sleeping together and…'

Jamie held up her hand and laughed. 'Oh its nothing like that, Miss Sarah. When I was in Afghanistan sometimes me and other women soldiers would cuddle up like that at night. You know, against the cold and all.'

'Oh.'

Jamie laughed. 'They ain't going dyke, no worries.'

'I wish you wouldn't talk like that.'

'Sorry.'

The two remained silent for a few minutes. Out to the west, toward the coast, there was a great flash of light.'

'What was that?' Jamie asked.

'Hate to say it, but it looked like a nuke.'

After another moment they heard a loud bang and then a low steady rumble. The trees before them swayed in a soft breeze that came with the sound. The white light changed to a fireball no larger than a quarter in the distant sky.

'I'll get the radio,' said Jamie.

Jamie came back out with the radio she turned it on to static. After several minutes of fiddling with the dial … she found a voice.

'Yo, Y'all, the president just took out those bitches!' said the DJ.

'Oh no, not K-R-A-P,' said Sarah.

'It's what I found.'

DJ Tin-dog continued, 'Yo, the Jai demanded she surrendered ya'll. Can you believe that!?'

'Oh!' remarked Sarah.

'That big explosion out over the Pacific, yo. That was one our nukes! Take that, alien biatches!'

'Oooh-Rah!' Jamie clapped her hands.

'Now, to celebrate, yo we're gonna play some..'

'Oh God, turn it off,' Sarah pleaded.

Jamie dutifully switched off the radio…

Elspeth watched as Benjamin brushed his long, wet curly locks out of his face and looked up the road. He blinked his eyes against the drizzle. He consulted his map and then turned to his three companions. 'The map says this road leads to the top of this hill.'

'Is there anything up there?' asked Elspeth. She pulled the straps of her designer pack against her sore shoulders.

Benjamin blinked again and looked down at the dirt road. 'Well, these tire tracks are pretty fresh. So something is up there.'

'Yep,' said Ethan.

Elspeth wanted to stay on the main road. She looked over to Ginny who grimaced at her. There weren't many vehicles on it anymore, but it was less scary than going into the woods, where there were animals and who-knows-what.

Leaving Seattle and camping after the aliens attacked was supposed to be fun, or at least fulfilling. She had hoped to blog about the experience and then publish an Indie book, but the wireless connection had been iffy at first and non-existent later. She had rarely been able to recharge her MacBook. Bringing a computer along on a weekend camping trip was one thing, but on a survivalist expedition into the mountains quite another. Even worse, she was down to her last week of birth control pills, and for all his professed sensitivity, Benjamin did not take no easily.

'I think we should stay on the road,' Elspeth said.

Ginny nodded in agreement.

Benjamin groaned. He always hated it when Elspeth didn't want to do what he wanted.

'Maybe we should talk about it?' said Ethan.

Elspeth felt a sense of relief. She wasn't alone in this. 'All right,' Benjamin huffed, 'We'll talk.'

The group sat at the side of the road in the rain and spent a good hour debating the merits of staying on the highway or taking the dirt road up the mountain. Ethan broke out his camp stove and made herbal tea for everyone. Benjamin won the debate, he always did, and the group of four young professionals trudged up the narrow dirt road. As they ascended the hill, the road grew rougher and narrower and showed ruts. After more than an hour of hiking they came to a road block of sorts. Several logs were strewn across. The party picked their way over them. Around a bend they came to a sign that read PRIVATE PROPERTY.

'I think we should go back,' Elspeth said.

'Nonsense,' replied Benjamin. 'It's probably someone's summer house. I bet there's nobody up there.'

'Maybe they have weed,' offered Ethan.

They'd run out several days before.

They continued up the road. After fifty yards they saw another sign, YOU ARE BEING WATCHED, it read. ADVANCE SLOWLY.

'I really think we should go back.'

'We came all this way,' Benjamin snapped.

They trudged on several dozen meters until the road began to level off. Benjamin could just make out a clearing.

He turned around, 'Hey I...'

Before he could finish a woman said, 'Hold it there.'

Elspeth looked past Benjamin and saw a female figure in fatigues and a brown rain poncho. She wore a baseball cap through which a red ponytail was threaded. She also cradled a rifle in her arms.

'Hello there,' Benjamin said. He took a step forward.

'I said hold it,' the woman said.

Confronted with an armed redhead, Benjamin stopped. 'We're just looking for a place to camp.'

'OK,' said Jamie. 'Where'd you come from?'

'We came out of Seattle before the Jai blew it up.'

'Oh.' Jamie said. 'You got any weapons?'

Benjamin shook his head.

'You're traipsing through the woods in a situation like this and you're not armed?'

'Should I be?'

'Let's just say you have a lot more faith in humanity than I do.'

They stood in the rain for a few moments.

'Where you headed?' Jamie asked.

'Just trying to find a good place to camp out for maybe a few days.'

'Well,' replied Jamie, 'That ain't nowhere around here.'

'Oh,' Benjamin looked deflated. 'Can we at least come up, warm ourselves by the fire?'

Jamie took a look at Benjamin, Ethan, Ginny and Elspeth. She pursed her lips and snorted. 'Well, don't see why not. You folks don't look very intimidating to me.'

Benjamin had nothing to say to that.

'Hey Maggie!' Jamie shouted.

A teenage girl popped up from behind a clump of bushes behind them. She wore the same kind of clothes as the women standing in front of them. Several tree branches were in her baseball cap for camo. She held a rifle as well.

'Lead these folks up the road to the cabin.'

'OK.'

'I'll be following along.'

'C'mon you guys,' said the girl. Without another word she turned and led them up the road.

The girl, she could not have been more than 17, led them up the road silently. They came to a driveway, walked past a pair of SUVs and into a clearing. Elspeth saw a cabin and people, all of them teenage girls, except for two. One, playing a guitar under a lean-to, looked to be in her early 20s. Several girls sat around her singing, one played the table they were sitting at like a drum. Another, sitting on the cabin's wraparound porch drinking tea was in her 40s. On the porch a pair of girls, twins Elspeth could tell, each cleaned a small black rifle. Next to them, a plump Middle Eastern girl stared down the site of a shotgun.

'Got company, Ma' said the girl who led them up the mountain.

They were shown hospitality, but it was limited. They were allowed to dry their clothes over the fire, wash up, and Sarah even fed them each one package of Ramen noodles. The visitors sat at the picnic table and hungrily slurped their noodles while Jamie sat on the porch steps, her rifle draped across her knees, eyeing them suspiciously.

'So what's going on out there?' she asked.

Benjamin and Ethan slurped their noodles and Benjamin said. 'Scary out there. Lots of people wondering around with nothing to do and nowhere to go. Too many for the National Guard and State Police to handle. One of the reasons we got off the highway and headed up here.'

Jamie leaned forward a bit and asked. 'What's happening around here?'

Ginny interjected, 'Feds are setting up some camps. Lot of people coming out of Seattle.'

When they were finished the red head (Jamie was her name) told Elspeth that it was time for them to move on. As they were walking back to the woods, Elspeth remembered something and ran back to the cabin. 'Uh, Jamie?' she asked.

'Yeah?'

'You don't have any birth control pills, do you?'

'Huh?'

'It's just that I'm almost out and Benjamin, well he…'

'Have you thought about telling him NO?'

'He doesn't like that.'

'Honey, when I was in the Marines, at least once a week some horny jarhead would try to get into my pants. Usually I'd just tell 'em to fuck off. Sometimes that wasn't enough, so I kicked him in the nuts.'

'Oh.'

'Try that.'

'OK.'

'And one other thing. In a time like this, you might want to ponder the idea that there are more important things in the world right now than your lady parts.'

Elspeth thanked Jamie and the girls for their hospitality, and Jamie watched as she ran down the hill to catch up with Benjamin, Ethan and Ginny.

'Be careful' Jamie yelled after her ' and remember what I taught you!' …

'Well,' Jamie began as she shook the rain out of her baseball cap. 'Someone is moving down there.'

'What do you mean?' Miss Sarah asked.

'Down along the trail, a pretty big group of people. They came off the highway, like Elspeth and those folks from the other day, and up our road, but then branched east on one of the side trails.'

'Did you follow them?' Ms. Sarah asked.

Jamie shook her head. 'Not by myself. You want me to go check them out?'

Miss Sarah shook her head. 'Just keep an eye out if they come back our way.'

They had a dinner of Campbell's Soup supplemented with some rabbit meat. Then Jamie asked for permission to take out a patrol. As Sami cleaned the table, Hailey and Bailey got a campfire going in the yard while Madison brewed some tea and coffee in the kitchen. Reagan played some folk songs.

'I thought you didn't want to go by yourself?' Miss Sarah asked.

'I'll take Mackenzie.'

'Alright. You sure it will be ok at night?'

'Absolutely, Miss Sarah. We know the ground, and we'll be able to spot them 'cause of their camp fires. If there's trouble, you'll know.'

'I'm sure.'

After sundown Jamie took Mackenzie out on the trail. She carried an AR-15 and a sidearm, and gave Mackenzie a .22. She seemed disappointed but said nothing as they started on the trail. As they walked, Mackenzie followed Jamie as she moved deliberately down the trail, copying her movements as best she could, and mimicking Jamie's absolute silence. They halted at the trail fork.

Jamie sat on a rock, took out her canteen and offered it to Mackenzie. By the light of the moon Jamie watched the girl as she drank. Mackenzie kept a hand on her rifle, and Jamie had noticed that she seemed to enjoy their time at the firing range more than the other girls.

Mackenzie finished drinking and gave the canteen back to Jamie.

'You like that rifle, don't you?' Jamie asked.

Mackenzie nodded. 'It makes me feel…'

'Safe?'

'No,' she grinned. 'Powerful.'

Jamie grinned herself. 'You don't need no man around when you have a gun.'

Mackenzie nodded. 'I don't have to be scared anymore.'

'What… were you scared of before?'

Mackenzie nodded.

'Of what?'

'My dad isn't around, my mom works late, so I spend a lot of time home by myself.'

'Well,' Jamie said, 'Next time you're home by yourself, you won't need to be scared.'

'I like that.'

'I used to be scared too,' Jamie said. 'My stepdad, my stepbrothers....' she didn't elaborate beyond that. 'So I ran away from home and joined the Marines. Made 'em think I was 18. I was only 16.'

'How come?'

'I knew if I was a Marine, no one would mess with me. Then I saw how they treat women in Afghanistan, and how we couldn't do nothin' about it....' Jamie shook her head. 'Let's go.'

They stood up.

'Hey,' Jamie said, 'You want to carry the AR-15?'

Mackenzie enthusiastically nodded. Jamie unslung the rifle. 'Safety is here,' she pointed, 'and keep the barrel slung down to the ground.'

They walked on for several minutes until Jamie crouched down and motioned for Mackenzie to do the same.

'You hear that?' Jamie asked.

Mackenzie listened closely but heard nothing.

'Hold your breath,' Jamie said.

Mackenzie did so, and heard a few voices in the distance.

Jamie looked ahead. 'The trail rises here slightly for about a hundred yards, crests and then drops off. I bet whoever is there is at the bottom of the dip.' She looked at Mackenzie and then looked ahead again.

'I'm going up to the crest. You stay here. If I'm not back in ten minutes, head back to the cabin.'

'OK.'

In the moonlight, Jamie saw fear in Mackenzie's eyes. 'Unsling that AR-15, girl. Nuthin' to be afraid off now.'

Mackenzie smiled and placed the rifle in her lap.

Jamie patted her on the head. 'Good girl. I'll be right back.'

Jamie disappeared down the trail. Mackenzie held the AR-15 against the dark, feeling safe, and feeling like she didn't have to fear anything. A minute later Jamie came back, Mackenzie heard heavy, fast footsteps first.

'Gimme the AR-15,' she said.

Jamie took the rifle from Mackenzie's hands and gave her the .22.

'Stay right here, do you understand?'

'What's wrong?'

'You'll know in a minute,' Jamie gulped for breath. 'Wait 'till we get back and stay right here no matter what.'

'Ok....' Mackenzie said as Jamie went back down the trail. *What did she mean we?* Mackenzie wondered.

'What are you doing?!' Jamie shouted.

Mackenzie heard a male voice, and then another, but couldn't make out what they were saying.

'Step back, now!' Jamie shouted.

More muffled male voices.

'Stop! One more step forward...'

Mackenzie jumped as she heard two shots from Jamie's AR-15. A man shouted, but Mackenzie also heard a woman scream. Scared now, she pointed her rifle up the trail.

'C'mon! C'mon!' she heard Jamie shout.

Jamie came down the trail, and Mackenzie could see that she was carrying someone across her back.

'Who is...'

'Quiet!' Jamie snapped. 'Mackenzie, you head up the trail and get back to the cabin, quickly.'

The woman Jamie was carrying sobbed quietly.

'Here,' Jamie handed the AR-15 to Mackenzie.

Mackenzie took the rifle and said, 'What if you need it again?'

Mackenzie patted her hip. 'Still have my Baretta. Now get going.'

'Ok.'

When Mackenzie got back to the cabin, Miss. Sarah was kneeling at the edge of the trail, an AR-15 at her side. She stood up and asked, 'Mackenzie! What happened?!'

'I don't know,' Mackenzie said as she gulped for air. 'I heard,' she gulped again, 'gun shots and the Jamie was there, carrying someone...'

'Wait, she has somebody?'

'Yes.'

Sarah looked down the trail and saw Jamie running toward them.

'Jamie, what happened?!' Sarah shouted.

'I shot that bastard!' Jamie shouted.

Sarah pointed. 'Who is that?'

'Elspeth.'

They brought her inside the cabin and set her down on the couch.

'She's naked,' Sarah said.

'Yeah,' Jamie replied matter of factly.

'Jesus, she's freezing.'

Sarah grabbed a blanket and threw it over Elspeth. 'Reagan! Get my first aid kit.'

Sarah lowered herself down upon Elspeth and wrapped her arms around her.

'Just warm up, sugar, just warm up....'

Elspeth opened her eyes and started screaming and pushed Sarah off her. 'No! No!' she shouted.

'Elspeth, it's me, Miss Sarah. Remember me?'

'Miss Sarah?' Elspeth asked.

'Yes, you are safe. Whoever hurt you is gone, and you are surrounded by women,' she said. 'Women with guns.'

'Oh thank God,' Elspeth said. 'There were lots of them.'

'Not, no more,' Jamie said. 'I put two rounds into one guy's chest.'

Sarah asked, 'Was it necessary to kill him?'

Jamie nodded. 'I made my point.'

Sarah sighed. 'Alright. Reagan, get a bucket of hot water and some soap.' She turned to Elspeth. 'We're going to give you a bath, clean you up, honey.'

Elspeth and her group had run into them after leaving the cabin. As near as Elspeth could tell they were a random group of men who had come together after the destruction of Seattle. She thought one may have been a mailman, at least a few others seemed to have been highway workers. They were all pretty desperate. Elspeth cried as she recounted how they had met up on the trail, and how the lead man, dressed in a mailman's uniform, had hit Ethan on the head with a baseball bat. Benjamin ran into the woods. Over the next two days they had raped Ginny to death. That's when Jamie found them.

'Looks like we have a problem, Miss Sarah,' Jamie said.

Sarah thought for a moment. 'You go out there and stand watch?'

'I was going to do that whether you asked me or not.'

'You want to take a girl with you?'

'Mackenzie.'

'Alright.'

'And give her an AR-15.'

'If you think that's best, Jamie.'

'She'll be fine.'

'And Jamie?'

'Yes, Ms. Sarah.'

'Just fire over their heads. I don't want anyone killed if we can help it.'

'They're a bunch of rapists.'

'Do as I say, Jamie.'

Jamie huffed. 'Will do, Miss Sarah.' She turned to Mackenzie. 'Stick with me, kid.' The pair went outside.

Reagan sat next to the couch with a bucket of hot water and started to bathe Elspeth.

'In a few minutes I'll give you an examination.'

Elspeth nodded, 'Ok...'

'Now don't you worry. I was a combat medic in Desert Storm and again in Iraq.'

Elspeth looked down at the floor and started to sob. 'My friend, Ginny, she's still out there...'

'They killed her, yes?' Sarah asked.

She shouted, 'I don't want to just leave her there!'

Outside, as they settled down on the trail entrance, Jamie and Mackenzie heard Elspeth's screams.

Jamie slung her AR-15 over her shoulder and placed her hands over her ears.

'I hate that,' she said. 'The women, hell, the girls in Afghanistan would scream like that too.'

Mackenzie began to cry.

'Don't cry, Mackenzie,' Jamie said.

Mackenzie wiped the tears from her cheeks. 'Sorry.'

'Don't be sorry. It's ok to be upset about what they did to Elspeth. Just don't cry about it. Get a gun instead.'

'When I think about what they did to Elspeth, I just want to take this rifle here and…'

'Yeah, me too.'

She looked down the trail and wondered how she was going to broach the subject with Sarah.

After a few minutes, 'Jamie, what do we do here?'

'We just sit tight and listen.'

'Listen for what?'

'For sounds that don't belong. You've been here a while now, right? You know the night should be still. You know what animals in the woods sound like, you know how much or how little noise they should make. You know a man will make a lot more noise.'

'Ok.'

'If we hear anything that don't belong, we know we got a problem.'

'And what do we do then?'

'We?' Jamie said. 'You,' she pointed to Mackenzie, 'will run and tell Miss Sarah. I will stay here.'

'Ok,' she was quiet for a moment, then. 'Do you think they'll come?'

'What, the guys that raped Elspeth? I doubt it. We just killed one of them, and they ain't gonna come looking for us in the dark.'

'Ok.'

After an hour Mackenzie drifted off to sleep. Jamie put a blanket on the ground and sat crossed legged. She placed the butt of her rifle in the ground, leaned forward and dozed in a series of quick cat-naps. Sometimes a noise in the woods woke her up, other times Elspeth's screams jerked her awake.

As the sun came up Sarah came outside with a cup of coffee for Jamie. She took it and sipped.

'Sometimes I wish we had something a little stronger.'

'You know I don't approve.'

Jamie sipped again. 'Just helps, that's all.'

'Helps warm you up or forget about what happened to you when you were a runaway?'

'Yes.' She sipped again. 'We better go find those bodies.'

'I thought you'd want to. Those guys are out there.'

She looked down the trail. 'I know. Sooner or later they're going to come here.'

'What do you want to do?'

'Let's go get Elspeth's friends, bury 'em, and if we run into those guys, we'll run 'em off.'

'I don't know...'

'You really want a bunch of rapists around here?'

Sarah rubbed her face. 'Alright. But I'm going and you are staying here.'

'But...'

'But nothing. I'm taking Reagan and Maggie, I know they can handle guns.'

'But you need me out there.'

'I need you here. If something happens to us, you'll be in charge, and I know you can handle it.'

The three went out each with an AR-15, a pistol and a shovel. Sarah stuffed a pocket version of the King James Bible in her fleece.

They found the dead man at the edge of the clearing. Sarah walked up to him, threw her shovel to the ground and knelt down before him. This was not the first dead body she had seen.

'Alright, we'll bury him right here. Reagan, start digging please.'

'Sure, Mom.'

'Maggie, gather some rocks for the grave.'

'Ok.'

I'm going to see if I can find Ginny.'

Sarah stepped off the trail. The wood was covered in felled leaves. It only took her a minute to find Ginny. Her body was propped up against a felled tree, still naked. About twenty yards away was her boyfriend Ethan, still clothed, but his face was gruesomely bashed to a pulp. Sarah scooped Ginny's body up and carried her over to the clearing. As her daughters watched she lay her down on the ground. The woman had a black eye and choke marks around her neck and black bruises on her thighs. Sarah took a kerchief out of her pocket and cleaned up Ginny as best she could. With a small comb Sarah brushed out the knots in her hair and parted it on the side. By then Reagan had dug a grave about two feet deep.

'That will do,' Sarah said.

Sarah and Reagan gently placed Ginny in the grave and replaced the dirt. They then carefully covered the graves with rocks. When they were finished, the three lined up and Sarah said a few words, and then the Lord's Prayer.

'Alright, let's dig one for him,' Sarah said.

'But he helped kill Ginny,' said Maggie.

'Yes he did,' her mother replied. 'But it is still the decent thing to do. We are still Christians, dear.'

Reagan elbowed her sister. 'Mom's right. Let's get started.'

Out of respect for Ginny they buried the man on the other side off the clearing.

'Lord, we hope your justice finds this man, and we hope he finds the peace that eluded him in life. Amen.'

'Amen,' Reagan said.

She elbowed her sister.

'Amen,' Maggie finally said.

'Reagan, you come with me and help me bury Ethan. Maggie, start digging.'

Maggie rolled her eyes but did what Sarah said.

Mother and daughter walked into the woods together.

'Mom!' Maggie shouted.

Sarah and Reagan turned and ran back to the clearing. Waiting there was Maggie, her AR-15 unslung and held chest high, pointed at a half dozen men standing menacingly at the other end of the clearing.

Sarah and Reagan unslung their rifles and raised them at the men. They were a scraggily looking bunch, with blue jeans, overalls, sweaters and fleeces worn by weeks spent in the outdoors. They all wore beards in varying stages of overgrowth. One, dressed in a battered army jacket was a mere two feet away from Maggie, his hand extended.

'Mom, he wants me to give him my rifle,' she said without taking her eyes off him.

Sarah pointed her rifle at the man's chest and said, 'Get away from my daughter right now.'

He held up his hands and backed away several steps. 'Easy there...' he said.

One of the other men said, 'They must be the ones that killed Ted.'

'Let's get them,' said another. He was a big man in a plaid shirt and camo pants. He pulled a pistol out of his pocket. Another produced a sawed-off shotgun.

'Why would we kill a bunch of pretty girls like them?' another asked.

Sarah said, 'Maybe you don't see the rifles pointed at your chests.'

'She's right, they already killed Ted,' the one in the army jacket said. He looked at Sarah, 'There are a lot more of us back at our camp, lady. Why don't you just be on your way?'

'This is my land,' Sarah said 'and you're trespassing.'

'You think any of that still matters, lady?' the man said.

'It does while I walk the ground, God willing.'

Another man stepped forward. He was a big guy, but youngish. He wore a 'Zoo York' hoodie and an Angels hat. He pulled a knife. Then another man, older, said, 'Holy crap guys, I just realized who she is.'

'Who?' the man with the camo jacket asked.

'Don't you remember that woman who shot a couple of gangbangers who were trying to car-jack her SUV. Big court trial, whole national story, lead the cable news every night. That's Sarah Wayne.'

'That's right,' Sarah said. 'I'm Sarah Wayne. I shot those car-jackers. One of my girls shot your friend there,' she nodded to the new grave. 'And if you don't get off my land, my girls and I will shoot you too.'

'Lady, we got more friends,' he stepped forward.

'Not enough.'

Sarah squeezed the trigger and took the man's head off with a well-placed round. Behind her, Reagan and Maggie opened fire. The man in the Zoo York hoodie flew backwards as Reagan put two rounds into his chest, as did the man in camo pants as Maggie put one round into his chest. The other three ran back down the trail. Sarah sent a pair of rounds after them. All three women lowered their rifles.

'Should we go after them?' Reagan asked.

'You two bury Ethan. I'll head down the trail a little.'

'Mom…'

'Do it, honey.'

The two daughters began digging. Sarah slowly walked down the trail with her rifle pointed forward. She advanced up the trail step by slow step, breathing softly and pointing her rifle forward. She could hear shouting up ahead, but couldn't make out the words. After a dozen paces, the trail turned and rose again.

Here she encountered one of the men.

He lay at the side of the trail, his hand pressed against his side. His other hand he held up in the air toward Sarah.

'You shot me in the kidney,' he said through strained breathing.

'Do you think I feel bad for you?'

'We were just having fun,' he said. 'I mean, this whole thing is going down,' he nodded to the sky. 'It's all over. Might as well enjoy it.'

'Murder and rape?'

He breathed hard and shrugged. 'I was in Seattle when the Jai destroyed it. Thought I deserved something.'

Sarah leveled her rile at him.

'You're going to kill me? I see that cross around your neck. That's not very Christian.'

'No,' Sarah replied as she took aim. 'The unchristian thing would be to let you die in agony.'

She pulled the trigger…

The morning sky was a whirlwind of blues and whites as Lieutenant Mike Chiang drifted to Earth. He could hear jet engines and distant explosions, but it was the ground, quickly coming up to him, that grabbed his attention. He saw a mountain, and ridge below that, both tree covered. Chiang closed his eyes as the trees loomed. He felt his boots slam into branches and brambles and felt his body being pulled down to the trees. His chute ripped and he could feel himself falling. He twisted and fell onto a branch and then another and another until he slammed into the hard ground. Chiang tried to stand up but collapsed under the weight of his chute.

Chiang awoke to the sound and feel of his chute being pulled off him. He stirred to life when someone nudged him. He opened his eyes but could not see, he realized that his helmet had twisted around. He reached up, took his helmet off and blinked. He was confronted by two teenage girls. One had red hair and braces, the other had blonde hair and freckles. He stared up at their sweet faces for a moment. Chiang closed his eyes, rubbed them and looked up again. The girls were still there.

'Am I in heaven?' he asked.

The blonde looked at the redhead 'He's alive,' she said.

'I'm alive?'

'You are,' said the blonde.

'Can you stand?' asked the redhead.

'Lemme see.' Chiang unsnapped his harness and slowly stood up. He wobbled a bit, the girls caught both his arms. 'I'm Ok, I'm Ok,' he said. Chiang held his arms out and steadied himself. 'I'm Ok.'

'We better get him back to Miss Sarah,' the blonde said.

'Who is Miss Sarah?' Chiang asked. 'Who are you? Where am I?' He looked at the girls and saw that the blonde had a rifle slung over her shoulder while the redhead had a pistol on her hip. 'What are those?' he asked. 'What is this?'

'C'mon,' said the blonde. 'You sure you're ok?'

'You sure I'm alive?'

'You feel this?' The blonde kicked Chiang in the shins.

'Ouch!'

'You're alive.'

'Don't kick him, Piper,' the other girl said.

'Let's go,' said Piper. 'Take your parachute, we may be able to use it.'

Chiang gathered his parachute and followed the girls. They led him onto a trail that wound in several different directions so that Chiang became disoriented and lost. The trail eventually led up the mountain and topped off at a small clearing. Chiang smiled as he saw the clearing was filled with teenage girls. All the girls were doing something. A pair was chopping wood while another pair stacked it. One was dragging a bucket away from an outhouse. Two more were tending a fire over which hung a deer carcass. To his surprise, Chiang saw a young woman in her 20's, it seemed, at a makeshift rifle range, holding a .22. A slightly older redheaded woman stood next to her.

'That's it, Elspeth,' the redhead said, 'Just squeeze the trigger gently.'

'Wow, this is some set up you girls have here,' said Chiang. 'Who is in charge?'

'Miss Sarah,' said the blonde. 'C'mon.'

The other girls stopped what they were doing and watched as Chiang was led inside the cabin. 'Miss, Sarah, we found the pilot you sent us to look for.' The blonde said.

Sarah came down the stairs, stopped at the foot and looked Chiang over.

'Pleasure to meet you, Lieutenant. I'm Sarah.' Sarah extended her hand.

Chiang shook the woman's hand and said, 'Lieutenant Michael Chiang United States Air Force.'

'Are you doing alright, Lieutenant? Anything broken?'

Chiang stretched his arms and cracked his neck, 'Just sore,' he said.

'Please have a seat.'

Sarah led Lieutenant Chiang over to the couch.

'Can I get you a cup of coffee?'

'You have coffee?' Chiang asked. 'I haven't seen any in a week.'

Jamie made a cup of coffee and handed it to Chiang. He sipped gratefully.

'If I can ask, what is this place?'

Sarah explained the cabin and the Girl Scout Troop to Chiang.

'Aren't you worried about being out here in the woods with a bunch of teenage girls?'

Sarah smiled. 'You saw. We have guns.'

'And we can use them,' added Jamie. She shook her head, 'You Air Force fly boys.'

'Huh?' Chiang asked.

Sarah smiled. 'She's a Marine.'

Chiang shook his head. 'You Marines.' He sipped his coffee. 'Hey, did you hear?'

'Hear what?'

'About the Marines on Iceland.' Chiang went on to explain the 1st Marine Division's valiant last stand on Iceland, Jamie hooted and hollered as Chiang detailed particular actions such as; the shooting down of a Jai carrier ship, the 1/8 Marines death charge outside of Reykjavik, and the last minute arrival of British reinforcements which kept Iceland in allied hands.

'So we won,' Sarah said.

'Yeah,' Chiang replied, 'but that's when the Jai got mad and slammed the West Coast.'

'We saw it,' said Sarah. 'We experienced it.'

'How's the rest of the war going?' Jamie asked.

Chiang sipped his coffee again and shook his head. 'Not good.'

'The radio guys have been downright optimistic.'

'That's what the government wants you civvies to think.'

'Yeah?' asked Jamie.

'We're losing,' said Chiang. 'The Jai are wearing us down. They send a big air group…'

'Air group?' Sarah asked.

'Oh, a big carrier ship plus some bombers. They send one of these groups against something we have to defend. My squadron was defending Bellingham. They punch through the air cover and then press forward getting our ground defenses to reveal themselves. They take out the lasers around the big Pac-3 batteries.'

'Don't they get hurt?' asked Jamie.

'Sure. We take down a few bombers. But to shoot down those carrier ships requires a maximum effort. You need dozens of aircraft launching sustained missile volleys at them. We can't always mass enough jets in time. Even when we do we lose tons of fighters. We can bring those things down, but we need a lot of luck to do it.'

'I see,' said Sarah.

'Hey,' said Chiang, 'Sorry for being rude, but do you have anything to eat?'

'Oh, I'm sorry,' said Sarah. 'Jamie get him some oatmeal and granola. Hope that's good enough.'

Chiang nodded. 'I haven't eaten since yesterday morning. Rations getting a little short at our base.'

Jamie heated up some water over the fireplace as Chiang talked. 'That's how they took out the Great Lakes Battle-Group. That's how they took out the big silos at Minot.' Chiang shook his head again. 'I guess they got Bellingham.'

'How can it go on like this?' Sarah asked.

'It can't,' Chiang said.

'So we've lost?' Jamie asked.

'Not yet,' Chiang said. He slurped his noodles. 'Something's up, I know that. All kinds of rumors.'

'What?' Sarah asked.

'I don't know, but something big.' He slurped again. 'My squadron XO said he saw a couple of Russian officers on the base the other day.'

'Russian?' Jamie asked. 'What're they doing in America? This aint Red Dawn.'

Chiang shrugged. 'North Pole, maybe. The Jai have that big ship there.'

'Is there anything we can be doing?' Sarah asked.

Chiang shrugged again. 'Honestly, I don't know.' He finished off the noodles. 'You know…you could get me back to my base.'

Sarah thought for a moment. 'Well, we can get you down to the main highway. I bet we can find some National Guard troops, or state police at least.'

'That'll work. I can at least tell my CO I'm alive.'

'It's too late in the day to start now,' Sarah said. 'Tomorrow morning.'

'So, Sarah,' Chiang said, 'Why are you running an armed camp here?'

'Lieutenant, I have eight teenage girls alone in the woods. I don't know if you've been out there.'

'I haven't.'

'Well,' Jamie chimed in, 'we had some trouble.'

'I see.'

'That's why you ran into Piper and Madison down there.'

'Could they really handle things?'

'You saw their rifles,' said Jamie.

There was silence until Piper spoke. 'Michael?'

'Piper!' Sarah snapped. 'Lieutenant Chiang.'

'Sorry, Miss Sarah. Lieutenant Chiang?'

'Yes?' he replied.

'Do you have a family?'

'Uhhhh...no.'

Piper smiled. 'A single man, then.'

Chiang spent the night on the couch, with Jamie dozing at the foot of the stairs.

'I really don't think that's necessary, Jamie,' Sarah said. 'I doubt Lieutenant Chiang would try anything.'

'It's not Chiang I'm worried about. Bunch of teenage girls, dreamy fighter pilot just feet away...' Jamie shook her head. 'Piper.'

'Do you really think she would try something?'

'Well, Sarah Jane, I hear the girls talking. Let's just say Piper ain't exactly...'

'Oh.'

At 0630 hours the girls filed out of the cabin into the cool morning drizzle. They said the Pledge of Allegiance and then the Girl Scout Pledge, the last part of which was drowned out by a flight of jets flying low over the mountain. When they were finished, Sarah said, 'I'm taking Lieutenant Chiang down to the highway. I'll be taking two girls with me. Jamie, who would you take along?'

'Hailey,' Jamie said.

'Sorry Bailey, you stay here.'

'But I want to go with Hailey.'

Sarah shook her head. 'No way.'

'Why not?'

'Because if something happens to us, I don't want your parents losing both of their girls.'

'Jesus,' Chiang said.

'Who else?'

'I'll go!' offered Piper.

'No way,' said Jamie.

Jamie looked over at her protégé. 'Take Mackenzie, she can shoot.'

'Alright, Hailey and Mackenzie and I will take Lieutenant Chiang down to the highway. Everyone take an AR-15, a pistol, and a belt.'

'Why all the firepower?' Chiang asked.

'I want us to look mean in case we run into trouble.'

Chiang nodded.

Sarah took a .22 out of the locker. 'You too, Lieutenant.'

'Ok.'

They were about to start down the trail when Reagan poked her head out the kitchen window, 'Hey, Mom?'

'Yes, Reagan.'

'I put the radio on K-R-A-P, but instead of music it's just running an Emergency Broadcast message.'

'What does it say?'

'Just says major events are happening and people are advised to stay home.'

'That might be the rumors I heard about,' Chiang said.

'Maybe you should stay home?' Reagan suggested.

Sarah pursed her lips. 'Well, if some big battle is happening, then Lieutenant Chiang will be needed,' she concluded. 'We're going.'

'Don't risk your necks on my account,' said Chiang.

'Some things are more important than our safety, Lieutenant,' said Sarah. 'Getting you back to a fighter jet may not be much, but it's what we can do and it's our patriotic duty to do it.'

Chiang held his hands up in mock surrender. 'Alright, alright.'

'I want to come too,' said Elspeth.

'I think you should stay here, honey,' said Sarah.

'Why, Miss Sarah? So I can curl up on the couch and cry some more. I want to come with you. And I want a gun.'

Sarah looked over at Jamie who said. 'She's shot plenty with a pistol, she checks out.'

'Ok, dear,' Sarah said.

Through a light drizzle the five made their way down the drive and onto the trail.

'It'll be more than a mile to the highway,' said Sarah, 'I wonder...'

Someone said, 'Hello?'

Sarah looked around, trying to find the source of the voice. There was movement off the trail, and finally a lone figure emerged. It was Benjamin. He looked destitute in only a T-shirt, jeans and his Birkenstocks, his beard lacking its trendiness and irony, and one of the lenses from his black, horned rimmed glasses was missing. To Sarah's eye, he looked hungry and cold.

His eyes fell on Elspeth, 'Elspeth! You made it!' he exclaimed.

Elspeth screamed in rage and hurled herself at Benjamin. They entangled and fell to the wet ground. As the group watched on in horror, Elsepth sat astride her former boyfriend and clawed at his face.

'You bastard!' she shouted as her nails dug into Benjamin's cheeks. 'You just ran off and left me with those men!' She balled her fist in rage and punched Benjamin in the eye, breaking his horned rim glasses. Elspeth had punched him again before Lieutenant Chiang was able to get his arms around her and pull her away. Even then she kicked and punched and wailed in pain. 'You coward!' she shouted.

Benjamin put his hands to his bleeding face and writhed on the ground. Sarah rushed to his side. 'Now hold still, dear, and let me have a look.'

Sarah peeled Benjamin's hands away from his face. There were several deep gash marks in his cheeks, and his left eye was black. Sarah reached into her bag, took out a first-aid kit and treated Benjamin's wounds. He quietly whimpered until Sarah applied a medicated wipe to his cheek, then emitted a high pitched yelp.

'Pussy,' said Elspeth.

When Sarah was finished she asked, 'Can you walk?'

'I...I don't know.'

'Hailey, Madison, help him up.'

The two teenage girls got on either side of Benjamin and pulled him to his feet.

'We'll take you down to the road.'

'Send him back to the woods!' spat Elspeth.

'Now, honey,' Sarah said. 'From there, you're on your own.'

They walked down the trail with Benjamin up ahead and Sarah in the back with Elspeth.

'I hate him,' Elspeth grumbled. 'I hate him more than the men who raped me.'

Sarah put her hand on Elspeth's back and gave her a maternal rub, 'Never depend on anyone but yourself, dear.'

There was no traffic down on the highway. They walked north, passing random bits of litter, water bottles, food wrappers, and a few broken down cars. After several minutes they heard engines, and then saw an army convoy of a pair of trucks and a Humvee. They waved the convoy down. The Humvees pulled up to them and the trucks stopped after about twenty yards. A harrowed looking soldier got out of the passenger seat, saw Chiang and saluted.

'Lieutenant Michael Chiang, US Air Force,' he said.

The soldier saluted back, 'Sergeant Bill Rivers, California National Guard. If you don't mind my asking sir, what are you folks doing out here?'

'I was shot down yesterday, these good people here took me in for the night.'

Sarah stepped forward, 'Sarah Wayne, Girl Scouts.'

Rivers looked at the heavily armed girls. 'Girl Scouts?'

'Yep.'

'Sergeant,' said Chiang, 'I'm trying to get back to my fighter wing.'

Rivera thought for a moment. 'Well, hop in back of one the trucks here. We're taking supplies to the FEMA camp down the road. We can get a radio hookup. You can call your base.'

'Sounds alright.'

Rivers looked at Sarah. 'You folks can get some help.'

Sarah scoffed. 'We don't need any help.' She patted her AR-15. 'But this guy does.' She pointed to Benjamin. 'We'll leave him with you.'

Rivers motioned to the truck, 'Get in.'

The truck was filled with crates of MREs and two soldiers bundled against the cold and rain.

'How you guys doing?' Sarah asked.

One of the soldiers said, 'Cold, and tired.'

The other said, 'Yeah, we've been running supplies for 48 hours.'

'Where to?'

'Big camp down the road here, there's a bunch of others around Seattle. Lots of refugees.'

'Yeah,' said the first one. 'Hungry and scared. Yesterday, at the camp west of here, they swarmed the truck. We had to fire rounds into the air to get 'em to disperse so we could do our job.'

'That bad, huh?' asked Sarah.

The first soldier said, 'Well, I saw worse in my time in Iraq.' He shuddered.

'Hey,' said the first soldier, 'turn the radio back on, maybe we can get some news.'

The other soldier patted his breast pocket. 'Don't want the battery to die down.'

'Just for a minute, maybe there's some news.'

The other soldier huffed but turned the radio on. It was turned to KRAP and DJ Tin-Dog was in a high state, 'We're back on air, ya'll and got big news. The military has been bitch slapping the Jai up on the North Pole, yo. And now they're starting in on the South Pole too. Double action, ya'll.'

Sarah said, 'Sounds serious. What do you think?'

The soldier with the radio shook his head. 'Lady, I'm just a soldier in a truck.'

They saw the FEMA camp from the road, a collection of a dozen trailers surrounded by a tent city. The gate had a pair of concrete barriers blocking it, a half dozen soldiers and some State Police were standing guard. They were waved through and drove along a makeshift road between the trailers and tents. People looked out from the tents and came outside. They wore a motley array of clothes; Sarah saw ragged designer jackets and boots on many. The small convoy stopped before a large tent, also guarded by soldiers. Someone in a blue FEMA jacket came out and directed several men to begin unloading boxes. Sarah and the girls jumped down from the truck. She walked up to the FEMA official.

'I have a guy here for you.'

The FEMA man said, 'OK, the next tent over is where we process people.' He looked at the girls, 'What about you folks? You need processing?'

Sarah shook her head. 'They're with me.'

'Those your daughters?' the FEMA man asked.

'No, but they are under my care,' Sarah reached into her pocket and took out the girl's legal papers and handed them to the FEMA man.

He looked the papers over. 'They are minors?'

'Yes both 16. As you can see, those papers give me temporary legal guardianship over the girls.'

The FEMA man read through the papers, shaking his head. 'These are minors…I don't think I can let you take them back out there.'

Madison stepped forward, 'I'm not staying here.'

Bailey got behind Madison, 'Me neither.'

'Girls,' said the FEMA man, 'It's for your own good.'

Chiang stepped forward and said 'This is ridiculous. I saw their cabin. They're perfectly fine up there.'

The FEMA man looked over his shoulder to where a couple of state police were standing, 'Sergeant!' he waved them over before looking back at Sarah. 'Besides, I don't think those guns are very safe. They're not even supposed to be here in camp.' By then a state police sergeant had arrived. he was a large man in a blue nylon windbreaker emblazed with the state police logo. The brim of his hat was pulled down close to his eyes.

'Problem, Garry?'

'Yes. This woman wants to take these minors out into the woods. With all the guns I see, I'm worried that it won't be a safe, healthy environment.'

'Safe?' Sarah replied, incredulously for the first time. 'They've all been checked out on those guns, the safeties are on.'

The policeman looked at the girls. 'May I see one of the rifles?'

'Of course. Hailey, give your rifle to the sergeant here.'

Hailey unslung her AR-15 and handed it to the sergeant. He took the rifle, examined the trigger and safety and looked down the barrel. When he was finished he handed it back to Hailey.

'Looks ok. Looks like someone taught her how to care for a rifle.'

'Thank you, Sergeant,' said Sarah.

'These girls are not hers.'

'No?' the sergeant asked.

'They're under my care,' said Sarah. She pointed to the papers the FEMA man held. 'Those are legal documents, Sergeant.'

'Well, let's have a look.' The sergeant took the papers and leafed through them. 'Hailey?' he asked. Hailey held up her hand. 'Madison?'

'Here.'

He looked at Elspeth. 'What about you?'

'I'm 23.'

'Alright....well, these papers look legal. Got a seal, signatures,' he handed the papers back to Sarah. 'You're free to go.'

'Thank you, Sergeant.'

'But…' Garry objected.

'You really want more people, Garry?' the sergeant said. 'If you had any brains you'd be trying to get this woman here to take a few children off your hands.' He waved. 'Good luck folks.'

The chastised FEMA man looked at Benjamin, 'What about him?'

'He's staying with you.'

Sarah looked around at her girls and then at Chiang. She extended her hand. 'Well, I guess that's all for us. Elspeth dear, anything you'd like to say to Benjamin?'

'No,' she growled.

The FEMA man pointed to a desk in front of several privacy screens, 'Over there.'

His arms folded against the cold, Benjamin walked over to the table. A woman came out from behind the privacy screen and wrapped a blanket around Benjamin before leading him behind the screen.

'Miss Sarah?' Madison asked.

'Yes, honey?'

'Do you think we can try to find out about our town?'

'Of course,' she turned to the FEMA man. 'You have any news about Seattle and its suburbs?'

Annoyed now, the FEMA man pointed to the back of the camp. 'There's an information desk back by those blue tents,' with that, he walked away.

The tent city was set up so that it created straight avenues. The tents were all large and marked MULTI-FAMILY. A porta-potty was on the side of each as was a large plastic water tank, each open against the drizzle. Many people had set out empty coffee cans or plastic cups to collect rainwater as well. Despite the rain, children played in the avenues. As they walked past, Sarah looked inside the tents. They were lined with cots and folding chairs. People huddled around wood burning stoves, dressed in multiple layers of clothing and draped in blankets. Many read books or played cards. Sarah saw that the hair of the women looked ragged, the men had scraggily beards. Children looked decidedly unkempt. Sarah snorted. At the last tent everyone had seemingly stopped what they were doing and were gathered around a transistor radio.

The camp information desk consisted of several tables, a ham radio, and several accordion files. A lone woman sat at the desk, conversing on the radio. When she finished she looked up at Sarah and the girls.

'Can I help you folks?' she asked. 'I'm Roberta.'

'We're trying to find out about our town. It's about ten miles outside of Seattle.'

'Well, let's break out the map and have a look.'

She reached into one of her accordion files and took out a map. She unfolded it, revealing a large, detailed map of Seattle and its surrounding areas. The woman took out a pen and ran the tip along the map. 'Let's see…'

'East of the valley, east, northeast.'

'Ah! There it is.'

'Bingo,' said Sarah.

People began running back and forth between the tents. 'I wonder what all that's about,' Roberta said. 'Well, it's well outside the zone of destruction. Let me see if there are any updates on it.' She took out another accordion folder. 'We've gone low tech here,' she smiled ironically. 'Got all the FEMA directives in here alphabetically…' She took out a sheet of paper marked SHELTER IN PLACE ORDERS and scanned it. 'Ah, here it is. Last month. Issued with a shelter in place order.'

'Shelter in place?' Sarah asked.

'Just Fed speak for stay put. Of course folks mostly do what they want…'

'So what does all that mean?' Sarah asked. 'It means your town is fine. At least the Jai haven't destroyed it. '

Sarah smiled. 'Well, that's a relief. And I know my girls will feel the same.' She turned to Madison. 'See dear, I'm sure your folks are alright.'

Madison asked, 'Any chance we can call them?'

The woman at the desk laughed. 'Sorry. The cell network is down and the Feds have taken over the land lines.'

Sarah patted Madison on the back. 'Sorry, dear.' She asked the woman, 'Can we go back?'

'There's nothing preventing you from…' Roberta was interrupted by one of her colleagues, 'Hey Roberta, turn on your radio!'

Roberta turned around, 'What for?'

The other woman beamed, 'The president is about to speak!'

Roberta turned on her radio. DJ Tin-dog was positively ebullient, 'Yo, the Preezy of the Untied Steezy is about to speak ya'll, and rumor has it…oh snap here she is.'

The president announced that she had demanded and received the surrender of the Jai. Sarah looked around at the jumping, shouting people in the camp. She waved Elspeth, Madison, and Baily to her. 'Come girls, join hands.'

They formed a prayer circle, Elspeth seemed reluctant.

'It's OK, dear, you just close your eyes and pray to whomever you want.' Sarah cleared her throat. 'Lord, we thank you for this victory over the heathen invaders…'

When she was finished, Sarah put an Amen to it and opened her eyes.

'Well, girls, we better get going.'

As they walked to the gate, Chiang ran out from the police tent. Chiang walked with Sarah and the girls to the gate.

Chiang took her hand, 'Thanks for taking me in.'

Sarah winked at him. 'Good luck. C'mon girls. If we hustle we can get back to the cabin by dark.'

As Chiang watched, Sarah and the girls walked down the highway, rifles slung over their shoulders, clad in fleeces, camo pants and windbreakers, their heads hooded or covered by baseball caps made their way down the road. One of the policemen standing guard said, 'They gonna be alright by themselves?'

Chiang shook his head. 'I wouldn't mess with them.'

CHAPTER 4

ORTHODOX COLD

'Let's turn over the engine, Hollander. Get some heat in here.'

'No,' replied Lt. Hollander.

'C'mon, it's cold out here.'

Hollander zipped his fur lined leather coat up to the neck. 'I said no. We can't waste the gas.'

'The chief won't know.'

'I said no, Ryan,' replied Hollander.

Officer Ryan put his gloved hands under his legs to try to warm them up.

Hollander looked down Route 401. It was iced over and the fallow fields on either side of the road were gigantic blocks of frozen snow. The winter sun pierced down through the ozone depleted atmosphere and beat down upon the large sheet of white, forcing officers Hollander and Ryan to don sunglasses. Ryan mumbled as the wind blew a hard gust that rocked the police cruiser slightly. Up the highway, about half a mile was the gray outline that looked almost like a city in the distance. It was actually an electric substation used to regulate power for Livermore and several towns further south. It had been dark for months. Just before where the road curved to the left, was the burned out shell of a Jai ship that had been shot down during last autumn's titanic fighting. If the light glinting off the hull flickered, it meant that people were coming down the road.

'Jesus,' Ryan mumbled. 'How cold is it out there?'

Hollander looked at the dashboard thermometer, 'Two.'

'Two degrees?'

'Yep.'

'C'mon, Hollander, there aint nobody coming down the road today, not in this. Let's get out of here.'

'Chief says we stay here and watch 401.'

Ryan knew there was no point in arguing with Hollander.

They sat in silence for ten minutes before the radio squawked. 'Hollander?' It was the chief.

Hollander picked up the receiver, 'Yeah, chief.'

'No one's coming down the pike in this weather. Get over to the east grain silo, it's about to open.'

'OK, chief.'

Hollander started the police cruiser and gingerly drove down the highway to the east grain silo. It rose out of a snowed over field. Behind it was a dilapidated red barn and beyond that an old farmhouse. The occupants, an old couple who had lived in Livermore their entire lives, had died early on in the winter. They never stood a chance. The town confiscated the land and used the silo to store grain. Two police officers were at the silo and there was a line of people waiting. Each had a bucket and a rifle slung over their shoulder. All were bundled against the cold. Their faces were invisible beneath scarves, hats and sunglasses. They stamped their feet and rubbed their hands.

Hollander shut off the engine.

'Aww c'mon,' said Ryan.

'Stay with the cruiser,' Hollander said.

Hollander got out. He brought his nightstick with him but left the shotgun in the car. He put on a fur cap and walked over to the silo.

'Morning, Lieutenant,' the two officers said in unison.

'Morning boys.'

Hollander looked down the line of people. At the head, a man held a bucket to the silo spigot, which let out a trickle of grain. The man operating the spigot counted to ten and stopped. 'Next!' he shouted.

A man hobbled forward and held his bucket over the spigot and got his ten seconds of grain.

'A little more?' he asked. 'I got five kids.'

'Move on,' Hollander said.

'Hey, five kids,' said the silo operator.

Hollander shook his head. 'No exceptions.' He looked at the pleading man. 'Sorry, sir.'

'Well, what the hell am I supposed to do?!' he shouted.

'Move on, sir,' Hollander answered.

'Listen up folks!' Hollander shouted. 'Ten seconds, that's it. Don't ask for more.'

The wind gusted again and knocked several people down to the ground.

'Ok?!'

There were grunts.

'Well, when the hell is the government going to deliver more grain?!' someone demanded.

'I don't know, folks' replied Hollander. 'Just go about your business.'

Hollander stood by with the other two officers, who stamped their feet and walked in circles. More people gradually came to the back of the line. After a time, there was pushing and jostling. One man pushed another, who went flying to the hard cold ground. Hollander ran to the fight and placed himself between the two combatants. He felt a fist smash into his face. Hollander pulled his nightstick and slugged his assailant in the gut. He then pushed him to the ground and fell on the man. Hollander handcuffed him and stood him up. The scuffle had knocked the man's scarf from his face.

'Tommy?' Hollander asked.

'Hey, Rick,' he said.

'Idiot,' Hollander said. 'Let's go.'

'You're arresting me?'

'Shut up,' said Hollander. He pointed Tommy toward the cruiser. 'You have the right to remain silent…'

'Who do you think you're kidding?!' someone shouted. 'You think that still matters?' Hollander ignored the heckler. 'Any more trouble, and I'll make more arrests, got it?' he said.

He put Tommy in the back of the cruiser and drove him downtown. Most of the buildings in town were boarded up. Great snowdrifts lined the sidewalks and few people walked the streets. The jail was on the far end of town overlooking the Green River. It had been frozen over for six weeks. A circle of ice fishers squatted in the middle of the frozen river. Several fish hung on a line beside them.

Hollander walked Tommy inside the police station. Inside the secretary sat at her desk, shivering despite wearing several layers of clothes.

'Hey Elaine,' he said.

'What's this?'

'Booking.'

'What for?'

'Disorderly.'

Elaine reached into her desk and took out a form. 'We're out of fingerprint paper.'

'What happened?'

'Using it for toilet paper.'

'Now how are we going to fingerprint people?'

'I guess we'll go without.'

'But… ahhhh. Alright.'

Hollander processed Tommy and threw him in one of the cells.

'Hey its, cold in here,' Tommy said.

'It's cold everywhere,' replied Hollander. 'Hey Elaine, get a blanket for Tommy, would ya?'

'Sure.'

Hollander walked back to the front. 'Hey, where's the chief?'

With her thumb Elaine pointed down the street. 'Meeting with the mayor.'

'What about?'

Elaine folded her arms inside her coat. 'He didn't say.'

'Alright.'

Hollander went back out to the cruiser and got it. He started the engine.

'Thank God,' Ryan said. He threw the heater to full blast.

'Let's get back to the silo.'

The line there was longer but orderly. Hollander and Ryan sat in the cruiser and watched as one by one, the residents of Livermore got their grain. At eleven sharp the silo closed, only those on line at the time of closing were allowed to fill their bucket. As the line dissipated, a small figure wrapped in several layers of clothing sauntered up to the cruiser. Hollander rolled down the window. The figure removed a scarf and sunglasses revealing a young woman's face.

'Hey officer,' she said. 'How about a ride?' The wind gusted again, blowing several locks of blonde hair into her face.

Hollander shook his head. 'Sorry, Mandy, can't do it.'

'I can make it worth your while.'

'Get going.'

Hollander rolled up the window.

'Why not?' Ryan asked. 'She won't tell no one.'

Hollander glared at the police officer. 'You've done it before, haven't you?'

Ryan said nothing.

'Is that what we've come to?' Hollander asked.

Ryan shrugged.

'Let's take a turn around town.'

They drove down the streets filled with twentieth century, post war houses and the occasional Victorian and rarer Federal. Thin wisps of smoke emanated from chimneys. Cars, covered in snow and ice, remained idle in drive-ways. He saw one house with a pile of garbage in the front yard and stopped.

'That's Mrs. Jenner,' Hollander said. He opened the door.

'What are you doing?' Ryan asked.

'I'm going to talk to her.'

Hollander walked up to the small house and knocked. Mrs. Jenner opened. Hollander could see through her layers of clothes that the fat, middle-aged woman had lost a lot of weight since Arrival. She looked tired and mean.

'What do you want?' she scowled.

'Mrs. Jenner, what is that pile of garbage in the front, here?'

The wind gusted and flew the door wide open. Hollander grabbed the handle.

'I'm cleaning my attic out, trying to find clothes and blankets.'

'OK, but clean that stuff up or I'll have to cite you.'

'Cite me?'

'Yes, ma'am.'

'What am I supposed to do with a ticket?'

'I expect you to pay it.'

'Anything else?'

'No, ma'am.'

Mrs. Jenner closed the door against a fresh gust.

'I'll stop by tomorrow, ma'am!' Hollander yelled through the door.

When Hollander got back in the car, Ryan asked, 'Is it really that big of a deal?'

'It's a public ordnance violation.'

'Jesus, Hollander, these people barely have enough to eat.'

'Yeah, and if we stop ignoring the law this town will fall apart.'

The radio squawked again, 'Hollander, the chief wants you back at the station.'

Hollander picked up the receiver. 'Alright.'

Hollander went right to the chief's officer. The walls were bare of pictures and frames and his desk was empty of paper, they had all been used for kindling. Hollander wondered when the desk would get put to the torch. The chief was old. He'd been getting ready to retire when word of the Jai was released. Before Arrival he'd been a youthful sixty. Now he looked like he was pushing seventy.

'We've got big trouble,' he said. The cold air cast his breath in a pall around him.

'Trouble?'

'I just got back from the mayor's office. The day after tomorrow, Livermore will be taking in refugees from up north.'

'What? Why us?'

'Because the state says so. The governor called the mayor personally. He got the word from FEMA. You know how they've been pretty much a dictator since Arrival.'

'How many.'

'A few hundred?'

'The day after tomorrow? They give us forty-eight hours notice?'

'They've been doing it with as little as twelve hours in most places. Governor gave us extra warning cause the mayor was his big political supporter, and this is an election year.'

'Oh, for Christ sake, where are we going to put them? We've got dozens of out-of-towners already.'

The chief sat back in his chair and put his hand to his chest.

'You OK, chief?'

'I'm fine. Heartburn. And we're out of Rolaids.' He leaned forward. 'You know I took this job four years ago after thirty years in the St. Louis PD. Thought it would be a nice gig before settling down. Bought that nice old farm house off the highway...' the chief shook his head, 'Jesus, I didn't want this.'

'What are we going to do?'

'The Mayor is calling a meeting tomorrow.'

'People aren't going to like this. Should we turn out the force?'

'God no,' said the chief. 'A lot of police there will just rile people up. Just you, ok? You have a calming effect on people.'

'Okay.'

'I want you to make the rounds with our guys. Tell 'em what's happening.'

'Sure.'

'And tell them to keep it quiet.'

'Okay.'

Hollander walked back into the waiting area. Elaine had taken out a small transistor radio. He heard the dull, steady drone of a news reader.'

'Anything interesting?' he asked.

Elaine shook her head. 'Just reports of rebuilding. Oh, and the Jai launched some missiles at Canada for some reason.'

'Anything about help for us?'

Elaine shrugged. 'Cincinnati.'

'At least they're almost in Kentucky,' Hollander said.

Hollander did his afternoon rounds through town. He passed several people carrying dead squirrels and other rodents. One lucky hunter nabbed a muskrat. In the front yards of several houses, Hollander saw groups of people gathered around barrel fires or grills over which pots were hanging. They stamped their feet and held their hands over the fires. Some even danced to improvised bucket drum kits, anything to keep warm. Stone soup parties had become a regular occurrence since Arrival.

When he got home, despite the cold Hollander took his boots off outside and carried them in. He didn't dare leave them on the porch. Someone would swipe them. The downstairs was awash in orange light from the fireplace. On the couch in the corner was a pile of blankets. Beneath them, Hollander knew, the boys were curled up sleeping. In front of the fireplace was the queen-sized bed from the master bedroom. Hollander had dismantled it and reassembled it down stairs when Livermore lost electricity. There was a pile of blankets on the bed. Beneath them was Mrs. Hollander. He looked over at the boys, who would wake up sooner or later and get in the big bed. Hollander got in bed without bothering to take off his clothes. It was cold. Besides, he wanted Delia to himself for at least a little bit.

He snuggled up against Delia and put his arm around her. She shifted her weight against him, reached behind her and patted his cheek.

'Kenny got a squirrel with his .22.'

Hollander smiled. 'Good.'

'The teacher didn't show.'

'Again?'

'Again.'

'They're supposed to be coming to the students since we shut the school.'

'Mmmmph…' she said.

'What did you do today?'

'Tried to stay warm.' Delia squeezed her husband's arm. 'Checked in on Cathy and the girls.'

'How 're they doing?'

'Not good. I gave Cathy a box of Cheerios.'

'Was that our last box?'

'We have another.'

'How was your day?' Delia asked.

'Not good. Trouble at the silo. And we have trouble coming to town I…'

'Mommy…' Kenny said from the couch.

'C'mon on over, sweetie,' Delia said.

Timmy, came over a few minutes later. The Hollanders huddled against the cold.

William Stroock

Hollander woke up with the sun; they all did now. He went to the enclosed part of the porch, where he kept the firewood since wood outside started disappearing. He got a big fire started for the morning, three logs fueled by kindling and now, his wife's old college text books. Delia fixed breakfast, cold cereal and milk from one of the town's many dairy farmers.

The boys ate their breakfast quickly and then dressed in snowsuits and heavy boots. Kenny grabbed his .22 rifle from the gun case and several shells. Timmy dragged his red wagon outside. In a spate of ingenuity, the boys had fitted it with skis.

'See you later, Dad!' Kenny shouted as he and his little brother made their way out the backyard.

'You gonna get another squirrel?!'

'You bet, Dad!'

'Hey! I spotted it!' Timmy shouted.

'Spot another!' Hollander shouted back.

Delia packed Hollander's lunch in an old pail and gave it to him. It felt lighter than normal. He looked inside and saw a small roll.

'Running low on flour?'

Delia nodded. 'You have to work. I can give you another.'

Hollander shook his head. 'You need to eat too.'

He looked out the window and followed the boys as they made their way down the road. 'They headed to the woods again?'

'Yes. They'll stay out there until they get cold and then some.'

'They're having a great time,' he said.

She smiled. 'They'll still have to do their studies when they get back.'

'What about their teacher?'

'If she doesn't show again today I'll assign them something.'

'OK.'

'Find out where she is, please.'

'OK.'

He looked for the boys but couldn't see them. 'I better get going.'

Hollander took his wife in his arms and kissed her. As she squeezed him, he felt her ribs.

'Don't give all the food to the boys.'
'I know.'
'You have to eat too.'
'I know.'
He kissed her again.
'I'll be late,' he said as he went out the door.
'I know.'

Hollander put on his sunglasses against the sun's glare. His walk of nearly a mile over packed, frozen snow took him through the center of town. People were already out, many dragging sleds or wagons behind them, all wearing several layers of clothing. He saw one middle-aged couple wearing Winnie the Pooh and Piglet Halloween suits. They were warm, at least. Hollander nodded and waved but did not stop to chat. He learned early, that they would only ask him for news and information about when the electricity was coming back or chew his ear off with their problems.

He passed Mrs. Jenner's house and saw that she had started a bonfire with the debris she had piled outside. Several people had gathered around the fire to keep warm. Hollander walked over to Mrs. Jenner's house. She sat in a cold metal folding chair on her porch wearing nothing but a thin mu-mu style gown.

'Mrs. Jenner, get inside!' Hollander shouted to her.

'It's my porch and if I want to sit out here I will.'

'But… ' Hollander looked at Mrs. Jenner and saw there was no point in arguing. He turned to the half dozen people gathered around the fire. They nodded to him.

'Hey folks. When this fire dies down, help put it out, throw some snow on it, okay?'

They nodded.

Hollander walked to the porch steps but did not ascend them. 'Mrs. Jenner. If I had my book with me I'd cite you.'

'For what?'

Her skin was red and raw from the cold.

'You need a permit for a fire like that.'

'Permit!' she screamed. 'A permit. I barely have enough to eat. I aint got no help from the town. I can barely keep warm and you're talkin' to me about permits!'

'Yes, ma'am.'

'You come back tomorrow, Officer Hollander. I'll show you! I'll show you!'

Hollander held out his hands. 'I'm not dealing with you like this Mrs. Jenner. Permit next time.'

Hollander checked in at the station and then went out back to the motor pool. Ryan was already waiting in the cruiser, though he hadn't started the engine. Hollander twirled his finger in the air as he walked up to the car, Ryan gratefully reached over to the driver's side and started the car.

Hollander got in and rubbed his hands.

'I think it's even colder today,' he said.

'It is,' Ryan replied.

Hollander drove the car out of the motor pool.

'Where we headed?' Ryan asked.

'Take a turn around town. I want to stop by Ms. Becker's place.'

'The teacher?'

'Yeah, she hasn't come by my house.'

Ms. Becker rented half of an old Victorian, long since converted into a two family home, near one of the dairy farms on the south side of Livermore. When he'd last had the night shift, Hollander had driven past it often, to keep an eye on the dairy farm, and had seen candlelight flickering long into the night. Ms. Becker was a confirmed bookworm, and had more than once bragged that she didn't care about losing the electricity because she still had her books.

They pulled into the driveway. In the distance they could see a man trudging through the snow toward one of the cowsheds, a shotgun slung over his shoulder. Further still, they could see two figures, both of them armed against pilferers.

Hollander got out of the car.

'Leave the engine on?' Ryan asked hopefully.

'Alright.'

Hollander walked up the porch and knocked on the door. After waiting ten seconds he knocked again. 'Miss Becker!' he shouted.

Finally the door opened. Emma Becker looked like a mess. She was wrapped in several blankets, her hair was unkempt and stringy, her face red and puffy as if she'd been crying a long time. Her eyes looked red through her black, horn-rimmed glasses.

'Officer Hollander, please come in.'

The apartment was cold, of course, but also messy. Ms. Becker, Hollander knew, was a meticulous organizer. The fireplace looked like it hadn't been used in a while despite the stack of wood before it. Her town issued bike rested against it. Books were scattered about, Hollander saw several Jane Austin novels, the complete *Twilight* series; *Orange is the New Black*, he looked away in embarrassment when he saw *Fifty Shades of Grey*. Reams of white paper were stacked before her old-fashioned manual typewriter. Ms. Becker had made it known that'd she'd been keeping a meticulous journal since Arrival.

'Is everything alright, Ms. Becker?' Hollander asked.

She nodded meekly.

'We haven't seen you around town the last few days.'

'I've been a little sick.'

'Catch something?'

'No...'

'Then what's wrong?'

'It's just that....'

'What?'

'You see, my medication ran out.'

'Medication? What like Amoxicillin?'

'No...Prozac.'

'Prozac?'

'Yeah.'

'How long have you been taking Prozac?'

'Since my boyfriend dumped me senior year..' tears started to well up in her eyes.

'Of college?'

'Of high school!' she sobbed.

Hollander rubbed his face.

'Ms. Becker, we do not have time for all of this.'

She sobbed more.

Hollander grabbed Ms. Becker by the shoulders.

'Now look here. You are paid a food and fuel credit by the town to teach our children. If you don't want to do it anymore, we can find someone who will. Got it?'

Ms. Becker looked at him through her tears. 'Yeah.'

'I expect to see you around town today.'

'Okay.' she sniffled.

Hollander looked her over one more time and then headed out the door.

'Everything good?' Ryan asked.

'Yeah she's just having some sort of breakdown, ran out of medicine.'

'Ran out of medicine?'

'Yeah, like the whole world revolves around her feelings.' Hollander shook his head. 'Let's get out of here.'

They took several turns around the town. A grateful Ryan luxuriated in the heat. Hollander didn't mind it himself. At 11:40 the radio squawked. It was the chief.

Hollander picked up the receiver. 'Hollander here.'

'It's getting pretty crowded at City Hall. Drop your patrol and get down here.'

'OK, chief.'

Hollander parked the cruiser at the station and walked the block down to city hall.

The room was usually about half full, but today it was packed. Every seat taken and people were standing along the walls. As there was no heat inside the town hall, everyone was bundled up. At least a dozen people had on fur lined camo hunting clothes. All of the men and some of the women had side arms and/or rifles with them. Partly for protection. There were some rogue groups outside of Owensboro Hollander thought, but mostly in case they spotted something they could shoot and eat.

At ten after noon, the mayor entered the meeting room. He stopped and shook hands with people in the aisle seats, answered questions as best he could, and asked them questions about how they were doing. It took him nearly ten minutes to make his way to the stage. Mayor Thomasson had thinned out like everyone else, and his wavy hair was graying a bit. He wore a heavy overcoat which he had unzipped revealing a three-piece suit. He had been the town lawyer before running for mayor, unopposed. Hollander knew via the chief, that Thomasson had bigger political ambitions. The chief was up on the stage, as was the Director of the Department of Public Works (a waste Hollander thought, as nothing was working) and the school superintendent.

There was no loudspeaker of course, so Mayor Thomasson simply stood at the front of the stage and projected his voice, 'Hey folks, it's good to see so many of you here.' He reached into his coat pocket and took out a slip of paper upon which he had scribbled some notes.

'First thing, as always if residents of Livermore have a complaint, please take it to the specific, relevant agency.'

'You're the mayor!' someone shouted.

Mayor Thomasson ignored the heckler. 'Next, those needing firewood can apply at the Department of Public Works this afternoon. Supplies are extremely low this week.'

Thomasson cleared his throat. 'To that end, we need people for the firewood detail. You will be paid with twenty percent of the wood you chop. See Public Works if you're interested.'

The mayor took a deep breath and exhaled, filling the space around him with white air. He reached into his pocket and took out another piece of paper. This one was crisp and white, and had a federal seal on it.

'This letter is from FEMA.'

There were groans in the audience. Livermore hadn't seen a FEMA agent in months and had received no help from the federal agency whatsoever.

'It informs me, as mayor, that tomorrow we will be receiving federal refugees.'

There was shouting this time. Someone shouted, 'What the hell are we supposed to do with them?'

It took the mayor more than a minute to get the room quieted down. 'Listen folks, we don't have a choice in the matter, OK!'

There was more shouting from the audience. From the stage, the chief motioned for Hollander to come up. He trotted to the front and stood in front of the stage and held his hands up, 'C'mon, people!' he shouted, 'Let the man speak!'

Finally the people stopped shouting.

'As I said, we have to take them. The letter also notes that the refugees will come in federal transport, whatever that means, and will be accompanied by the Kentucky National Guard.'

'How many?!' shouted Burt Hopkins. He owned the biggest dairy farm in town. Naturally, his voice, and views carried weight.

'Doesn't say,' responded the mayor.

There were more protests from the audience. One man, Frank Sellers, who was known by Hollander and the town to be something of a rabble rouser and agitator against all things not-Livermore shouted, 'We aint seen shit from the feds, now they saddle us with a bunch of refugees!'

Sellers got the audience stirred up again. He turned and shouted, 'We gonna take this!? Let's blockade 401 and turn them back!'

The chief stood up and tapped Hollander on the shoulder and pointed to Sellers.

Without a word Hollander walked over to him. 'Sit down, Frank,' he said.

'This is still America, you can't shut me up, officer,' Sellers said.

'I'm not trying to shut you up, just sit down,' he said firmly.

Sellers sat down.

'Look, folks,' said the Mayor. 'I told all this to the governor when he told it to me. We have no choice. Anybody tries to stop the feds, I'll have him thrown in the Klink.'

The chief spoke. 'What are you going to do, people? Go up against the National Guard?'

Given the reality of federal force being used to forcibly make them take refugees, people calmed down and listened. It was agreed that they'd house the refugees, however many there were, in the high school. The mayor asked for donations of food and clothing. Hollander knew the people of Livermore had little to spare, but most would try to give something. Hopkins spoke.

'Look folks, we can give them milk, that's something. I have the cows but I need some help with the labor. I suppose these newcomers can help with that. I bet I can find a cow to slaughter for them. I bet some of the other farmers can too.'

Hopkins looked out to the dairy farmers scattered throughout the audience, many of whom nodded.

Sellers shouted, 'You had extra milk and you didn't give it to us?!'

Hopkins was a big man, he scowled at Sellers and said, 'I don't see you milking my cows. I'll get some help, I can make do.'

The dairy farmers commiserated in the back of the room.

'So look folks,' said the mayor, 'We're going to take these people in and do right by them the best we can. I'm not asking for much, just what you can do. You don't live in some big city, you live in small town Livermore, and don't you forget it.'

More questions were coming from the crowd such as; what other towns would be forced to take in people, and how long were they going to stay. He didn't have the answers and dismissed the meeting.

Hollander stayed at the front of the stage, watching the people leave. They talked amongst themselves, from the snippets he picked up they weren't happy. Few milled about outside, it was still cold. Sellers did though, he stood in a circle of a dozen men and women and ranted against FEMA, the Kentucky National Guard, and the mayor.

Hollander walked over to the group. 'Move along folks. Get home, it's cold.'

'We have the right to peaceably assemble!' Sellers shouted.

'Go home, Frank.'

Sellers didn't move.

'Wanna get busted for vagrancy?' Hollander asked. 'There's no heat in the jail you know.'

Sellers and his crowd reluctantly dispersed.

Hollander shook his head. 'Like he doesn't have bigger things to worry about.'

'You say something Lieutenant?' Ryan asked.

'Nah,' Hollander said. 'Let's take a turn around town.'

William Stroock

They started at the river to check on the ice fishers and worked their way into town from there. They saw a rising, billowing plume of smoke near the center of town.

'Oh, great, Mrs. Jenner again,' said Hollander. 'Let's go over there.'

When they got to Mrs. Jenner's the house was in flames. Mrs. Jenner stood in front of the burning house, the wind blowing her mumu against her portly frame. Hollander got out of the cruiser. 'Mrs. Jenner, what the hell are you doing!?' he shouted.

'What am I doing?!' she shouted back. 'I'll show you what I'm doing!' She backed up a few steps and ran forward and dived head first into the flames.

He couldn't have saved her even if he tried. There was no water pressure for the fire department to use, so the EMTs waited for the fire to die before retrieving what was left of Mrs. Jenner's body.

When Hollander got home he smelled meat cooking and saw two skewered squirrels and a chipmunk over the fire. In the kitchen the boys did homework by candlelight. On the couch, with Delia, was Ms. Becker. Her eyes were swollen from crying. The young woman looked up at Hollander and said, 'I had better get going.'

She quickly gathered her things and hurried out the door without so much as acknowledging Hollander.

'What did I do?' he asked.

'She says you were mean to her.'

'Oh for Christ sake, I told her to do her job.'

Delia stood up and put her arms around her husband. 'I didn't say I agreed with her.'

Hollander hugged her. 'Jesus, if you had seen what I saw...'

'I heard,' she gently ran her fingers through his hair.

Hollander reluctantly let go. 'The boys, bring those back?'

'And cleaned them,' Cathy said. 'Almost ready, I'll get you a plate.'

'Don't bother,' Hollander said. 'Ryan had some jerky he made from a couple of raccoons he caught, I'm OK,' he lied.

The family ate in front of the fire, roast squirrel and chipmunk and ten potato chips each. Hollander had a few pieces of chipmunk just to satisfy Delia, but otherwise let his family devour the meal. Hollander watched Delia to make sure she didn't give any of her food to the boys. Later that night with Delia warm and content against Hollander, his stomach growled, but he didn't care.

Hollander was awakened by frantic knocking on the door.

'They're here!' Ryan shouted.

Hollander got up from bed and walked to the door. 'What time is it?' Hollander asked.

'Just after six,' Ryan replied. 'They're here already.'

'Who?'

'The refugees. The Feds brought them into town before anyone knew it. They're at the high school now.'

Hollander rubbed his face. 'Great.'

'The chief wants us down there right now.'

'Any trouble?'

'Sellers is already down there.'

'Wonderful.'

The boys hadn't stirred but Delia was up. 'What's wrong?'

'Refugees are here already.' Hollander said as he pulled his boots on. 'I gotta go.'

Hollander and Ryan drove down to the high school. In the parking lot were two battered military busses, two army trucks and several Humvees. Soldiers stood at the entrance to the lot and the school, and around the trucks. Some took boxes out of the trucks and carried them inside. At the entrance was the mayor and the chief, standing with an army officer. Sellers and three other men stood just off the school property before a line of soldiers, all of whom held rifles at their sides.

They drove in and parked by the chief's cruiser. Hollander and Ryan walked up to the entrance.

'Mr. Mayor, chief,' Hollander said.

Both men nodded. The chief spoke. 'This is Captain Jones, Kentucky National Guard. Captain, Lieutenant Hollander.'

The two shook hands. 'You picked a hell of a time to bring people in, Captain.'

William Stroock

'Not my choice Lieutenant Hollander. The authorities seem to think transporting folks in the early morning will avoid trouble.'

Hollander shrugged. 'I suppose so.'

'A few weeks ago we brought a bunch of busses into Paducah and a riot broke out. Had to clear it out with bayonets.'

'You gonna stick around and help us out with these people?'

'You going to feed us?'

Hollander laughed.

'We're going back through Owensboro and patrolling the Ohio.'

'What for?'

'Governor wants us to keep unauthorized persons from crossing into the state. That's what we do, at least until we get Federalized again.'

'But you settle people here?' the Mayor asked.

'Doesn't make sense, does it?' Captain Jones nodded toward Sellers who glowered at the men and women in the parking lot. 'Looks like you have some trouble.'

'Yeah,' said Hollander, 'Sellers is a bit of a blowhard.'

'I'd keep an eye on him. Over in Henderson a bunch of locals ran some refugees out. We had to go resettle them by force. Couple people got shot.'

'I don't think that'll happen here,' said the mayor.

Hollander cleared his throat, 'Lieutenant, Mr. Mayor, Chief, if you don't mind I'd like to go inside and introduce myself to the refugees.'

'Go ahead,' said Captain Jones, 'But they're not the most social people.'

'What do you mean?'

'You'll see.'

Hollander went into the high school. Several soldiers milled about the lobby and the hallway to the gym. Hollander nodded to each. The gym was lit only by candles. He could see the risers had been pulled out. Several Livermore Public Works employees were setting up cots and passing out blankets. Hollander was taken aback by the children. Dozens of boys ran wild through the gym, chasing, pushing and tackling one another. They all wore dark pants, long sleeve shirts, and sneakers. Many had funny looking curls of hair on the side of their faces. Then Hollander saw the men. They wore the same clothes as the boys. All had beards and most sported the same funny strands of hair on their faces. Then Hollander saw the kipas upon their heads.

A gaggle of boys ran circles around one of the stacks of MREs until one tripped and toppled the boxes. The boy got up and resumed running, his friends chased him. A couple of men talking nearby pointed to the MREs and laughed. One of the public works guys walked over and restacked the boxes. Hollander turned away from the boxes and looked for someone in charge that he could introduce himself to. Near center court he saw a circle of men, they had shawls over their shoulders, some had funny strips of leather strung along their arms. They all read from open books and bobbed up and down. As Hollander walked over he could hear the men speaking a strange, guttural language.

Must be Hebrew, he thought.

One man seemed to stand apart from the others. He was large with grey hair and beard. He wore glasses and a heavy black overcoat. To Hollander's eyes he clearly looked in charge. Hollander stood discreetly aside as the men went through their prayers. When they were finished the large man said 'Amen'. Hollander stepped forward to introduce himself, but before he could the large man walked right past him.

Hollander asked, 'Was he in charge?'

The other men looked away from Hollander and talked amongst themselves.

Hollander looked around, seeing no one to talk to he left the gym.

That night he told Delia about the new arrivals.

'Oh,' she said, 'I bet they're Orthodox Jews. My roommate at UK was Jewish, not Orthodox though.'

'They weren't very talkative,' Hollander said.

'Yeah, she said they're kind of shy and keep to themselves.'

The next morning Hollander was walking to work when he saw a boy coming out of a small yellow shotgun house. He recognized the boy, one of the Mexican kids from the apartment houses on the south side of town.

'Hey, Manny!' Hollander shouted.

Manny didn't stop, or even acknowledge Hollander. He saw that the kid had a couple cans of tuna in his hand.

'Hey Manny, hold on!'

Manny finally stopped and turned. His face was a patch of brown beneath layers of wool and nylon. His family had come up from Mexico a few months before Arrival, and he was enduring his first Midwestern winter. He shivered against the cold.

'Where'd you get the Tuna?'

'Traded for it.'

'Traded what?'

'Corn.'

'Family doing OK?'

He nodded.

'Alright, get out of the cold.'

Manny hustled down the street back toward his family's apartment.

Hollander looked at the shotgun house. It was one of several owned by Mrs. Crabtree, the heiress to a once powerful family in town. He knew it had been rented for several months before the war, a single man, as Hollander recalled, but he didn't really know him. He worked at the Perdue plant, as had Manny.

When Hollander got to the station he saw that the chief seemed to be in a good mood. 'Chief, that's as close to a smile as I've seen you come to in months.'

'Well, we're having another meeting tomorrow.'

'What for now?'

'Power company rep.'

Hollander lifted his eyebrows.

'Oh really? That might be good news.'

'Well, let's hope so. Until then, I want you to head down to the high school, talk to the folks there.'

'Sure, what about?'

'One of their rabbis was in here already complaining. Said folks around town were bothering them. Fella by the name of Kaplinski.'

'Alright, I'll head over there now.'

When he got to the high school, Hollander's cruiser was swarmed by a dozen Orthodox boys. None of them wore coats despite the cold. They gathered around Hollander when he got out but none actually spoke. They bounced and hopped around as if they'd never seen a police officer before. Rabbi Kaplinksi was at the entrance, wrapped in a large black coat and what seemed to Hollander like a comically oversized fur hat. Hollander waved and walked over to him.

Without greeting him Kaplinksi said, 'You must keep these shiksas away from us?'

'I'm sorry, Rabbi, the what?'

'Shiksas.'

'What's a shiksa?'

'A non-Jewish woman.'

'Are they bothering you?' Hollander asked.

'Yes, several walked past the school.'

'Did they cause some kind of problem?'

'We don't want to see them.'

A gust of wind blew past, waving the rabbi's prayer curls in the air.

'I'm sorry, I don't see how they would be a problem. Who was here?'

'A pair of shiksas walked into the school and went into the office, here.'

'Ohhhh,' Hollander said.

'You must mean the staff. We have a teacher going around town to instruct students, I bet that was Miss Becker, and one of the secretaries? Was it Mrs. Ferry?'

'I did not stop to talk to them.'

'Well I'll...'

'Just make sure they stay away.'

With that, Kaplinski went inside the school.

Not wanting a scene, Hollander walked back to his cruiser. As he drove off he felt and heard a snowball hit the back window. In the rear view mirror he could see the kids gathered in a group, waiting to see what he'd do. Hollander drove on.

That night Hollander walked into his house shaking his head. He was too tired to even take off his boots outside, and simply slumped into the easy chair in front of the fire.

'Where are the boys?' Hollander asked.

'They're taking Miss Becker home.' Hollander looked at Delia. 'At night?'

'They both have rifles. They'll be fine. It's Miss Becker I'm worried about.'

Delia went to the kitchen, got a can of soup, and poured it into the kettle over the fire.

'The boys will have a great time.'

'True.' Hollander rubbed his face. 'Wait? Was this Miss Becker's day for us?'

'No,' replied Delia. 'She came over here after having some trouble at the high school. Do you know what they did?'

'I went over there already. The chief said Rabbi Kaplinski came down to the station to complain about…what did he call them…?'

'Shiksas?!' Delia said incredulously.

'How did you know?'

'Because a gaggle of little Orthodox Jewish boys hounded Miss Becker from the moment she walked on campus till the moment she left, calling her, Shiksa among other names. And your Rabbi was watching the whole time.'

Hollander held up his hands. 'Don't blame them on me. They threw snow balls at my cruiser.'

Delia softened a bit. 'You're right. I'm sorry.'

The soup was ready. Delia poured it into a mug and handed it to her husband.

'You're running yourself ragged,' she said.

'Thanks.'

He quickly ate the soup. Delia took the cup and put it in the kitchen. She sat back and sat in Hollander's lap.

'You feel good,' he said.

Delia smiled. 'So do you.'

Hollander mumbled. 'It's too cold for any of that…'

Delia brushed a hand through his hair. 'Just close your eyes.'

'Ok…Big meeting tomorrow,' he mumbled.

The town meeting began promptly at 9:00 am. There was a man up on the stage with the mayor, Hollander didn't recognize him. To Hollander's eyes he looked to be about fifty. He was large, long limbed and had short, gray hair atop his head. He wore blue jeans, heavy work boots and a thick, blue coat with a fury hood. The mayor introduced him, 'This is Tom Casper, he's a representative of the power company.'

Before the mayor could finish, a great chorus of boos rang out from the auditorium. The man stepped forward and held up his hands but it was no use. People booed, and then they shouted, and then they screamed. Hollander watched Casper, who simply returned to his seat and waited. He had done this dozens of times already, Hollander realized. When the mayor finally got the crowd quieted down, which took about five minutes, Casper stood up again and walked to the edge of the stage.

'I'll make it real simple folks. We're coming.'

This time the audience cheered and clapped for more than a minute. When the deluge subsided Casper spoke again. 'Now don't get too excited folks. We're coming, we're not here yet. It'll be at least a few weeks. Honestly, probably more.'

'But you are going to get the power back on?' someone in the audience asked.

'Yes,' he said unequivocally. 'We've got the trucks. We've got the gas. We've got the lines. We've got the poles. We've got the equipment we need to fix the substations. We have everything we need except one thing. Manpower. We need your help folks.'

There was a murmur throughout the room.

'We need folks to clear the lines. If you see busted poles, take 'em down. If you see downed lines, just coil them up by the side of the road. The juice isn't on yet so there's no danger there. If there's debris around the poles, clear that. If you do that, it will make our job a lot easier, and your power will get on a lot faster.'

There was more murmuring in the audience. Hollander saw lots of men nodding heads. Mr. Hopkins walked to the back with a few other dairy farmers and talked. He walked up to the stage and spoke with Casper for a few minutes, no doubt getting tips on pole removal. Finally, Hollander heard someone shout, 'Hey what about the Jews?!'

He turned and saw Sellers standing near the middle of the seats.

'What about the Jews?!' he repeated.

'What about them?' the mayor replied.

'They ain't doin' anything. They're getting all this free stuff from us and the Feds. Least they could do is pitch in.'

There was renewed murmuring in the audience. The mayor looked over at the chief, 'You know, he's right,' he said. The two men spoke for a moment.

'They're our guests here and...'

'Alright, Sellers,' the mayor said. 'The chief will go down there today.'

'Good!'

Sellers sat down. The people sitting with him were the same half dozen people Hollander had seen with him the other day.

'Hollander!' the chief shouted across the room. He pointed to him and motioned for him to come over to the stage. Hollander walked over. 'You and me are going to head over to the school in a bit.'

'Sure thing, Chief.'

When the meeting was finished the chief and Hollander drove over to the school. The National Guard trucks were gone, but standing in front of the door were a quartet of men, all clad in black and white, kipa and prayer curls. Hollander and the chief walked over.

'Watch Sellers,' the chief said.

'He's just a blow hard,' Hollander replied.

'Yes he is. But he's a trouble maker, always has been. Remember a few years ago when he plastered the town with Gadsden flags?'

'I don't begrudge the man his politics.'

'Neither do I, but just watch him. Hot head like that. Times like this.'

When they got to the door the four men sitting there stood up. One stepped forward a few steps and said, 'Can I help you?'

'Just wanted to talk to the rabbi,' the chief said.

'Which rabbi?' the man asked 'We have more than a dozen.'

'The head rabbi,' said the chief. 'Rabbi Rosenzweig.' He walked forward, the Jewish man held out his hand.

'You can't go in,' he said. Hollander noticed how he said everything in a rapid fire, clipped fashion that seemed to cut the words off. He also wasn't looking the chief in the eye.

'Son,' the chief said, 'I'm the Chief of the Livermore Police. Get out of the way.'

The man and his compatriots reluctantly moved. The chief and Hollander walked into the school and went down to the gym. On their way they heard loud, rhythmic chanting. Inside they saw a few hundred people bobbing back and forth and popping up and down every few seconds to the chants. The room was divided by a rope strung from one end to the other, several blankets and tarps hung on the rope, creating a rough screen between the two sides. On one side was men, on the other women and children.

A black coated man walked over to them and held up his hands, 'You two cannot be in here!' he said over the chanting. 'Please leave.'

'Who are you?' asked the chief.

'I am Rabbi Kaplinski and you two cannot be in here.'

'How much longer is this going on?' the chief asked.

Kaplinski held out his hands again and held them against the chief. The chief pushed him away. 'You put your hands on me again I'll run you in.'

Kaplinksi stood back with a look of surprise on his face.

The chief stepped forward now, 'I asked you how long?'

'Uhhh, these are our afternoon prayers. They will be completed shortly.'

'When you're finished, tell Rabbi Rosenzwieg we need to see him.'

Kaplinksi said nothing.

'Got it?'

Kaplinksi nodded.

The chief pointed to the door. 'We'll be right out there.'

They took seats outside the gym and folded their arms against the cold.

'How come none of these guys will look you in the eye?' the chief asked.

Hollander shrugged.

A few minutes later the chanting stopped. Then, Hollander and the chief waited but Rabbi Rosenzwieg didn't appear. After ten minutes or so the chief said, 'Let's go in and see him.'

They walked back into the gym. Kaplinksi was standing just inside the entrance. 'Where's Rabbi Rosenzwieg?' the chief asked.

'He's in the office.'

'He has an office?' the chief asked.

Kaplinski pointed to the bank of offices at the end of the gym. Hollander didn't recall those being unlocked.

The two police officers started toward the office, Kaplinksi held out a hand to stop them.

'You can't go over there,' he said.

They swatted Kaplinksi's hand away. 'Let's get one thing straight,' he said. 'I am the chief of police. You got it?'

'But, you have to go through the women's section. You can't go there.'

'What did I just tell you, Kaplinksi?'

Hollander shuttered. When the chief used a last name like that without a salutation, it meant he was angry.

'C'mon, Hollander.'

As the pair walked through the gym, people looked away from them, most of the women turned their backs and grabbed their children to keep them away. A large tarp had been draped on the office window and another on the door window. Through the cracks a couple of candles flickered. A pair of men sat against the wall. When they saw the chief and Hollander approaching they stood up. One said, 'You can't go in there.'

Fed up with the intransigence the chief walked past them and knocked on the door.

'Not now!' a great voice bellowed.

The chief opened the door. Inside the rabbi sat at the office eating a plate full of eggs, more than Hollander had seen since Arrival. But that's not what grabbed his attention. The walls were lined with makeshift shelves cobbled together with wood planks and cinder blocks. Upon them sat hundreds of hardcover and leather-bound books, most had funny writing on them, which Hollander supposed was Hebrew. There was a cot in the corner upon which rested a twin mattress and a camp stove.

Rabbi Rosenzweig looked up from his plate. 'I said not now.'

'Rabbi,' began the chief. 'I'm here to talk to you.'

'Can't it wait?'

'Afraid not.' The chief told him about the looming power restoration. 'Basically, we could use your help. If you could send some men out to clear the debris, well we'd all be real thankful.'

Rabbi Rosenzweig pursed his lips and rubbed his beard in deep contemplation. 'I don't think so,' he said.

'Why not?' asked the chief.

'Between prayer and religious study we won't have time.'

'It's just going to be a few hours,' said the chief.

'I'm sorry.'

The chief stood dumbfounded for a few moments, as if he was waiting for Rosenzweig to laugh and tell him it was a joke and of course they could get out and help. Finally, the rabbi spoke. 'By the way, the bathrooms need cleaning.'

'Well, there are mops and buckets in there.'

'Yes, but where is the staff?'

Hollander could see the chief run his fingers, ever so gently, across the handle of his nightstick. 'let's go, Hollander.' he said.

The chief walked quickly out of the gym, Hollander could barely keep up. His face was dark, and jaw was clenched. He was livid, Hollander knew, but too professional to give the rabbi a tongue lashing. When they got back to the car he finally let loose a barrage of curses ended with, 'What the hell was that!? I mean, Jesus Christ!' He punched the steering wheel. 'What the hell?!'

When they got back to the station, word had arrived about another death. This time it was Mrs. Crabtree. Hollander had known her all his life, and when he was a teenager had made money mowing her lawn and shoveling her driveway.

'You go over there?' the chief asked.

'I'll take care of it.'

Hollander drove over to Mrs. Crabtree's house. Her neighbor, a middle-aged man who had run a gas station in town, waited on the front porch. He was bundled up against the subfreezing weather and wearing heavy sunglasses against the sun.

'Hey, Davey,' Hollander said.

'Good afternoon, officer. Mrs. Crabtree is up in her bedroom.'

'How'd you find her?'

'I've been checking on her a few times a day, at least. You know, I'd come over, start a fire for her, stuff like that.'

'Uh huh.'

'I knocked on her door, there was no answer. So I forced it open, you can see the door knob knocked off there.'

'Got it.'

'I called for her, but no answer. She's in her bed under about five blankets. I guess she just popped off last night.'

Hollander went inside Mrs. Crabtree's house and up to her bedroom. He saw a bit of spittle, frozen now, on her mouth. She was already cold. He picked her up and carried her out to his patrol car where he lay her gently on the backseat. He covered Mrs. Crabtree with a blanket.

Back at the station, Hollander filled out paper work and got a toe tag. He then drove her up to the cemetery. He pulled up before the maintenance shack. There was supposed to be a town worker there, but Hollander didn't see him. He'd most likely left because of the cold. Hollander opened the shack and put Mrs. Crabtree's' shrouded body on the last turn of a makeshift shelf. Several bodies were above. The ground was frozen and there was no diesel for the cemetery backhoe.

When he got back to the station the chief said, 'I want you to take a group of guys on cleanup tomorrow.'

'Sure.'

'We'll have volunteers meet here in the morning. Head out to 401 and clear out what you can.'

'Ok, Chief.'

The next morning was cold and sunny, with the rays bouncing off the frozen snow.

When Hollander got to the police station, a dozen men clad in heavy coats, work boots and each carrying a shovel or an axe waited out.

'You fellas ready?' Hollander asked.

One stepped forward. It was Charlie Bass. He was a local contractor, and had done some work for Hollander. He'd done some work for most people around town. Most of the men with him had worked with him as well.

'Ready when you are, Officer!' Charlie said cheerfully.

They piled inside the police van, not out of enthusiasm, but because it would be warm, Hollander knew. Hollander rode shotgun in the van, Ryan drove. They went slowly up 401 until they came to the burned out Jai ship. Hollander got out of the van and took a look.

When it had crashed the previous November, the Jai ship had come down in one of the cornfields adjacent to the highway. The ship's momentum took it through the field and across 401, taking out several telephone poles and chewing up several feet of concrete. The ship itself was large, larger than a B-1 or Stealth bomber. Soon after it crashed, the National Guard had come and gone over the Jai ship, stripping it of everything of value and recovering the crew, all of whom were found dead.

Hollander didn't really have to do anything. They filed out of the van, Charlie clapped his gloved hands and said, 'Alright fellas. Let's get these telephone poles cleared out of here.'

The men gingerly piled out of the van.

'We'll chop off the telephone poles, ok?'

'C'mon, Mr. Bass, one of the men said. 'It must be ten degrees out here.'

'Well keep moving then and you'll keep warm.' The assembled volunteers looked at Hollander who said nothing. Even through their sunglasses and bundled faces, their skepticism showed. He reached inside the van and grabbed an axe. 'I'll pitch in too.'

The cold and hungry men made short work of the half dozen telephone poles. When they were done, one of the men walked over to a drainage ditch a hundred feet off the road to relieve himself.

'Hey!' he shouted. 'There's a body over here!'

Hollander ran over to the ditch and looked in. Lying at the bottom on his back was a body.

'That's not human,' Hollander said. 'It's a Jai.'

Because of the cold, the body had hardly decomposed at all. The grey skin was frozen over as were the eyes and hair. The Jai's face had been gashed open and red blood had frozen black down his chin and neck.

'C'mon,' Hollander jumped down into the ditch. 'Help me carry him to the road.'

They hauled the body back to the van and dropped it. It landed on the cold asphalt with a loud, frozen thump.

'I aint riding back with that thing,' Ryan said.

'Relax I'll call for a car to come get it.'

'Phew,' he said.

Charlie clapped his hands. 'In the meantime, you guys walk down both sides of the highway and clear debris off the road and away from the poles.'

There was more moaning.

'Hey!' Charlie shouted. 'The power company is coming right down this road. You want the lights turned back on or not?'

The men worked sluggishly but steadily for another hour until the cold got to be too much even for the perpetually enthusiastic Charlie.

'I think that's it,' he said. 'We stay out here much longer we're going to lose some extremities.'

'Alright. You guys finish up,' Hollander said. 'I'll go start up the van. It will be nice and warm for you.'

The men cheered at that.

When they got in the van, the men took off their gloves and opened their coats to let the heat get to them.

'Nice work today, fellas,' Charlie said. He elbowed Hollander and leaned over to him, 'Can we hang out here a little while? Don't use much gas just to idle.'

'Yeah, the guys earned it.'

Hollander leaned back in the driver's seat a little and listened while the men talked. Most seemed happy to be out of the house. More than a few complained about trying to keep their kids happy and busy. One of the younger guys complained about his recently pregnant wife. When one of the older men asked why he'd knocked her up at a time like this he simply replied, 'Hey, no TV, no internet, there's nothing else to do.' The older men nodded.

Someone else said, 'Or you could go yellow.'

Another said, 'Shut up, I did what I had to do.'

'Yeah at the yellow shotgun house.'

Hollander turned around in time to see the two men throwing punches at each other. He dived into the back of the van and got between them. The next thing he knew, Hollander took a punch to the jaw.

'Oh crap!' someone said.

The other men in the van tackled the two brawlers. Charlie grabbed the instigator by the hair and shouted at him.

To Survive the Earth

'Alright!' Hollander shouted.

'Instead of going home, you both are coming to the station with me!'

There was a groan from each.

Charlie offered to drop them off and drive the rest of the men home. Hollander agreed. If you couldn't trust Charlie...

Back at the jail, Hollander tossed both men into a cell together. The first, Jim, who had thrown the first punch, was a younger guy and single. The second, Ron, was older and married.

'What's going on?' Hollander demanded. 'And if I don't get answers you'll spend a few days here while we sort things out. Lucky for you guys, I can't tell which of you actually punched me.'

'Look Jim,' Ron began, 'You better just tell him.'

After a little more cajoling, Jim finally spoke. 'I work with him at the Perdue plant.'

'Who? Hollander asked.

'Terry. He was a new guy at the plant.'

'And?'

Ron spoke, 'Let's just say he's got a lot of food stored up and he don't like girls.'

Hollander looked at Jim, who blushed and hung his head.

'I see and he's giving food for...'

'Yes.'

'Alright.' Hollander patted Jim on the shoulder. 'Hard times. you gotta do what you gotta do.'

Ron was about to speak but Hollander glared at him, 'Don't say a word. Both of you get out of here. You can walk home.'

'What was that all about?' the chief asked when Hollander came out of the cell.

'We got a little sex for food problem.'

The chief shook his head.

'I'll take care of it.'

'Nice work finding that Jai body,' he said.

'One of the guys found it.'

149

William Stroock

'We've already called the Feds, they're on the way to pick it up.'
'I let the workers keep the wood from the chopped up telephone poles.'
'We got a problem other than prostitution,' the chief said.
'What's new?' a weary Hollander asked.
'Bob Sellers was here.'
'That's never good.'
'No,' replied the chief. 'Sellers is going to hold a protest at the school tomorrow.'
'A protest? In this weather?'
'Uh-huh.'
'What the hell for?'
'He's protesting the refugees and their refusal to work when they're getting all this federal help.'

Hollander shrugged. 'He's got a point.'
'Maybe he does, Lieutenant, but I couldn't care less.'
'Can't we stop him?'
The chief shook his head. 'He paid the fifteen dollars for the permit.'
'Where'd he get fifteen bucks?'
'No one is using money. He must have had it saved up.'
'Well, if it's just Sellers, I mean, how much trouble can he make?'
'That's the problem. He's got a group of guys with him and they're going all over town right now. Telling people the time and place.'

Hollander shook his head. 'Like he doesn't have anything better to do.'
'He's always been a troublemaker.'
'What do you think the Jews will do?'
The Chief threw up his hands, 'I don't know. Honestly, as long as they have their food and their housing, they may not care.'
'You want me down there?' Hollander asked.
The chief shook his head, 'I'll be down there with most of the men.'
'What about me?'
'I want you to keep an eye on the rest of town.'
When he got home, the boys were cooking an opossum over the fire.
'Hey, how 'bout that!' Hollander exclaimed.

Kenny and Timmy didn't look up. Instead they studiously turned the spit over the fire. Hollander walked over to the boys and patted them both on the head. 'Good work, boys,' he said.

Delia came in from the kitchen with a small bowl of cereal. She handed it to her husband. He handed it back. 'You first.'

'I already ate, Rick. You're working.'

Hollander tried to pace himself, but he quickly scoffed down the cereal.

Later that night, as they all huddled in bed underneath the blankets, Hollander actually felt and heard Delia's stomach rumble.

On his way to the station the next morning, Hollander passed the yellow shotgun house and decided to stop there first. He walked up the steps and knocked on the door. After a moment, a tall, thin man with floppy hair and glasses answered.

'Officer,' he said.

'Are you Terry?' Hollander asked.

'Yes I am.'

'You're new in town, right?'

'I came to work at the Perdue plant a few months before Arrival.'

'I thought so,' replied Hollander. Through his peripheral vision, Hollander saw a bedraggled looking youth coming down the sidewalk. Wrapped in heavy clothes and a blanket against the cold, Hollander couldn't tell what he looked like, but he seemed to be coming from the Hispanic apartment complex.

'Is there a problem?' Terry asked.

'Well….there might be,' Hollander said. 'We've heard some things about you and what goes on here.'

Terry was about to speak but Hollander held up his hands. 'Just listen, ok?'

'Ok.'

'Now, I don't know you, and since you came to town, I never heard anything about you. That's a good thing. But now I am hearing rumors about you, and that is bad.'

'Am I in some kind of trouble?'

'Well, this is an unofficial visit, so not yet.'

'Ok.'

'Like I said, I hear things, but I don't know them, and I don't want to know them either. Understand?'

'Yes.'

'My point is, what I think has been going on here, has to stop… right now. Understand?'

'Yes.'

'Ok, have a good day then.'

Hollander actually allowed himself a smile. *We can still do our jobs*, he thought. *We can still do good police work.*

Hollander's smile left him when he turned the corner at the police station. At least a dozen Jews were gathered out front. They wore what were to Hollander's eyes comically massive fur hats and long overcoats. They looked surly. Hollander said hello and nodded at a them as he walked past, but they didn't even acknowledge him. Inside, Hollander heard a man shouting in the chief's office.

'But you can't let them!' someone said. 'The rebbe forbids it.'

'What's a rebbe?' Hollander heard the chief ask.

'Rabbi Rosenzweig. Our Rebbe.'

'Look, Mr. Kaplinksi, Rabbi Rosenzweig is in no position to forbid anything. He, and you are guests here.'

'But you have to take us in.'

'And besides, Mr. Sellers has complied with the law. If he wants to have a protest, he can have a protest. And that's it.'

There was silence for a moment. Then, 'Just make sure there are no shiksa women.'

'Shiksa women?'

'Non-Jews. The Rebbe doesn't like them. They're not modest enough for us.'

'Modest enough? I don't even know what you're talking about. Now get out of my office.'

The door flew open and out stormed Rabbi Kaplinksi.

The chief stood at his office door and shook his head.

Hollander saw inside the chief's office. He had taken down most of the paneling for firewood, revealing the 2x4 studs beneath.

'The studs are next,' the chief said.

'I hadn't thought of that,' Hollander said. He thought of the woodshed in his backyard. The boys would probably enjoy taking it apart. Hollander shivered a bit against the cold.

'If you don't mind, chief, I'd like to get in my squad car.'

The chief said, 'Man, you know things are bad when even Lieutenant Hollander wants to get in the car to keep warm.' The chief's sallow face came close to actually smiling. 'Make sure you cover all the town. With all my man power at the school…'

'Right. Good time for someone else to make trouble.'

Hollander started the squad car and let it warm up before getting in. He walked down to the river. The ice fishing teams were there as usual. One man looked up from his hole and waved. Hollander waved back, but he couldn't tell who it was, not with the bright sun glinting off the ice. The teams looked a bit thin.

'Where is everyone?' Hollander shouted.

'Couple of guys are going to Seller's protest!' the man shouted back.

Hollander went back to his squad car. He went down the river road and stopped at Mrs. Crabtree's. The door was wide open.

'God damn it,' he said.

Hollander pulled the car over and called the station. 'Elaine, something's up at Mrs. Crabtree's. Door is open, I'm going to have a look.'

'OK.'

Hollander walked to the door and stepped inside. The entryway was left alone, and looking to his left he saw the living room was undisturbed. He walked through to the kitchen. The pantry doors were all open. Whoever had broken in had found nothing, an officer had already appropriated the food for the town relief pantry. He went back to the door and was confronted by two teenagers standing at the foot of the stairs. Each held a stuffed laundry bag in his hands.

'Don't move, you two.'

'One looked like he was about to run.

Hollander shook his head. 'Don't make me draw my service piece.'

The boys stayed still.

'Show me your faces.'

The boys took off their scarves. Hollander knew both of them, the Cleary brothers. Their father owned one of the dairy farms at the edge of town. They were both prone to making trouble, nuisances for the most part. There was really nothing wrong with them that growing up wouldn't fix.

'Now put the bags down slowly.'

The boys dropped the laundry bags.

'I said slowly.'

The oldest brother, Brad spoke, 'It ain't breakable, Officer Hollander,' he said.

He nodded to the bags. 'What's in them?'

'Just blankets, officer.'

'Yeah,' the younger brother, Joey said.

'Blankets?'

'Yes, sir,' they said in unison.

'Empty them,' Hollander ordered.

The boys dutifully emptied the bags, spilling Mrs. Crabtree's blankets onto the hardwood floor. 'She don't need them anymore,' Brad said.

'But we do,' Joey added.

'Is that all you took?'

'Yes, sir,' they both said.

'You rifled through Mrs. Crabtree's cabinets.'

'We were hungry,' Joey said.

'Yeah,' added Brad. 'She don't need food no more either.'

Hollander pursed his lips and sighed. 'Alright. You two are going to go down to Murphy's hardware to get a new doorknob, then you can put it on.'

'Yes, sir.'

'Then you're going to walk the key down to the station and give it to Elaine.'

'Yes, sir.'

'And you'll do it all today.'

Hollander smirked. They'd be walking back and forth the whole day, in the near zero temperatures, that would be punishment enough.

'Now take those blankets and get out of here.'

The boys scurried out.

Hollander got back to his car.

The car's radio squawked.

'Hollander,' the secretary said, 'The chief wants you over at the school ASAP.

'ASAP?'

'Yep, Lieutenant.'

'I'm on my way.'

When he got to the school, Hollander was greeted by two opposing mobs.

Sellers and his followers, were gathered around a couple of steel garbage cans, both of which were filled with flaming debris. They had two large banners. Written on long bed sheets one read 'Guests Pitch In' the other 'Ingrates Go Home'.

In front of the school was a line of Jewish men. Behind them was a phalanx of women, maybe twenty in all. They were frothing mad. Hollander watched as they shouted Hebrew obscenities and shook their fists at Sellers and his people. A few even spat.

With his Gadsden flag, Sellers walked back and forth before the crowd. 'Why do these outsiders get help when we get none?!' he shouted. 'Why do they receive aid and comfort when we receive nothing?!'

With each question the crowd shouted answers almost as if they were at a revival meeting.

The chief saw Hollander and waved him over to the line of police cars in the parking lot. Hollander walked over.

'This doesn't look good, chief.'

'No, both crowds are getting geared up for a fight.'

Hollander looked at both groups. 'Yeah,' he said.

'C'mon,' said the chief. 'You and me are going to go walk both those lines, try to dampen things down.'

Hollander and the chief interposed themselves between the two throngs of shouting protesters. He wasn't really worried about Sellers and his folks, they were known about town after all. Sellers may have been a troublemaker, but he had never been a problem. The man owned a home in town, and had managed the Walmart in Owensboro before Arrival.

'You think Sellers will start a riot?' the chief asked as they turned toward the Jews.

Hollander shook his head. 'No. In his heart, Sellers is just a blowhard. Likes spouting off, that's all.'

The Chief nodded to the Jews as they began their walk in front of them. 'What about these folks?'

Hollander bit his lip in thought. 'You see, chief, that's the problem. I know Sellers, and I'm confident I know what he will do. I don't about these folks.'

Sellers and his protestors were shouting slogans, albeit loud and enthusiastically. But as they walked past the Jews, the chief and Hollander heard nothing but bitter hatred, much of it shouted in Hebrew. Rabbi Kaplinksi was at the head of the group. He didn't even acknowledge the two police officers as they strode past.

'Let's go talk to Sellers,' the chief said.

The two men sauntered up to Sellers. 'How you doing Pat?' the chief asked.

Sellers beamed, 'Fine, just fine, chief. Just lawfully exercising our constitutional rights.'

'That you are,' said the chief.

As the chief chatted with Sellers, Hollander walked up and down the protest line, saying hello and asking how folks were doing

When he got to the end of the line, Hollander shouted, 'Hey chief, I'm going to go over to the school entrance; talk with Rabbi Kaplinski.'

The chief nodded his approval.

Hollander walked over to them and said, 'Morning folks, how's everyone doing?'

The shouting Jews ignored him.

'Everyone staying warm in there?'

Again nothing.

He walked over to Rabbi Kaplinski, 'Morning Rabbi.'

Kaplinski muttered something under his breath.

'Where's Rabbi Rosenzweig?'

'Working on his sermon. Today is Friday.'

'Funny,' said Hollander. 'Most of us haven't been paying attention to the calendar lately.'

'Well, unlike you, we have to.'

Hollander wondered what that was supposed to mean.

'Look, Rabbi. I'd like you to keep your folks under control.'

'What do you mean by that?'

'Why don't you folks just go inside?'

'Are you trying to shut us up?'

'Look, Rabbi, all I'm saying is there's no point in standing out here in the cold.' Hollander held out his hands and motioned for the people to go inside.

Kaplinski slapped Hollander's hand away. 'I will not be herded about.'

'Rabbi, you can't slap a police officer like...'

'We are not to be herded into boxcars.'

'Boxcars?' Hollander asked. 'What the hell are you talking about?'

'This isn't Auschwitz.'

Kaplinski turned around and shouted in Hebrew to the rest of the assembled people. Hollander heard several people say Auschwitz and a moment later the chant went up 'Auschwitz! Auschwitz!'

Hollander held up his hands to the crowd.

'Folks! We just want you to settle down and move back a little!'

Rather than move back Kaplinski stepped forward and shoved Hollander. 'Back away from us!'

'I warned you, Rabbi.' Hollander reached behind him and took his handcuffs off his belt. Hollander grabbed Kaplinski's arm.

An outraged cry went up from the Jewish crowd. Before he could handcuff Kaplinski someone pushed Hollander away, so hard that he took several awkward steps across the concrete. Then he was hit in the face by a chunk of ice. Hollander had enough crowd control experience to know he had already lost control of the situation. He turned around and jogged back several dozen feet. The chief ran over to him with several officers.

Hollander told him what happened.

'Where's Kaplinski now?'

As the chief spoke, the angry mob tossed snowballs at them.

'I think they took him inside,' Hollander said.

'Well, we've got to go get him.'

Hollander pointed at the mob. The men in the front row stood menacingly, but behind them the frumpy women were hopping mad. 'If we go through those people we'll cause a riot.'

'Excuse me, chief,' it was Sellers. 'You gonna let them do that?' he pointed to the Jews, who were now ripping the high school moniker off the wall.

'Get back over there,' the chief said.

'But if we did that...'

The chief cut him off. 'I don't have time for this right now, Sellers.'

'Well look at them!' Sellers shouted, 'They're lighting the sign on fire.'

'Get the men ready,' the chief said to Hollander. 'Get everyone in a line right here.'

'Ok, chief.'

Hollander gathered the half dozen officers on hand as the chief ran back to his car. He switched on the loud speaker. 'THIS IS THE LIVERMORE POLICE. GO BACK INSIDE AT ONCE OR WE WILL BE FORCED TO MAKE ARRESTS.'

The mob booed and hurled snowballs at the chief's police car.

'I REPEAT. GO INSIDE.'

Hollander turned to Sellers and said. 'You better get out of here before they decide to take things out on you.'

Someone smashed one of the windows at the school entryway.

'I'm not going anywhere!'

'Sellers this is not time for one of your lectures on the Constitution.'

'I don't care about that. You've always treated me fair, Lieutenant, never gave me a hard time even while I was giving you a hard time. I'm staying.' Hollander looked to the assembled protestors. 'C'mon, folks, we don't have to take this!'

He walked over to one of the massive snow banks lining the parking lot and made a snowball. The other protestors, getting his meaning, did the same. In unison they lobbed snowballs at the phalanx of Orthodox Jews in front of the school. Because the sidewalk and parking lot had been meticulously cleared, the

Jews had no ammo in the snowball fight. As they were barraged with packed snow, they ducked, and finally fled inside the school. Sellers and his army of snowball throwers sent a few more barrages after them, until they simply peppered the doorway.

Holding his hands out to show he was no threat, Hollander walked toward the protestors. 'Ok, Mr. Sellers, you all have had your fun, and you've made your point.'

Sellers smiled. 'I think we have.'

'Time to head home.'

Sellers nodded. 'I think so. We'll march though.'

'Just stay out of the street.'

'I know! Don't want to get cited.'

Hollander waved as the protestors began their march out of the parking lot. He walked back to his cruiser and started the engine. He watched the protesters as they marched away, and then looked at the pile of snowballs amassed at the front door. Hollander chuckled. Then he cackled. Then he laughed uncontrollably.

Before knocking off for the day Hollander took a turn around town. When he got to the highway out beyond the cemetery he saw several trucks parked outside the substation. He called the station.

'Elaine, I see several trucks on the north side of 401 here.'

'Yeah, we just got word!' she replied enthusiastically. 'Power company is here!'

'Well, that is good news.' Hollander allowed himself to smile.

He drove up to the substation and got out of the cruiser. Outside of the substation was a half dozen utility trucks. Two had already deployed buckets to the nearby telephone poles. Hollander looked further up the highway and saw another truck with its bucket deployed. Inside the substation several men worked.

One of the men outside the substation walked over to Hollander. He was heavily bundled against the approaching night and wore a hard hat. Hollander saw he had a sidearm on his belt as well.

'Hello there,' the man said as he walked up to Hollander. 'I'm Wilkins,' he pointed to his men. 'This is my crew here.'

'Glad to see you!' Hollander said as the wind kicked up.
'Not sure how you guys managed it, but our boss said get out here quick.'
Hollander shrugged.
One of the utility trucks started up and slowly went south down the highway.
Wilkins said, 'Bob and Gary there are going to drive down the highway and survey the main line, check for damage.'
'A few days ago we took out a few poles that had been damaged. Rest of the lines are up though.'
'That's good to hear. Now we need to repair the line to this substation here. The substation itself is ok. So when we get that line repaired, we can run power from Owensboro down here.'
'So we'll have power?' Hollander asked hopefully.
'Assuming the lines into Livermore are up, yes.'
'God, that's great!' Hollander said. 'You need anything?'
'The company is taking pretty good care of us,' Wilkins said. 'Can't start sending out bills until folks get power. We sleep in the trucks but got enough gas to keep the engines running.'
'Well, if you guys want a warm shower afterwards, come into city hall, we'll do what we can for you.'
'Appreciate that.'
'Hey, Wilkins!' One of the workers shouted from the substation. 'We need you over here.'
'Excuse me.'
Hollander couldn't keep the smile off his face as he walked home. Seller's protest was the talk that night around the stone soup parties. Hollander was so ebullient he actually stopped and chatted with a few of them, happy to be the one to deliver the good news about the power company. The party goers were so ecstatic they gave him a couple of cups of soup to take home.
The Hollanders slept well that night on warm, full stomachs.
Before dawn Hollander woke up.
'What was that?' he asked.
Then he heard a pair of gunshots. And then another pair.
'Oh Christ,' he said.
He jumped out of bed and got dressed.

'What's wrong?' Delia asked.

Hollander heard shouting.

'Gun shots.'

'Oh Lord,' said Delia.

When he got outside, the wind lashed Hollander's face. He looked around and heard the shouting again.

That sounded like it was coming from Sellers' place, he thought.

Hollander ran up the street toward Seller's house. When he got there a crowd of people was already gathered out front. Sellers was standing on his front porch, waving a shotgun in the air.

'What happened Sellers?' Hollander asked.

'I'll tell you what happened. Two of those Orthodox goons tried to break into my house.'

'What?'

'One of them is right here, I caught him trying to kick in my door.'

Hollander walked over to Sellers. He took out his flashlight turned, and shined it on the porch. Before him was a body in a long beard, prayer curls and greatcoat. Seller's shotgun had torn a great gash in his chest.

'See, he has a screw driver in one hand.' Hollander looked, sure enough, there it was. 'And there's a Leatherman on the second step there.'

Hollander shined on the body on the step and saw the Leatherman.

'Go behind the house, Officer, there's another carcass waiting.'

Hollander trudged through the icy snow to the back. Hollander's flashlight revealed another body, clad in a greatcoat. He had a knife and a screwdriver. He shined the light on the window and could see several deep indentations. The glass, of course, had been blasted out by Seller's shotgun.

Hollander came back around to the front. By then, a police cruiser pulled up. Ryan got out.

'Alright Sellers. First thing, you're coming down to the station.'

He nodded.

'And I'll have the shotgun.'

'Ok,' he handed the shotgun over to Hollander. 'But no cuffs. I know my rights, I know the law.'

'No one's arresting you.'

'Ryan, call for another car to keep an eye on things here,' Hollander said.

'Sure, anything else?'

'Yes. Get the EMT guys and then call the county coroner. We'll play things by the book.'

Hollander turned to the crowd. 'Look folks, head on home. Get out of the cold.'

'What happened?!' someone shouted.

'What does it look like?!' Hollander shouted back.

'Hollander!' Ryan shouted. He held up his mic, 'chief wants you.'

Hollander filled in the chief on what had happened.

'That's just great,' the chief said. 'Now, why the hell would two Orthodox Jews be trying to break into Seller's place?'

'Jesus, chief, I don't like this.'

'Get down here with Sellers. I've already called out all our guys.'

'What for?'

'We're going down to the high school and we are making arrests.'

'Who? Rosenzweig, Kaplinksi? I'm not sure we have the evidence, chief.'

'I don't care.'

By the time Hollander got back to the station the sun was starting to peak over the horizon. He walked Sellers inside, and they saw a dozen police officers donning riot gear and loading shot guns.

The chief saw Sellers and said, 'We really don't have time to deal with your situation right now.'

'Well, that just chokes me up,' Sellers replied sarcastically.

'I expect you to stay here with Elaine.'

Sellers shrugged. 'Ok.'

'Chief,' Hollander said. 'I'm not sure going down there in riot gear is the best idea.'

'I already cleared it with the mayor.'

Hollander thought for a moment. 'Alright,' he said. 'But let me talk to them first, okay?'

'What for?"

'Just let me go in there first. If there's trouble, you come in with the cavalry. Trust me, Okay?'

Ryan said, 'Hey, you don't have to go down to the high school. They're coming here.'

'What?' the chief asked.

Ryan pointed to the window. 'Look outside, there must be a hundred of them coming up the street.'

Indeed, with Rosenzweig and Kaplinksi at the fore, dozens of Orthodox Jews marched up the street, many of them carried led pipes, several held snowballs in their hands.

'This is not good,' the chief said ominously.

The two rabbis led the Orthodox mob to the foot of the station. Kaplinksi shouted, 'We want the bodies of our dead! They are to be treated according to Talmudic law!'

The mob shouted its affirmation. Smiling, Rosenzweig leaned over to Kaplinski and said something. Kaplinski shouted, 'And we want that killer, Sellers!'

The crowd hissed and shouted. Snowballs flew out from the mob, slamming into the station's windows.

'Where are the bodies?' the chief asked Elaine.

'The coroner's van pulled into the back fifteen minutes ago. They're still in the garage.'

More snowballs came out from the mob, as did the beginnings of a chant.

'What are they yelling?' the chief asked.

'Sounds like...' Hollander strained.

'Me,' Sellers said, 'They want me.'

'He's right,' said Hollander. 'They're shouting GIVE US SELLARS.'

Hollander said, 'Let me see if I can talk some sense into them.'

He walked outside and held up his hands in a peace gesture. 'Look folks I...'

Before he could finish the mob pelted Hollander with snowballs. He ducked and ran back inside.

The chanting grew angrier and louder.

'Well, what now, genius?' the chief angrily asked.

Looking out the window, Hollander saw the crowd advance menacingly toward the station entrance, their chant shortened simply to 'Sell-ers! Sell-ers!'

'You don't think they're going to try to bust in here?' Ryan asked.

The chief said, 'Sure looks that way.'

'I ain't going down without a fight,' Sellars said. 'Give me a shotgun.'

The chief looked out of the window, snowballs slammed into the window, and then a rock. 'Ryan,' he said, 'issue Sellers a shotgun.'

Ryan walked over to the arms locker and took out another shotgun. He handed it to Sellers, who took several shells from a box on the front desk and loaded them into the shotgun's breach.

'I just don't get it,' said the chief. 'Who the hell do these people think they are?'

Hollander looked out to the mob, which had now advanced to the station's front steps. He chambered a round. 'Doesn't matter what religion, I guess,' he said. 'Religious fanatics…' he shook his head.

'Ok, men,' the chief said. We'll step outside and fire a blast over their heads. I say again, over their heads. Except me. I'll fire a couple at their feet.'

'Might send some buckshot off the steps into the crowd.'

'That's their problem,' the chief said. 'Sellers, you stay here. If we go down, you have my permission to act as you see fit.'

'What about me?' Elaine asked.

The chief took out his revolver and handed to her.

'Thanks,' she said.

The chief kicked the door open and led the bulk of the Livermore Police Department out onto the front steps. He arrayed them in a line and shouted. 'In the air! In the air. Fire!'

The eight police officers loosened a volley of buckshot into the air as the chief fired one into the steps. The men in the front line, startled by the display of force ducked and dove to the ground. Many more ran away. Some in the middle collided with those in the back, creating a tangled, writhing mass in front of the station. Hollander heard Elaine shouting something through the window, but couldn't make it out.

'Another!' the chief shouted.

Another buckshot volley crashed out from the blue line.

Elaine shouted again.

'Another!'

The mob disintegrated in all directions, save for Rabbi Rosenzweig who sat on his behind, his face bloody. As the mob dissipated, Hollander grabbed the Rabbi and hustled him inside the station.

That's when he noticed how bright it was inside. Then he realized what Elaine was shouting. 'The power's back on!' She shouted. 'The power's back on!'

Hollander looked around. The overhead fluorescent lights were on as was Elaine's desk lamp. Her computer, unused for months, was showing the blue screen of death. He ran over to the electric baseboard heater and felt air flowing out.

The chief, though, was concerned only with Rabbi Rosenzweig. He angrily slapped a pair of handcuffs onto him and hauled him up to his feet.

'You can't treat me like this!' the rabbi exclaimed. 'I'm the head of the Lubbuvitch community here!'

'I really don't care,' the chief said. He walked him to the back of the station and threw him in a cell.

CHAPTER 5

CRAZIEST IVAN

Captain Ivan Dimitryiev felt his leg throbbing. He felt blood trickling out of his lips, mouth and ears. That's how he knew he was alive. He was floating. He opened his eyes and saw nothing, he realized, because the bridge was dark. It was cold too. That final Jai missile hit had taken out *Brezhnev's* power plant.

'Hello?' he asked.

He heard nothing.

A minute later he floated into one of the bridge's bulkheads and then smacked into a cold, fleshy lump. He wondered who it was.

'Anybody?' he asked.

There was no response.

Dimitryiev's head ached. He wondered if it was because of a head trauma or diminishing oxygen. He floated in the dark for a long time. Long enough to realize that he had to take a piss. He pissed in his pants.

I hope I die before I have to take a crap, he thought.

Dimitryiev shivered against the cold.

Why wouldn't the Jai finish us off? He asked himself. *Why let the ship float in space?*

Dimitryiev shivered again and folded his arms against himself. He floated in the pitch black. He bounced off bulkheads, he bounced against cold lumps of flesh, his bridge crew. In time his teeth chattered with the cold. He floated and slammed the left side of his face into the bulkhead. He winced in pain and pushed himself away from the bulkhead only to fly across the bridge and slam into another bulkhead, sending a flash of pain shooting through his broken leg. He screamed gutturally and against his will he began to cry.

I don't want to die like this! He thought.

Dimitryiev composed himself after a minute and asked himself, *Then how did you want to die?*

His mocking laughter filled the dark, silent bridge. 'Who gets to choose that?' he asked aloud.

I am Captain Yuri Dimitryiev, and I earned a better death than this! He replied to himself.

Dimitryiev sobbed again.

He drifted off to sleep and not long after woke up to a clanking sound. There was another such sound, and then the bridge was bathed in white light. Dimitryiev slammed his eyes shut against the glare. Suddenly someone grabbed hold of his leg, He screamed in pain. He yelled and cursed as he was pulled across the bridge and out into the corridor. Dimitryiev looked around and saw three men in strange spacesuits. They weren't men, but Jai. Floating between two of the jai was a Russian space suit.

Through a speaker in his helmet, one of the Jai said in English, 'On.'

He pushed the spacesuit toward Dimitryiev.

'On.'

Dimitryiev took the suit. He had been on several spacewalks and knew how to check and use a suit. He checked the air tank in the back and saw it was full and functional. Seeing no other choice, Dimitryiev put on the suit and donned the helmet. When a light on the helmet indicated the suit was sealed he pressed the oxygen button. They pulled him through *Brezhnev's* smashed decks to the airlock. The Jai attached a harness to Dimitryiev's suit. When the airlock opened they attached him to a pulley line. A motor took him out into space.

Dimitryiev spun and bounced against the pulley line, occasionally catching glimpses of Venus, thousands of miles below. He grabbed the line and righted himself. Dimitryiev saw that he was being pulled toward a Jai carrier ship. He saw a trio of blast marks on the hull, the laser scars *Brezhnev* had burned into the ship during the battle. Dimitryiev then slowly turned himself around so that he could see *Brezhnev*. He stared at the ship until the pulley brought him to the carrier-ship, into a storage bay and into a small chamber he assumed was an airlock. A door opened and out came a Jai. He detached Dimitryiev from the line and pulled him inside the door. The Jai set Dimitryiev on his feet and pressed a button on the wall. Gravity slowly came on.

'Wait!' He shouted.

Dimitryiev fell to the floor and grabbed his leg in pain. The Jai helped him up. He opened the inner door and helped Dimitryiev inside. He was in a small room with a bench and hooks on the wall. He sat Dimitryiev on the bench. The Jai, still in his space suit motioned for Dimitryiev to take his off. He quickly got out of his suit and hung it on the hook. Dimitryiev sat, and enjoyed the feeling of warmth, the first he'd felt in….he didn't know how long he'd been floating on the bridge. He realized he was starving. Dimitryiev looked around the room for some sort of com, but didn't see one.

'Anyone listening?' he asked.

There was no response.

'Well, at least it is warm.'

Dimitryiev leaned back against the wall and closed his eyes. He was about to drift off when the door opened. In walked three Jai. They spoke Jai to one another. One of the Jai, wearing a blue uniform got down on his knee and examined Dimitryiev's leg. He winced as the Jai poked and prodded at him. The Jai doctor spoke to his compatriots. One asked, 'You speak English?'

'Da,' replied Dimitryiev.

'Where …is leg broken?'

Dimitryiev pointed to his thigh.

The Jai doctor took a large splint out of his bag and strapped it to Dimitryiev's leg. He pressed a button on the splint. It filled with air and tightened. Dimitryiev felt a wave of pain, but the splint straightened and held the broken bones in place. The doctor said something else to the other two Jai.

'You will be able to walk with a…cane,' said the translator.

The doctor gave Dimitryiev a cane.

'You come,' said the translator.

Dimitryiev put his weight on the cane and stood up. Gingerly he made his way out the door and followed the Jai translator down the crowded and cluttered passageway. Boxes were stacked in odd spots, as were panels and rolls of wires. Dimitryiev saw signs of wear and tear on the bulkheads, and the hatches.

Much of the paint was chipped. Corners looked worn as if countless objects had slammed into them. To Dimitryiev's navy-man eye the ship was long, long overdue for rest and refit.

They led him to another passageway lined with small folding doors. In the middle they stopped. Here the translator opened the doors and motioned for Dimitryiev to walk in. He did so and found himself standing in small living quarters. There was a bunk, a chair, a desk and shelves on the walls. These were empty.

'You will live here,' said the translator.

Dimitryiev looked around the sparse surroundings. 'Mine?'

'Yes,' said the translator.

'Why?' Dimitryiev asked. 'I am a prisoner?'

'Yes.'

'Where is the rest of my crew? Where will they stay?'

'You are the only one,' said the translator.

'Me?' Dimitryiev asked. 'Just me?'

'Yes.'

Dimitryiev held his head in his hands and cried himself to sleep…

He awoke some time later. Dimitryiev sat up on his bunk and rubbed his face. *Crying yourself to sleep like a love struck teenager….*he shook his head. He looked around the cabin again. and then lay back down. After a few minutes the translator popped in.

'You are awake,' he said. 'Are you hungry?'

Dimitryiev sat up. 'I suppose I am. I can get something to eat?'

'Yes. You can walk down this corridor and find, what is the English…word… room.'

'I may just go?'

'Yes.'

Dimitryiev shrugged.

'I have…duties now.' The translator left.

He looked around the compartment. 'This is not what I expected,' he said to no one.

Feeling hunger pangs in his stomach, Dimitryiev stood up and hobbled out of the compartment and made his way down the corridor. The last room on the left was larger than the others, Dimitryiev looked inside and saw a large center table with several seats. It was ringed with counters strewn with bowls and cups. On the left side of the room was a stove and several trays of food.

Two Jai, both in blue overalls sat at the table. As the Jai officers ate, they looked down at small electronic devices set next to their plates, their bony fingers tapped them. Dimitriyev could see light reflecting off their pale, white faces. The Jai looked up and stared.

'May I enter?'

The Jai nodded left to right and returned to their electronic devices.

Dimitryiev hobbled into the wardroom. He put his cane forward to brace himself and slipped awkwardly to the floor. He yelped as a shot of pain went up his leg. The Jai nearest Dimitryiev got up, grabbed his left arm and helped Dimitryiev up. He then helped him down into the seat nearest the door. The other Jai said something. The first Jai walked over to the stove and got a tray of food. He placed it in front of Dimitryiev. The tray had four compartments. One held a brownish white goulash, while the other three had what looked like fruits and vegetables. He looked at one of the fruits, red and round.

'These are tomatoes,' he said.

The Jai said nothing. Dimitryiev took a spoon and gingerly tried the goulash. It wasn't bad and he quickly devoured it and then the other food. He looked at the two Jai and mimed holding a cup to his mouth.

'Water?'

The first Jai got a small cup and filled it from a dispenser in the corner. Dimitryiev gulped it down and asked for more. The Jai refilled the cup and gave it to Dimitryiev.

Another Jai walked into the wardroom. The two other Jai looked at him and held up their hands. Dimitryiev recognized a salute when he saw one. He gingerly stood up and snapped off a salute.

The Jai wore blue pants and a white shirt. There was a bright red emblem in the shape of an animal over in the center of his chest. He was taller than the average Jai, taller than Dimitryiev who topped two meters. The Jai's face was whitish-gray with deep lines across his forehead. He had no hair, whether by choice or age Dimitryiev couldn't tell. The Jai looked at Dimitryiev, 'You are… Captain…Dimitev?' he said in the halting, pausing style typical of the Jai.

'Dimitryiev,' he corrected.

'I am Captain Gee-a-nah. Please sit….I know you are… hurt.'

Dimitryiev nodded in appreciation and sat down.

Gee-a-nah walked over to the buffet and fixed himself a tray of food. He sat down across from Dimitryiev. The other two Jai quickly finished their meals and left the two captains. Gee-a-nah put a spoonful of food in his mouth chewed and swallowed. Then he said, 'As a captain you deserve good treatment, so you will get that.'

Dimitryiev nodded.

'You will be treated with respect…by my crew.'

'I see.'

'In return, I expect you to help.'

'In what way?' asked Dimitryiev.

'I would like to talk to you about the battle. About Earth.'

'I will not betray secrets. I will not help you learn about *Brezhnev.*'

'Brezh…nev?'

'My ship.'

The captain nodded his head left then right.

'You will have to do that for yourself,' Dimitryiev said.

Gee-a-nah put another spoonful of food in his mouth and thought for a second. 'That is fair…'

'One other condition.'

'Yes?'

'You no doubt are planning to keep *Brezhnev*, yes?'

'Yes.'

'The bodies of my crew must be treated with solemnity and respect and I insist on proper burials and services for them.'

'What would this entail?' Gee-a-nah asked.

'Services, rites in the tradition of the Russian Orthodox Church.'

Gee-a-nah nodded. 'It is agreed then.'

'Yes.'

William Stroock

The Jai captain was silent for a few moments. 'You seem…reconciled to your new situation.'

'What choice do I have?' replied Dimitryiev. 'And at this moment, it is all I can do to make sure my crew is properly treated.'

'They are all dead,' said Gee-a-nah.

'They are still my responsibility.'

'I understand completely.'

There was silence as the two captains ate.

Finally, Dimitryiev said, 'You seem very permissive of my presence on your ship.'

Gee-a-nah thought for a moment. 'What could you do to this ship?'

Dimitryiev smiled, 'I could sneak onto the bridge. Kill the crew. Ram the ship into one of the orbiting stations.'

Gee-a-nah bared his teeth, 'I do not think you could do so.'

'Probably not. So then, what is my status aboard this ship? Am I a prisoner?'

Gee-a-nah thought for a moment. 'Let us say that you are on…temporary attached duty.'

'Temporary? Is it possible I could be repatriated to Earth?'

'It is not my decision. But I do know that we would want to get our prisoners returned and you are the highest…ranking human we have ever captured.'

'Another honor,' said Dimitryiev sarcastically, 'In addition to losing *Brezhnev*.'

'Now, Captain Dimitryiev, you will please tell me about yourself.'

Dimitryiev cleared his throat, 'Well, there is not much to tell. I have been in the Russian Navy my entire life.'

'What did you do before taking command of…*Brezhnev*?'

'I commanded a destroyer in the Black Sea Fleet.'

'And before that?'

'Various sea duty. I taught at our naval academy'

'Where are you from?'

'Novosibirsk. In the middle of Russia. I wanted to see the ocean, so I applied to the naval academy.'

'I see.'

'I'm afraid I am not very interesting, Captain.'

'Do you have a family?'

Dimitryiev shook his head. 'I never had the time for that.'

'A situation I know myself.'

'Besides, Russia after the war was not a good place to start and raise a family.' Dimitryiev looked bitterly at Gee-a-Nah.

The Jai Captain said, 'As I remember, Russia used nuclear weapons, not we.'

'Did we have a choice?'

'There is no shame in nuclear weapons,' said Gee-a-Nah. 'You destroyed one of our ships over your…what is the place…called…Caucasus, yes that is the name.'

'And you responded by smashing the infrastructure in European Russia.'

Gee-a-Nah nodded. 'Yes, a move I questioned.'

'Why?'

'Because had we won, we would have wanted that infrastructure.'

Dimitryiev nodded in agreement.

'We were surprised by the ferocity of Russian…resistance.'

Dimitryiev laughed. 'You are not the first invader to be surprised thusly.'

'How so?'

Dimitryiev explained Napoleon and Hitler to Gee-a-Nah.

'Ah yes…we have heard of this Hitler. He made quite an impression on your planet.'

Stoked with Russian pride, Dimitryiev explained the Great Patriotic War. Gee-a-Nah listened intently.

When Dimitryiev was finished, Gee-a-Nah said. 'That was…fascinating and I would like to hear more, but unfortunately…'

Dimitryiev held up his hand, 'You have duties.'

'I knew a fellow captain would understand.' Gee-a-Nah stood. 'Now, Captain, I was wondering, would you like to write a report for us?'

'About what?'

'Your view of the war. Your view of us.'

Dimitryiev thought. 'I cannot tell you everything.'

'Of course.'

'But I can give you my impressions, Russia's impressions.'

Gee-a-Nah nodded, 'I would like that.'

Dimitryiev looked down at his pants, remembering that he had pissed them before. 'I would like to get my uniform cleaned.'

'Of course.'

'Gee-ah-nah stood. If you will excuse me, Captain.'

'Yes.'

After Gee-ah-nah left, Dimitryiev finished his food and hobbled back to his quarters. A sailor came by and collected his uniform, leaving a green jump suit in its place. He also dropped off a bound ream of paper and a pen. He sat down at the desk, thought for a moment, and penned a quick intro.

> The following is intended for informational and scholarly purposes only. Captain Ivan Dimitryiev, late of the *Brezhnev*, professes his loyalty to Russia and the Russian Navy.

He read the statement over and began writing. After two hours, he had penned a quick summation of the Russian view of the war.

As he was reading over the report Dimitryiev realized he had to use the bathroom. He wrenched himself up and made his way down the corridor until he found a door. There was Jai writing on it. Dimitryiev looked at a Jai sailor coming down the passageway and pointed at his crotch and then the door. The Jai bobbed his head left and then right, a Jai equivalent of a nod, Dimitryiev knew. He opened the door into the Jai bathroom. There was a shower stall and in the corner, what could only be a toilet. Everything seemed to work the same as on a human ship. Dimitryiev used the equipment without incident.

When he got back to his quarters he found his uniform folded on his bunk. His insignia and ribbons were placed next to them. Dimitryiev took his time getting dressed. The uniform, he realized had been dry cleaned, or whatever the Jai equivalent of dry cleaning was. When Dimitryiev was dressed he affixed his rank to his lapel and his campaign ribbons to his chest. The lines of ribbons he had amassed was not unimpressive; ribbons for the Georgia War, for two different campaigns during the Jai Invasion, another pair of subsequent actions against the Jai the following decade.

Satisfied, Dimitryiev sat down and read his report.

From the beginning of the war, Russian forces were concerned with keeping the Jai from penetrating Russian airspace and making a landing within Russia. As such, high command committed a majority of the Russian military to an early battle with the Jai on and over the Russian Arctic coast. While casualties were heavy, high command was satisfied with the toll exacted from the Jai. Over the Kola Peninsula, Russian air divisions launched repeated attacks on the trio of Jai carrier-ships assailing St. Petersburg. Over Sverdlov Island, land and submarine launched missiles shot down a Jai carrier-ship and damaged another. However these battles led to the near total destruction of Force Sverdlov Island, and Force Kola Peninsula.

The commander of Russia's forces then recommended an all-out nuclear assault led by our arsenal of S-24 Ballistic Nuclear Missiles. The president agreed and ordered the attack. While another Jai carrier-ship was destroyed, the S-24s failed to penetrate the considerable air and land based defenses on the North Pole, and the pole-ship there survived.

From this point the war followed a pattern: Jai raids on the Russian interior; Moscow and Smolensk, for example, followed by Russia counter-attacks. The Jai mounted a considerable effort to degrade Russian land forces prior to a ground invasion. These efforts were highly successful…

Dimitryiev handed the paper to Gee-a-Nah. The Jai captain looked at the paper and laughed. 'I did not think to say.'

'I'm sorry?' Dimitryiev asked in confusion.

'I do not recognize the words or….characters. You wrote in Russian, did you?'

Now Dimitryiev laughed. 'Of course.' He reached across the table and took the paper back. 'I will re-write it in English.'

William Stroock

Gee-a-Nah said, 'This gives me an idea....do you think you could...conduct...Russian classes?'

'Well....'

'You will need duties aboard ship.'

'Well, I suppose I could write in the morning and teach in the afternoon.'

'Excellent!' Gee-a-Nah beamed.

Dimitryiev spent the rest of the evening re-writing the report in English. He was wondering if he should turn in when there was a knock on the door. A Jai officer poked his head inside.

'Who are you?' Dimitryiev asked.

'My name is Gin-hi,' he replied. 'I am...I believe your rank would be...ensign.' He spoke the same way the captain had, Dimitryiev noticed, halting and pausing.

'Yes, Ensign Gin-hi?'

'Excuse me, Captain. Captain Gee-a-Nah says we are viewing a movie in the wardroom and invites you.'

Dimitryiev raised his eyebrows. 'Movie, well, that could be fun.' He nodded. 'Please tell the captain that I will be there.'

Most of the ship's officers were gathered around the table in the wardroom. Their attention was fixed on a large screen in the wall above the sink.

Captain Gee-a-Nah stood. 'Good, Captain Dimitryiev. Please sit.' He motioned for Dimitryiev to sit next to him.

'Thank you for the invitation,' Dimitryiev said as he sat down.

'It is my...pleasure. You are going to view...quite a show.'

The movie took about an hour, actually an hour and eleven minutes by Jai standard time. Like everything else about the Jai, the movie was manic, with tons of action in every frame, bright lights, lots of noise. It seemed to Dimitryiev more suited to a hyperactive, meth addicted Japanese teenager than a ship full of naval officers. Still, even though he did not speak their language, Dimitryiev found himself engrossed in the film. It was as easy to follow as a Hollywood summer blockbuster, a guilty pleasure of Dimitryiev's.

The movie, Gee-a-Nah translated the title into English as, 'The Forlorn Hope', was a modern film. Gee-ah-Nah said it had been made about twenty years before the expedition left Jai. At first, Dimitryiev found himself concentrating on the Jai military equipment, it looked similar to what he had seen on Earth. 'The Forlorn Hope' was about a band of Jai soldiers who launch a suicidal counterattack. It was filled with heroic speeches and Jai soldiers encouraging one another as enemy fire decimated their ranks. The combat sequence took up most of the movie, but was interrupted by flashbacks to the home life of the half dozen principle characters. Aside from the differences in small details, the home scenes were eerily similar to what an earth movie would show.

When 'The Forlorn Hope' was over, the assembled Jai turned in their seats and looked at Dimitryiev.

'What?' he asked.

Gee-a-nah said, 'They want to know what you think.'

'Why me?'

'You are human,' Gee-ah-Nah said. 'This is considered one of the best movies in our…culture and they want to know what you think of it.'

Dimitryiev smiled slightly. Then he stood up and clapped his hands. The assembled Jai cheered.

He slept well that night, not waking until early morning, ship's time, at the hand of Ensign Gin-hi.

'We have taken *Brezhnev* into tow.… Captain Gee-ah-Nah thought you would want to see.'

'Yes, very much so.'

When Dimitryiev was ready, Gin-hi brought him to the bridge.

'I am glad…you are here, Captain,' said Gee-ah-Nah.

The bridge was laid out similar to the bridge in a human navy; command consoles, a captain's chair in the center, and a large view screen forward. Dimitryiev felt a stab of violent pain as he saw *Brezhnev* moving across the screen. His lips quivered and face twitched, but Dimitryiev managed to keep himself from weeping.

Brezhnev was being towed by two Jai tugs, their engines glowed white as they pulled her across the view screen.

'Where are you taking her?' Dimitryiev asked.

'Her?' replied Gee-ah-Nah.

'*Brezhnev.*'

'The ship will be docked at one of our orbital space stations.'

'I see.'

'Captain Dimitryiev, I am not an expert in…human characteristics, but I must ask…are you unwell?'

Without taking his eyes from the view-screen Dimitryiev said, 'Surely you understand?'

'I do. Would you…like to leave?'

'No.'

It took a few hours for the tugs to tow *Brezhnev* over to the orbital station. Dimitryiev watched and remembered the years he and his crew had learned the ship, their excitement at beating the Americans back into space after the Battle of Luna and most painfully, their misplaced optimism leading up to the joint Russian/Chinese attack on Venus.

'Damn Chinese,' he said.

Gee-ah-Nah looked over at Dimitryiev. 'Sorry?'

'Nothing. What will you do with her?' Dimitryiev asked.

'We will go through *Brezhnev* and learn all we can about the ship.'

'What of my crew?'

'Fear not,' said Gee-ah-Nah. 'All bodies will be recovered and placed in the station's morgue. I will personally bring you over there so you may perform… whatever ceremonies you wish.'

'When?'

'Tomorrow hopefully.'

That night's movie was called, according to Gee-ah-Na 'The Big Trek'. Dimitryiev told him that in English, 'Great Trek' would probably be more appropriate. It took place further back in the Jai past, in an era when they were just mastering spaceflight. The movie followed an iron willed space captain who piloted a ship full of refugees. Dimitryiev watched as the ship was launched from the Jai home world by a trio of massive solid fuel rockets similar to those used by the old American and Russian space programs. The film shifted rapidly between several characters and plot points, but always back to the ship captain who by will alone seemed to get the ship to a planet in the Jai solar system.

'You have more than one inhabitable planet in your solar system?' Dimitryiev asked.

'Yes. This movie is about the…colonization of the other such planet. It is like your Mars. Further away from the sun and cold, but with a…breathable atmosphere.'

Dimitryiev smirked. 'Our Mars?' Dimitryiev smirked. 'You occupy it.'

It seemed the people aboard the ship, translated most nearly into *Trekker*, were forced to leave Jai after losing a great war. Over the course of the film, Dimitryiev saw that even though they were refugees, all the Jai aboard ship had hand held devices, mostly games or music players, a generation or two behind those available on Earth prior to arrival. The bulkheads featured view screens, speakers and in many places strings of lights, blinking manically in different patterns. Midway through the film Dimitryiev leaned over to Gee-ah-Naa and said, 'You Jai need a lot of stimuli.'

'Stimuli,' said Gee-ah-Naa, not quiet getting the inflection right for a question.

'Many things before you. Lights, images, sound.'

'Ah yes. It seems to us that you humans need much less than we.'

'I think so,' replied Dimitryiev. 'Your children must be difficult to control.'

'Actually, they are not,' he replied. 'The need for outside things, stimuli, comes during growing up period. I think you call it…'

'Adolescence?'

'Yes.'

When the film was over, Dimitryiev and Gee-ah-Nah remained in the wardroom discussing the film.

'How long ago did the events portrayed take place?'

'About four hundred of your years.'

'And the colonization of the planet Ijaz succeeded?'

'Oh, yes. I am from Ijaz, most of my crew is as well. As I said, cold, but habitable. Our home planet Jai, is much warmer. I have…been there, But I could never…adapt to the climate.'

They spent much time discussing the movie and other aspects of the Jai solar system. Most of the Jai lived on Jai, with the population of Ijaz being roughly one tenth of the former. After more than an hour the two retired for the night.

William Stroock

The next day Gee-ah-Nah took Dimitryiev in a small, cramped shuttle from the carrier ship to the orbital station. After they departed the ship, Dimitryiev asked, 'So what was this great war that the Trekkers lost?'

Gee-ah-Nah said, 'It was a war between the forces of the growing world king and those that did not want the king.'

'World king?'

'Oh, not really a king more a...'

'World government?' asked Dimitryiev.

'Ah, yes, world government. Those that did not like the world government lost. Many fled to Ijaz.'

'How many?'

'Many thousands in fact...'

Dimitryiev lost interest. As the station orbiting Venus' North Pole loomed, Dimitryiev could see *Brezhnev* moored alongside. He remembered with pride the way the ship, bristling with weapons, had led the Russian squadron out of the space station, the optimism with which the officers and crew had performed their jobs. When he saw the great gash ripped in *Brezhnev's* hull by a Jai laser Dimitryiev's pride changed to pain.

The shuttle drew closer to the station until it filled the view screen. It was composed of several compartments linked together by long passageways. He could clearly see weapons blisters on each side of the station and additional docking portals. In the berth next to *Brezhnev,* a great construction project seemed underway, with the old dock being swapped out for a larger dock housing an exo-skeleton around it. Dimitryiev knew what he saw. It was the difference between a berth for say, a destroyer and one for an American air craft carrier.

When they docked, Dimitryiev and Gee-ah-Nah were met at the airlock by the station commander. He led them through the station to the morgue. Most of the Jai crew had seen humans before. Still they paused what they were doing and watched as Gee-ah-Nah and the station commander led him through the orbital station.

They stopped at a small door. The station commander spoke to Gee-ah-Nah who translated.

'This is the morgue,' he said. The bodies of your crew are inside. 'We… recovered thirty-seven bodies.'

'Just 37? I had a crew of 53.'

Gee-ah-Nah spoke to the station commander. The two bantered back and forth in the quick, sharp style of the Jai language. 'He says there were several great…gashes opened in the hull of *Brezhnev*. Many obviously…floated out.'

The commander spoke again.

'Some may have been…burned up.'

Dimitryiev nodded. 'I understand.'

The commander slid a small panel at the top of the door, revealing a pane of glass. Gee-ah-Nah stepped in front of the glass and said something to the commander. 'I know you humans are more….what is the word?…sensitive about your dead than we. You should know there is no gravity in the morgue. Each of your crew is wrapped in a plastic bag and tied to the wall.'

Dimitryiev nodded.

'Also, it is kept at the temperature at which water freezes.'

'Of course.'

Gee-ah-Nah stepped aside. Dimitryiev leaned forward and peered inside. He quickly turned away.

'What do you intend to do with the bodies?'

'We cannot bring them aboard the station itself. Health.'

Dimitryiev nodded.

'The commander says they have gotten the name identifications of your crew.'

'I would like those.'

'You will have them. And then we will have to…I am trying to find right word…'

'Jettison the bodies.'

'Yes.'

Dimitryiev nodded. 'But not before I say some words for my crew.'

Gee-ah-Nah nodded his head left and right in agreement.

'I would like to be alone.'

Gee-ah-Nah said something to the station commander, who said something back. The two seemed to bicker for a few moments. Before leaving Gee-ah-Nah said, 'He doesn't trust you.'

Dimitryiev snorted. He stepped forward again and looked through the window. Thirty-seven cold lumps, his crew, floated in the morgue. He forced himself to look for a few seconds before turning away. Dimitryiev said a few words. He wasn't a religious man and his crew was mixed, with many Russian Orthodox Christians but more than a dozen Asiatic Muslims; Dimitryiev managed a few prayers in each religion. When he was finished he turned to Gee-ah-Nah and said, 'I am ready.'

Gee-ah-Nah spoke to the commander, and pressed a button on his collar and gave the order to open the bay door. The hooks holding the Russian bodies retracted and a burst of air sent them flying into space. When the bay door closed, Dimitryiev nodded to both Jai and said, 'Thank you.'

On the trip back to the ship, Dimitryiev simply leaned back in his seat and closed his eyes. Once docked, Gee-ah-Nah walked Dimitryiev back to his quarters.

'I will leave you,' he said.

'Thank you.'

Dimitryiev sat in his chair and looked at the desk of papers before him, his write up of the war and English translation. He thought of his crew and felt tears welling up.

No point in crying like a teenager, he thought. He took a deep breath and pushed the chair away from the desk. Dimitryiev thought for a moment about writing something else.

But who would read it? Dimitryiev thought. He shrugged, who cares.

Dimitryiev got out a new piece of paper and began writing.

Later, at dinner, Dimitryiev showed what he had written to Gee-ah-Nah. He read for a few moments and then held up his hand, 'Now this is…interesting…' Gee-ah-Nah read aloud, 'Lieutenant Gennadi Pleshkov was a fine officer with years of…experience in the Russian Navy having served….' He moved on to another page, 'Commander Anvar Mohadev was a brilliant tactical weapons commander…' Gee-ah-Nah read on for a few minutes.

'This is…fascinating, Captain.'

'It is, my crew,' Dimitryiev said.

'I would like to keep this, Captain.'

'Of course,' Dimitryiev replied. 'Make copies. I would like one.'

'Yes.'

'Now, if you don't mind, I am very tired and would like to rest.'

'Goodnight....Captain.'

Dimitryiev retired to his small cabin and lay down. Then he began to quietly weep. Not out of sadness, but out of the loss of a great burden, finally relieved.

The next day there was great excitement as they docked with another Jai ship. The visitor was a small cruiser of a type Dimitryiev had never seen. It docked for several hours, and unloaded several dozen small metallic containers before leaving. Throughout the day there was, what seemed to Dimitryiev to be excited talking amongst the crew, in the Jai manner. He was picking up the language, at least some words, and he thought he heard 'new shipment' and 'fresh fish' several times.

At dinner that evening, Dimitryiev was indeed served fresh fish. Though not any he recognized, his meal looked like a typical bottom feeder. Long and cylindrical, with a spongy exterior. It looked like an eel perhaps. Dimitryiev's knife cut it easy enough, and it was edible with the orange/yellow sauce that the jai provided.

When Captain Gee-ah-Nah arrived he sat and looked his plate over.

'Ahhhh,' he said. 'We have not...had this in several months.'

'I do not recognize it,' Dimitryiev asked. 'Is this fish native to your planet?'

Gee-ah-Nah looked up from his dish. 'What? Oh, you mean you people on Earth still don't know?'

'Know what?'

Gee-ah-Nah gave a Jai laugh. He pointed to the fish with his fork, 'This is native to your solar system, it comes from one of Jupiter's moons.'

'Really?' Dimitryiev said in amazement.

'Yes, really. I believe you call it...' he searched for the name, 'Europa.'

'Of course!' Dimitryiev said excitedly. 'Many thought there might be life on Europa.'

'Yes. Underneath a few kilometers of ice is a vast fresh water ocean. Its floor is teaming with life.'

'Fascinating.'

'When we lost the first part of the war, we had to…scramble, to find sources of food and water. We immediately investigated your Europa. We have a large base there. We farm it…for aquatic life…and water…'

'May I see some photos?'

Gee-ah-Na bobbed his headed left to right.

That night, Gee-ah-Nah gave Dimitryiev access to one of the ship's computers and showed him their files on the sea life of Europa. The computer worked much like an Earth computer, with windows, icon, and a cursor. Apparently, the Jai had long ago conquered the technology, the captain was not even familiar with the old key stroke format of early Earth computers. The screen was three-dimensional

Gee-ah-Nah showed him pictures of Europa's sea floor. Like earth scientists who believed Europa might have life theorized, the floor was rent open with gashes opening up to the moon's hot core. The vents produced super hot water creating the conditions for life. Dimitryiev saw a kind of green plankton growing around them.

'Do the plankton get enough light for photosynthesis?'

'Barely.'

Gee-ah-Nah showed more photos. These showed bottom-feeding creatures similar to crustaceans on earth, tubers living in shells, and eel like creatures swimming about the vents.

'Is there any other kind of life?'

'None that we can find, just these basic sea creatures' replied Gee-ah-Nah. 'So, sorry. No intelligent…life in your solar system, other than us now.'

Dimitryiev scrolled through more pictures, close-up of the various forms of life.

'We can harvest that indefinitely,' he said. 'I will leave you.'

Dimitryiev looked at every photo he could find. He could not yet read Jai so he scrolled through them pretty quickly.

Later, in bed, Dimitryiev couldn't stop thinking about his conversation with Gee-ah-Na. After tossing and turning he finally realized why. The

Captain's words echoed, 'No intelligent…life in your solar system, other than us now….we can harvest these indefinitely…when we lost the first phase of the war…'

Dimitryiev spent the next day instructing several of the ship's officer's in Russian. He did not see Gee-ah-Na again until dinner.

'So,' he began over a meal of Europa Eel, 'You harvest these eels and other life from Europa?'

'Yes.'

'How? I mean, how do you get through the ice?'

'Well, said Gee-ah-Nah, 'I am not completely familiar with the process, but the ice is thinner at the…equator, of course. We have a base there. It drilled through the ice. At first, we actually…sent probes to harvest fish, but now, I think, there is…a big aquarium. A farm, you say.'

'Is this your only food source?'

Gee-ah-Nah nodded his head right to left, 'We have farms on Mars where we grow Earth crops. We ran out of most kinds of Jai food long ago.'

'So vegetables and fish,' said Dimitryiev.

'Yes,' replied Gee-ah-Nah, 'No, what do you say…? Beef. Yes. No beef.'

'Now that you mention it,' said Dimitryiev, 'Your crew does look a little emaciated.'

'What is this word?'

'Oh…thin.'

Gee-ah-nah smiled.

Dimitryiev said, 'The meal portions are the same even though you have more food.'

'We received our normal allocation,' Gee-ah-nah said. 'Most of the rest is being stockpiled.'

'I see.'

That night, Dimitryiev was about to drift off to sleep, when he put everything together.

In the morning he rose as usual and took his breakfast in the wardroom exchanging pleasantries with the Jai officers there. Then, before his scheduled Russian language class, Dimitryiev took his leave and walked the ship. When

Geeh-ah-nah asked Dimitryiev what he was doing, he said, 'I wanted to strengthen my leg and stay healthy. I do not want to lay about.'

The Jai captain nodded his understanding.

To avoid suspicion in the coming days Dimtryiev made it a habit to walk several laps around the ship in the morning and then again after dinner. He began recognizing much of the crew and exchanging pleasantries, in Russian with his language students. He didn't stop at the station he was interested in. That would be too much of a risk. But he walked past it several times during the day and was able to look in. Usually only one Jai was on station there. But for what Dimitryiev wanted to do, there was the matter of learning the equipment therein. Before he turned in, Dimitryiev looked on his cabin computer and sure enough, operating manuals for the entire ship were on the hard drive. But he didn't click through. Dimitryev had no idea if his actions on the computer were being monitored, and if they were, he couldn't risk being seen reading up on the ship's systems. The implications were too obvious. Besides, his understanding of the Jai language was too rudimentary to make sense of a technical manual.

That night in his bunk Dimitryiev pondered the problem of learning how to use the Jai equipment. He already knew how to do what he wanted to do on *Brezhnev*, or any Russian ship for that matter. Russian ships were designed for simplicity, so that a poorly educated young man could learn and master his task in a short period of time. The Americans had a phrase for it he knew, 'designed by geniuses to be run by idiots.' In his time aboard Spear, he had seen little to make him think the Jai were any different. He had understood most of the symbols on Spear without incident. The lavatory worked the same aboard as it had on *Brezhnev*, why not their communications room?

Yes, that is my only chance, he thought.

There was no point in waiting.

He stayed awake until the ship's day crew was off duty and replaced by a skeleton night crew, and waited an hour after that to ensure most were asleep. He rose and hobbled out of his cabin. He walked down the corridor, passing a single Jai who was himself on the way to the lavatory. Dimitryiev nodded and smiled.

Without pause, he walked into the communications room. One Jai was on duty there, his head buried in some kind of hand held electronics device. He didn't look up until it was too late. Dimitryiev gently closed the hatch and sealed it. The Jai said something in his own language but did not stand. Dimitryiev smiled and then punched him in the face. The Jai fell to the floor. Dimitryiev fell on top of him and punched him in the face again and clasped his hands around the surprised Jai's neck. He brutally squeezed. The Jai flailed hopelessly as Dimitryiev felt cartilage bend, then he heard a sickening snap. The head went limp. He wheezed and then stopped breathing. He maintained his grip on the jai's neck until he was sure he was dead. Then he pushed the Jai away and sat in his chair.

Dimitryiev surveyed the communications equipment. There were several dials and switches, each with a small illustration to show what it was. He fumbled with several buttons until he brought a display up on the comm set's monitor. He was confronted with row after row of Jai writing. Each was short, amounting to only a few words. A button allowed him to scroll down. He was in luck. Many of the words were illustrated by icons. There was Venus, and below that, icons for land and space stations, there was Mars with the same arrangement. At the bottom was a blue-white circle which had to be Earth. He scrolled down and highlighted the Earth icon. By the microphone were several buttons, each with writing below them. He pressed each, trying to discern their function. After one button, the Earth icon blinked.

Could it be? he wondered.

Dimitryiev heard static emanating from the microphone.

Yes, he thought. *This is it. I am patched into Earth. But to whom?* He picked up the microphone. There was a button on the side, similar to a CB and pressed it. The static stopped. He let go and the static started again.

Very well, the radio is activated and pointed to Earth, now what?

He looked at the screen. Below the main screen was a smaller console with two buttons. One button had a single line on it, but the other had several, radiating from a single point like rays of light. It looked a bit like a wireless icon. He pressed the button and it lit up.

If I am doing this right, I am on a broad, general frequency pointed toward Earth.

He took a deep breath and pressed the button on the microphone.

'Any Earth military personnel, any Earth military personnel, come in please.' He waited. When nothing happen he repeated. 'Any Earth military personnel come in please. This is Captain Yuri Dimitryiev of the Russian Navy Ship *Brezhnev*. Please respond.'

Dimitryiev waited. It would take several seconds for the transmission to reach Earth.

There was static and then, 'This is Moon Base Victory, who is this?'

'Moon Base Victory?' said Dimitryiev. 'American?'

After several seconds pause, '…Yes, U.S. Navy. Who are you?'

'This is Captain Yuri Dimitryiev, Russian Navy Ship *Brezhnev*.'

'…Get out of here,' said the typically irreverent American. 'Stop clogging up this line.'

'With whom am I speaking?'

After a pause, Aother voice spoke. '….This is Lieutenant Commander Rick Martinez. Get off this line.'

'Commander please listen,' said Dimitryiev. 'I am a Russian naval captain, late of the *Brezhnev*.'

'….This is a Jai communications signal. Do you think I will fall for this?'

'I am Russian.'

The wait was several seconds longer than the rest, no doubt as the Americans discussed what to do. '…Prove it.'

'The last Soviet premier was Mikhail Gorbachev, before him Chernenko, before him Andropov, before him Brezhnev, before him Khrushchev.'

'…Give me a break, any Jai could have learned that.'

The communications room intercom came on, a Jai voice spoke. Dimitryiev ignored it. 'I do not have much time, Commander. Here,' he recited in Russian, the words to the old Soviet national anthem.

'…Keep, going.'

'I am from Novosibirsk. My father was Pavel Dimitryiev. I graduated from the naval academy in 2001 with high honors and a degree in mathematics. You can confirm this with my government. I was never married. My eyes are blue, my hair blond.'

The intercom spoke again.

'…Alright, Captain, if that's who you are. What do you want?'

'You know of our failed attack on Venus yes?'

'…Yes.'

'My ship was boarded and I was captured. I'm in the communications room of a Jai ship, the *Spear*.'

'…That's incredible.'

'It's true. If I'm lying it does not matter. If it is true I have information for you. For all of Earth. Are you recording?'

There was pounding on the hatch, and Dimitryiev saw the handle spinning as whoever was on the outside turned it. The door opened, a Jai officer stood there, alone. Obviously sent down to investigate whatever had happened. Dimitryiev brought himself to his feet. The Jai approached, Dimitryiev socked him with a two handed fist right under the chin. The Jai went flying out into the corridor. Dimitryiev grabbed the handle and slammed the door. He sat back down.

'Listen carefully, they are coming for me. The Jai are receiving reinforcements from their home world. I saw them building a massive dock over Venus to house a large ship.'

'…Ok.'

'I do not know when it will arrive. But I think soon. They are stockpiling food for the arrival of more Jai. I saw them do this. They have a farm on Europa.'

'…Europa?'

'Yes, Jupiter's moon. It's an ocean. They get fish there.'

'…I don't believe it.'

'Believe it. I ate one. It is their main food supply. I….'

The entire console before Dimitryiev went dark.

The hatch opened. A Jai pointed a rifle at Dimitryiev. Behind him stood Gee-ah-Nah. The Jai with the rifle clubbed Dimitryiev in the stomach. He fell to the floor in a ball.

'What did you do?' Gee-ah-Nah asked.

Dimitryiev looked up and smiled. 'I will not tell.'

'No matter. We will find out.'

'I know.'

'I imagine you contacted Earth.' Gee-ah-nah shook his head left to right. 'Even after we saved your life.'

'You destroyed my ship and killed all my crew.'

'And you shall join them soon.'

Dimitryiev put a hand on the chair and slowly pushed himself to his feet. He laughed. 'Of that I am very glad.' He stood at attention. 'Captain Gee-ah-nah, whenever you are ready…'

Connecticut

Melody answered the door.

'Oh!' she said. 'I remember you. You're Peter's friend.'

Rodden nodded.

'Please, come in.' She opened the door 'What brings you here?'

'Well, I had a bit of news…' Rodden looked down and saw that Melody carried a big bulge on her stomach.

She blushed and smiled. 'Five months now.'

'Ah.'

'He's in the living room by the fire place. You know, with the power out and everything.'

'Sure. I'll find my way.'

Rodden found Cosgrove throwing a log on a burgeoning fire in the cottage's small living room. 'Hey!' he shouted.

Cosgrove stood up, 'Well, well. To what do I owe this pleasure?'

The two men shook hands.

'Just thought I'd pop by. I have some news.'

'Have a seat,' he said.

The two men sat down on the loveseat before the fire.

'Sorry about the cozy arrangement, but the power is in and out and you've come during one of the out times.'

'There's a reason for that,' Cosgrove said.
'Oh?' Wait a minute,' Rodden said. 'What's with Melody?'
'What do you mean?'
'Well, I mean…'
'Yes, I knocked her up. It ain't rocket science.'
'I thought you swore you'd never…'
Cosgrove waved his hand.
'Don't tell me you're settling down?'
'Shut up,' Cosgrove said. 'Is this why you came down here?'
'No,' replied Rodden. 'This is why.'

He reached into his pocket and took out a slip of paper. It was a memo, marked classified.

'How did you get this? If they find out…'
'My C-O knows. You remember Del Carmen?'
'Tommy Del Carmen? That whack job we served with on the old *Truman*? Sure.'
'He runs my section now. I told him I wanted you to take a look at this. He said no problem.'

Rodden handed the memo to Cosgrove. He read quickly, moving his lips and muttering as he did so.

'I don't believe this. A base on Europa?'
'A farm.'
'A fish farm. How did they even know to look there?'
'Give me the memo back.'
'Alright.'

Rodden took the memo. 'Now, what I am about to tell you…'
Cosgrove waved his hand, 'Yeah, yeah, I know.'
'Good. Now, remember that failed Ruski attack on Venus?'
'Sure. And I think it ought to give you space-boys a bit of pause, don't you?'
'That's not the point. Turns out the Jai captured a Russian captain.'
'Now how the hell do the intel boys know that?'
'Because this captured Russian managed to get hold of a radio and contact our big base on the moon's north pole.'

'Oh c'mon, it's a ruse.'

'That's what the DIA guys thought. Then they looked at a transcript of the call. This Russian said there was a Jai fish farm on Europa. So the DIA guys pointed some powerful telescopes at Europa.'

'They find a fish farm?'

'They did. Or a big base, anyway. The Jai are doing something up there.'

'Hmmm,' said Cosgrove, 'why would they tell us about their fish farm?'

'They wouldn't.'

'No they wouldn't, would they? So how did this Russian guy get to a radio?'

'I have no idea, and don't over think it. We don't care.'

'Good point.'

'Now, there's something else this Russian guy told us, and it's a problem.'

'Yeah?'

'He said the Jai are coming.'

'To attack Earth? Good, they don't have the fire power. We'll make mincemeat of them.'

'No, Pete. Another Jai ship is coming to the solar system, from their home world.'

'Jesus. Do we know when? How long? How much?'

'No, and we haven't been able to spot it either.'

'And if this Russian captain was right about Europa…'

'There's no reason he'd be wrong about an approaching ship from the Jai homeworld.'

Rodden shook his head. 'Nope.'

'So they're coming?'

'They are,' Rodden replied. 'And we're going.'

'What?'

'That's why your power is out lately. Atomic Boat is sucking up all the electricity.'

'You mean we're going up into space.'

'No, I mean we're going to attack Mars, and soon.'

'Jesus Christ, are we even ready?'

'Hardly.'

'Oh and the Indians are hitting the big Jai base on Ceres.'

'Why not concentrate everything on Mars?'

'That's above my pay grade, my friend.'

'Do they even have enough personnel assembled?'

'Nope. That's actually why I came down here.'

'Don't even think about it.'

'Well, if you want a post on one of the ships, it's yours.'

Cosgrove looked over at his five months pregnant young wife. 'Can't do it. I did my part already.'

Rodden nodded. 'I know.'

'Why don't you go?'

'I can't?'

'Why the hell not?"

Rodden reached into his coat pocket and took out his radiation detection badge. The indicator button had turned from green to red. 'Because I have cancer,' Rodden patted his stomach. 'It's bad, and it won't be long.'

CHAPTER 6

THE BATTLE OF CERES-EUROPA

In his cabin, Captain Vijay Rao sat on his bunk and read passages from the Bhagavad Gita in the original Sanskrit. The language had been a hobby of his as a young naval officer before the war and he liked to stay in practice, even if mission planning took up most of his time. Reading the Bhagavad Gita cleared and focused his mind. He had always read it before a big activity or event; his academy graduation, his wedding, and even his first command as a frigate in the old Indian Navy. He read them again now:

> ...the great army drawn up by Drupada's son and one of your wise students Great heroes who throw the arrow in the same way as Bhima and Arjuna in battle wanted to fight, and Virata, and Drupada with the great chariot.

Task Force Ceres is certainly that, Rao thought.

Rao read on about the great discourse on the eve of battle between the warrior Arjuna and Kirshna until he heard a respectful knock on his cabin door.

'Captain, Commander Patel says it is time.'

'Thank you,' he said to the old orderly in the passageway. 'I will be at the bridge shortly.'

Rao stood up and smoothed the wrinkles out of his whites, put on his gold braided captain's hat and headed for the bridge. Unlike the great *USSS Wasp* and

Hornet, he walked through the passageways. The ship's fusion drive powered gravity was somewhat weaker than a standard G, but Rao had long ago gotten used to the awkward feel. 'Getting your space legs' they called it, now.

Upon his arrival the bridge crew stood. He dismissed them with a wave. Commander Patel relinquished the captain's chair in the center of a U shaped bank of stations. Rao sat down and gazed upon the assemblage of Indian technological might; computers and flat-screens in control of the most mammoth warship the subcontinent had ever built. Irrespective of its mission, *INSS William Slim* was a point of pride for the nation still smarting from the drubbing the Jai delivered it during the late war. She was a statement as much as a warship.

William Slim was big, more than three hundred meters long. At her aft were four white streams of nuclear fire, each powered by an Israeli made MK-II fusion drive, half again as powerful as the old Mk-I's that had powered *Wasp* and *Hornet* at the Battle of Luna. A quartet of railguns were mounted forward. Two more were mounted amidships, both port and starboard. Missile racks lined *William Slim's* keel. They were not the old T-SLAMS Captain Masters had used to smash Jai bases on Luna, but high tech space missiles designed in India. She did carry old fashioned A-bomb casters, low tech had its place, even in a technological behemoth like *William Slim*. She outgunned the old *Wasp* and *Hornet*, and could probably take them both on. No one really knew how she stood against the ships of the doomed Sino-Russian fleet that was destroyed at Venus.

Rao turned his attention toward his main flat-screen. It showed Task Force Ceres' dispositions. *William Slim* had the lead of course, followed by two 'cruisers' in the old wet navy lexicon, *INSS Jacob* and *INSS Indira Gandhi*. 10,000 kilometers behind them cruised *INSS Manekshaw*, a space assault ship carrying the First Gurkha Regiment.

Ceres loomed less than two million kilometers away. But as *William Slim* drew closer, her bridge crew focused on the tactical net of Task Force Mars. Four squadrons, a great fleet of the English-Speaking-Peoples closed in on the Red Planet, all under the command of the legendary American, Admiral Maha Ganesan.

'Captain,' said the Comm Officer, Lt. Peri, with the enthusiasm of a child seeing his favorite football player scoring a goal, 'Task Force Mars is beginning its attack.'

Rao pressed a button and changed his flat-screen to Task Force Mars' tactical readout. 'I see.'

'May we listen in? The British Squadron is engaging.' asked Patel.

Rao nodded.

'Comm,' ordered Patel, 'switch to Squadron Royal Navy.'

'Yes, Commander,' Ensign Peri replied.

Rao heard the voice of the British squadron commander, Captain Obidejo, whom he knew socially.

'All ships, report,' Obidejo ordered.

'*Warspite* has the lead.'

'*Victory* on station.'

'*Ajax* on station.'

'Copy, *Victory* and *Ajax*. Follow me past the pole-station. Fire pattern as follows; *Warspite* will bombard the pole, *Victory* to bombard the station and *Ajax* in reserve will organize its marine boarding parties for the station.'

'Affirmative.'

'Affirmative.'

'We are going in,' said Captain Obidejo. 'Follow me.'

Rao motioned for Peri to switch off Task Force Mars' feed.

'I can't listen anymore,' he said. 'If I wanted to feel this powerless I'd watch a cricket match.'

'Yes, sir.'

'Commander Patel,' he said to the exec, 'Listen in on the battle though. Give me updates.'

'Yes, sir,' she replied. Rao looked at Patel, she didn't seem pleased at the prospect.

No doubt Patel had visions of glorious naval battles for herself that did not include keeping tabs on a battle for her skipper. Like all the other young officers on the bridge she lionized Admiral Ganesan, who had quickly become a legend in India after she skippered *USS Hornet* at the Battle of Luna. She was treated like a cult figure by millions of young Indian women; one whose deeds should be emulated. Indeed, two thirds of Rao's bridge crew were female. Rao looked at the pert, eager faces and suddenly felt old. He couldn't help but think of the Bhagavad Gita:

"I see those
Who are about to fight-
Those who have gathered here,
Wishing to do loving service in battle."

They seemed so young to Rao, a new generation of Indians. They were well travelled. Most had lived for long periods in the United States or Britain, many in places like Dubai and Singapore. They weren't nationalists, at least not the way Rao had always been. While all spoke English and Hindi of course, many were not fluent in the language of their native state (Rao still dreamed in his native Tapori). Patel for example didn't know her native Gujarati tongue. The young officers didn't have hang-ups about colonialism. Rao had once had a conversation with Lt. Maruvada, the Sensor Officer, who actually argued that the British Raj was great for India and expressed her admiration for Lord Bentinck. Then there was Captain Thapa, commander of *William Slim's* contingent of Gurkhas, who liked to argue that Ghandi was a short-sighted, little man, and the British never should have left. Rao wasn't obsessed with anti-western colonial sentiment like some old-timers, after all he commanded a ship named after an Englishman, but even he was not prepared to go *that* far. Of course, Rao would much have preferred if the ships were named after ancient Indian heroes, Arjuna, perhaps.

What's the term the Americans adopted? Rao thought. *Gung-ho, that's it.*

Most of the young officers had been children during Arrival. Rao had been there.

Arrival + nine days

'Fire,' ordered Lt. Rao.

INS Kalkata's forward gun cracked.

'Forward gun fired.'

A 76 mm shell streaked through the air toward the coast, now just three kilometers distant. It exploded just behind the beach.

Lt. Rao could see a ball of fire. He wasn't sure what exactly they'd hit, only that it had been a Jai vehicle.

'Gun reloaded,' the gunnery officer reported.

'Fire.'

The gun cracked again.

'Gun fired.'

Another 76 mm shell arced through the air and impacted on the beach. Rao saw another explosion.

'Gunnery, this is the Captain.'

'Go ahead, Captain,' Rao replied.

'That is excellent, gunnery.'

'Thank you, sir.'

'Proceed.'

'Yes, sir,' replied Rao. 'Forward gun, fire for effect.'

'Yes, sir, firing for effect.'

Two more shells went toward the beach, each exploding in a fireball.

The Jai vehicles on the beach withdrew out of view.

'Plus 100 and fire for effect,' Rao ordered. 'Chase those Jai vehicles.'

The gun cracked once more.

Coming near *Kolkata* now, Rao could see several boats. Some had outboard motors, a few were recreational motor craft. He even saw a couple of rowboats with small put-put style motors. He picked up a small microphone and said, 'Bridge, gunnery... second wave of boats approaching.'

'Understood,' replied the XO.

Behind Rao, dozens of Indian Army soldiers leaned or sat against the bulkhead. Few had weapons. All looked waterlogged.

'Boats approaching.'

'Get those ropes down!' Rao shouted.

Sailors threw ropes over the railings; they were taken by bedraggled soldiers in the boat. One by one, they climbed the ropes and hauled themselves aboard.

'Get a count!' Rao shouted.

The forward gun fired again. This time the shell screamed through the air but exploded above the beach.

The gunnery officer said, 'It looks as if the Jai have ranged us.'

'Fire again.'

'Yes, sir.'

Another shell, and another explosion on the beach.

Rao spoke into his mic, 'Bridge, the Jai have our range.'

'Very well,' the XO replied. Down in the CiC the captain said, 'Get underway, five knots.'

Rao leaned over the rail and shouted, 'You better get up here. We are leaving!'

Behind him a waterlogged sergeant, his uniform in tatters said, 'What do you mean, leaving? We still have men on the beach!'

'The Jai have found us. If we stay we go down.'

The sergeant said, 'Then let me back in the water, I will take a boat to the beach and rescue my comrades.'

Rao shook his head.

'I said let me down.'

'No.'

The sergeant pulled a pistol. Before he could fire, one of Rao's sailors knocked the weapon out of his hand.

Now angry, Rao grabbed the sergeant by both collars and said. 'I have already seen the wreckage of *INS Vikrant*. I have no wish to join her at the bottom of the Indian Ocean. The Jai have found us. We leave or sink. Now go sit down.'

'Yes…Lieutenant.'

'Is it really that bad?' Rao asked. 'What happened?'

'I do not know everything,' the sergeant said. 'I was with First Armoured Division. We fought the Jai to a standstill,' he shook his head. 'We must have lost half of our vehicles. The Jai actually withdrew.'

'So why this?' Rao gestured to the shore which was already receding.

'The Jai cut through the division guarding our northern flank. The rest of us withdrew. Most of First Armoured Division escaped, but my battalion was trapped on the coast.'

The gun fired again.

'What does the army do now?'
'Withdraw.'
'And leave the west to the Jai?'
'They won, we lost. Accept it, navy.'

Task Force Ceres

'Captain,' said Commander Patel, 'we are entering the battle zone.'

Ceres lay less than a million kilometers away now. Rao brought up a real-time projection of the asteroid on his flat-screen

Satellite imagery had shown that over the past decade and a half the Jai had transformed Ceres into a fortress. They had other bases in the solar system, on Venus and Mars of course, as well as Europa and the rest of the Galilean Moons, but none boasted defenses comparable to Ceres'. Slag piles on the asteroid's surface showed where Jai engineers had dug deep underground tunnels. Other slag heaps in symmetrical patterns were visible across the asteroid. Intelligence was sure these were missile or laser batteries. For years American, British and Indian intelligence had intercepted electronic communications to and from the asteroid. These were encoded and the cryptologists hadn't had much luck breaking the Jai code. Given this, and the stream of ships heading to and from Ceres, the Americans believed that it was the Jai main base and Xetroch Nanreh's headquarters.

An orange arrow labeled 'grav-point' pointed to a spot behind Ceres.

Rao zoomed in on Pyramid, a four-mile high plateau topped mountain near the North Pole. A Jai satellite orbited above the target, and slag piles nearby suggested a pair of missile silos. Atop the mountain were several structures; laser or missile batteries, intelligence thought. Extending north toward the pole was a great protuberance running underneath the surface for more than a kilometer.

Pyramid was Task Force Ceres' main target.

'Sir,' Lt. Maruvada said, 'I am detecting new targets.'

A pair of red dots appeared on the Ceres display, both emanating from Pyramid.

Close ups of Pyramid showed a pair of massive doors and two large ships streaking into the sky.

'Ah,' remarked Rao. 'So they base ships in Pyramid.'

Two ships quickly gained altitude. 3D, radar, and infrared sensors analyses produced a three-dimensional image on Rao's flat-screen. They were smaller than Jai carrier ships and boasted a pair of barrels on the fore.

'More contacts, sir,' said Maruvada. 'Two more, this time on the South Pole.'

'Understood,' said Rao. 'What do you make of those, Lieutenant Commander Mukherjee?'

'Maybe a gunship, a flying weapons platform,' he replied. 'Those forward batteries look large. I think lasers.'

'Alright.'

'Two launches at the equator,' reported Maruvada.

'Speed?'

'All contacts accelerating at 1.11 Gs.'

'In unison then.'

'Yes, Captain,' replied Maruvada. 'More launches, two on each pole.'

'Eight, altogether now,' said Rao.

Rao considered the tactical display. During the Battle of Luna, Xetroc Nanreh had committed his forces piecemeal, fighting three separate engagements with Task Force Luna. It was like feeding a meat grinder as *Wasp* and *Hornet* dealt with each group of four Jai carrier ships individually. In closed briefings, even Admiral Ganesan had admitted Task Force Luna had been lucky in this respect. Had *Wasp* and *Hornet* gone up against twelve or even eight carrier ships at once, their task would have been far more difficult.

'So they have learned their lesson,' said Rao. 'They are going to stay close to Ceres, it would seem, eh Commander Patel?'

'Yes, Captain. I think so.'

Rao picked up his radio receiver and raised the skippers of *Nehru*, *Indira Gandhi* and *Manekshaw*. 'This is Captain Rao. We will attack according to plan.' Rao heard a trio of affirmatives from the other skippers in the task force. 'Captain Rao signing off.'

He pressed another button raising the engine room.

'Lt. Commander Alon.'

'This is the Captain. What is your status?'

'Ready whenever you are, Captain.'

'Good. We will accelerate to 2 gees.'

Lt. Commander Alon replied. 'Good to go.'

'Helm,' ordered Rao, 'bring us up to 2 gees.'

In the engine room, two of Alon's engineers, one Israeli the other Indian began the acceleration process. At one end of the ship's magnetic core, the Israeli engineer injected deuterium pellets, while at the other end the Indian engineer injected tritium pellets. Two more engineers; an Indian and Israeli, fired an ion laser which fused the pellets together, creating nuclear fusion.

Rao felt the acceleration push against him as *William Slim* gradually gained gravity. Slowly she pulled away from the other ships in the task force.

'Helm, set course for the grav-point.'

'Yes, Captain,' replied Ensign Gandhi. Her name was actually Patel, but on the bridge he called her Gandhi to avoid confusion.

William Slim accelerated and pulled away from the task force, eleven thousand kilometers, twelve thousand kilometers…

Rao ordered, 'Lt. Commander Mukherjee bring all weapon systems on line.'

'Yes, Captain.'

'Execute firing solutions for enemy targets.'

'Yes, sir.'

'Hit the Jai with every weapon at hand, Lieutenant Commander. Hold nothing back. We'll hammer Ceres as we fly by.'

Lt. Commander Mukherjee looked at his weapons techs, 'All right techs. Let's make some art.'

Rao actually smirked at that.

Mukherjee was a mathematician, a statistics major actually who did a lot of graduate work in chaos theory. He was an artist in his spare time dabbling with bright colors in abstract paintings. Rao had seen his work and found it incomprehensible even after explaining that he combined art and chaos theory. Of course, there was nothing more chaotic than an explosion and Mukherjee explained that he viewed each detonation as a work of art.

'Let's add some photos for my art files.'

'Two gees, Captain,' said Ensign Gandhi.

'No reaction from the Jai, yet,' Rao commented. 'They really do intend to stay close to Ceres.'

At 100,000 kilometers from Ceres *Manekshaw* maneuvered behind *Nehru* in preparation for the landing. Rao patched in to *Manekshaw's* comm as the launch officer readied the Gurkha assault troops...

'All boats, report status.'

'Alpha Boat, platoon aboard and ready.'

'Beta Boat, platoon aboard and ready.'

'Gamma Boat, platoon aboard and ready.'

'Delta Boat, heavy weapons platoon aboard and ready.'

'Very well,' replied the launch officer. 'Alpha Boat will lead; Delta Boat follows then Beta and Gamma.'

The Gurkha commander, Colonel Rai spoke next. 'Aayo Gurkha' he shouted. 'On to Ceres and victory!'

Colonel Rai's plan called for putting a battalion of marines on the surface, establishing a perimeter and using the heavy weapon's platoon to blast open the entrance and fight his way inside the tunnel. Once the entrance was secured, another company would clear the tunnel while still another would land and deploy above it against Jai escape attempts. There had to be more than one way out.

Rao had sat in on several planning sessions and had gotten to know the Gurkha's commander. Rai was convinced of the infallibility of the First Gurkha Rifles to the point of arrogance when dealing with Rao and the rest of the navy. Rao still recalled one particularly trying planning session...

'Just get us to Ceres, we can do the rest.'

'We can get to Ceres, but I do have to protect my task force.'

'But you must get us as close as possible.'

'Colonel, I assure you, my ships can unleash a bombardment that will cover your landing.'

'Frankly, Captain, I am wondering if that will be enough. I would like your ships to get us as close as possible.'

'I understand your concern but I also fear for unnecessary casualties for my crew.'

'They will be necessary to get my boarding troops on Ceres.'

'Excuse me?'

'Captain, as far as I am concerned the navy is a tool to project the army.'

Rao had gathered his wits about him and rather than give a lecture about naval power and its influence simply said, 'That may be true but I am in command of this task force and I will make these decisions.'...

Helm snapped Rao back to the present.

'Two point five g's,' Gandhi said.

Ceres was coming up fast, now. With the assault boats getting ready to deploy, Rao decided the time had come to engage.

'Weapons,' said Rao, 'target that cloud of satellites above the north pole.'

'Yes, sir.' Mukherjee said. He could barely hide his glee, like a child getting to take out a new toy and see what it could do, 'Caster, give me a volley of A-bombs.'

'Sir.'

The caster tech fired a volley of five A-bombs in a finger-five spread pattern.

'Fire another,' said Mukherjee. 'Lasers, escort those A-bomb spreads into target!'

The laser tech trained the ship's forward battery on the cloud of Jai satellites. He fired a quick burst at one satellite and then another.

'New, contacts,' Lt. Maruvada reported. 'Several launch plumes on the surface and now....'

Before sensors could finish *William Slim* took a laser hit from Ceres. She shook from the force of the blast, and then shook again as another hit her.

'Damage Control, where were we hit?'

'Forward, Captain.' *William Slim* shook again. 'No damage.'

Rao waited another minute and then patched himself into the squadron net. 'All ships, open fire, fire at will.'

Nehru and *Indira Gandhi* added their fire to *William Slim's*, filling space with lasers, A-bombs, missiles and railgun volleys.

Helm reported, '50,000 kilometers from the grav-point.'

Maruvada said, 'Two Jai gunships are moving against us.'

'I see them,' said Rao.

The gunships each fired a great forward laser, *William Slim* shook with the impact which left two great scorch marks on the front armor.

As *William Slim* drew closer, the Jai brought more fire to bear. Rao thought he understood the Jai's fire plan. He called Patel over to him.

'Alright, Commander, this is what I see. The Jai have used their satellites to establish a perimeter.'

'Right, Captain, I see it.'

Rao was about to speak but was interrupted by another jarring blast.

Damage Control spoke, 'I'm afraid we just lost a railgun.'

'Understood.' On the flat-screen a big explosion temporarily illuminated space.

'Just nabbed two satellites!' exclaimed Mukherjee.

Rao continued, 'The Jai are plowing the road, as it were, for those Ceres based missiles.'

'We could fire on them from this altitude but we'd never get through,' said Patel.

'Weapons, do you concur?'

Mukherjee replied, 'I do, Captain.'

'Very well.' *William Slim* rattled again. 'We shall push in toward the grav-point.'

'Yes, Captain.'

'Helm, accelerate to 3 gees.'

'Yes, sir.'

'Captain,' Patel said. 'Let us remain here and escort the attack boats in.'

'No.'

'Why not, sir?'

'That is what we have *Indira Gandhi* and *Jacob* for.'

'But sir, we have the most fire power.'

'Enough, Commander.'

Trying to emulate Admiral Ganesan, he thought 'Lt. Commander Mukherjee, target those two gunships over Pyramid.'

'Yes, Captain.'

The sensor read-out showed the Jai defenses reorienting toward *William Slim*, which was just fine with Rao. The ship rumbled again and then again, the last one so badly that it threw Rao against the arm of his chair. He rubbed his ribs in pain.

'That was a laser,' said Damage Control. 'We've been hulled.'

'Three gees,' said Helm.

'Whoa, there's a massive volley of missiles.'

'Where?' asked Rao.

'Originating from Pyramid. I make fifteen. I see another line of launch plumes… Make that thirty.'

Mukherjee ordered, 'Gunnery, target Pyramid and fire.'

William Slim's two forward laser batteries alternated fire on the surface target, kicking up rocks and dust as each laser impacted. While gunnery worked over the target, Rao brought up satellite imagery of the target. Pictures clearly showed silos in the Ceres rock, but they had no way of determining just how deep they were. If the silos where built like ICBM silos back on Earth, they would be able to take quite a punch, even from *William Slim*.

Mukherjee asked hopefully, 'Shall I give Pyramid a volley of missiles?'

'No,' said Rao, 'you'll never get them through all those layers of defenses. For now, just the lasers.'

'3 gees,' Helm reported.

'Captain at this rate we won't have much more time over the target.'

'I understand.'

Maruvada reported, 'Captain we are drawing Jai defenses away from the equator.'

'I see.'

'And we still haven't seen any of their carrier ships.'

'Another volley from Pyramid.'

Patel said, 'A few missiles are going to get through…'

William Slim rumbled again with the force of a missile explosion, and then another.

'Countermeasures, why are those missiles getting though?'

'We are taking fire from everywhere.'

'Prioritize those missile silos, Lieutenant Commander Mukherjee.'

'At the expense of other targets?'

'Yes. Do it.'

'Ok, Captain.'

Mukherjee issued orders to his technicians. 'Forward battery, target those perimeter missile silos.'

'Yes, Lieutenant.'

'Caster, I want a half dozen A-bomb spreads for each.'

'Copy.'

'Variable detonation points. Your target is not the surface but enemy countermeasures.'

'Understood.'

'You will create a gap in the Jai defense for the railguns.'

The caster spat out a half dozen A-bomb volleys, creating a series of blue nuclear fireballs above Pyramid. Railgun volleys came in behind them. Jai point defenses took out the first few rounds, but Mukherjee's railgunners kept firing behind the line of A-bombs until one volley got through. The super charged steel spheres slammed into Ceres, kicking up great geysers of rocky debris.

'Captain,' said Maruvada, 'I am detecting a substantial explosion about Pyramid.'

'Good.'

'There's another.'

Mukherjee slapped his hands together and exclaimed, 'Alright!'

'Keep firing!'

'Right, Captain.'

William Slim shook again.

Helm spoke, 'Captain we are entering the grav-point.'

'Got another silo on Pyramid, massive blast this time.'

William Slim shook.

Rao ordered, 'Helm, break to port.'

'Yes, Captain.'

He contacted Captain Chakravorti aboard *Indira Gandhi*, 'Captain, we are executing the gravity assist.'

'Understood, Captain.'

'Keep closing and land the Gurkhas.'

'We are on task.'

'Excellent, Captain.'

'Three point three gees now, Captain.' Reported Helm. 'Three-five… three-six…three-seven…'

Ceres' gravity seized *William Slim* and projected the great ship forward, adding dramatically to her acceleration, like a ball bouncing off a moving car. As the great ship picked up speed, the Jai engaged.

William Slim shook with the force of a laser blast from Ceres.

'Hulled again,' reported Damage Control. 'Amidships, just below number two railgun.'

'Is the gun operative?'

'Doing a diagnostic now…yes.'

'Four gees…four-one…'

'Helm, give me an estimate…'

'Approaching four point five gees.'

William Slim whipped around Ceres beyond Pyramid's horizon and shot back out away toward Jupiter.

Rao picked up his receiver and raised Captain Chakravorti.

'Captain, I want you to take the assault ship in.'

'Understood.'

'In the meantime *William Slim* will proceed to target.'

'Yes, sir.'

'I transfer tactical command of the task force to you.'

'Yes, sir.'

'Get the Gurkhas down and clear Pyramid.'

'It shall be done, I swear.'

Rao signed off, inwardly he shook his head at Chakravorti's dramatics.

He turned his attention to the damage reports that were coming across the flat-screen.

Two hull breaches, one railgun obliterated, two railguns heavily damaged.

'Alright,' Rao said. 'Damage Control get me repair estimates.'

'We are working on that now, Captain,' replied Damage Control. 'The hull breaches should be controllable.'

'The railguns, Damage Control. Prioritize them.'

'Understood.'

Rao patched into the task force's tactical net and readout and observed the battle. *Jacob* was maneuvering to screen against the two Jai carrier ships and trade fire with the North Pole base. A visual display in his flat-screen's bottom right corner showed a distant firework like display of orange lasers, tiny blue and yellow dots against the black of space exploding conventional and nuclear ordnance. *Indira Gandhi* lead the assault ship toward Pyramid. She alternated laser and railgun blasts against Jai batteries on the surface. Rao listened in as *Indira Gandhi's* weapons officer brought the ship's forward batteries to bear on the surface.

'Target....map reference three dash four-six, inclusive.'

'Identified.'

'Forward batteries fire.'

'Batteries fired.'

'Fire at will.'

'Another missile volley.'

Captain Chakravorti chimed in. 'Weapons, target that missile battery.'

'Affirmative. Railguns. Map reference four...dash three-three.'

Rao brought the map reference up on his view screen. It was a high ridge running across the Ceres' equator. The Jai had dug several deep silos within and most likely reinforced the rock with steel plates.

'Identified.'

'Fire.'

Rao followed the trajectory of the four shots. A jai battery on the surface fired an A-bomb but missed. The explosion obscured the shot. The blast cleared just as the shots impacted on the surface. Great geysers of rock and debris flew into space. For a moment Rao thought they had taken out the battery, but then it launched another missile volley.

'Reducing that battery is going to take some time,' he said.

'Railguns,' Captain Chakravorti said. 'Keep firing on that battery. Missiles behind them.'

Under cover of the sustained orbital barrage Rai's 1st Gurkha battalion landed on Ceres' surface seven kilometers from Pyramid. With the target looming in the background, engineers unloaded prefab equipment and quickly pieced together a small base camp of three buildings housing ammunition, spare parts and a dressing station for the wounded. The Gurkhas readied the base camp in under an hour. With that, Colonel Rai led his battalion against Pyramid.

Having already expressed his utmost confidence in his assault troops, Rai's attack on Pyramid bordered on suicidal. At first the Gurkhas tried to bum rush Pyramid's tunnel entrance in the hopes of overwhelming the defenders. Jai gunners cut the lead platoon to bits and inflicted heavy casualties on the two follow up platoons trying to relieve the first. In under an hour Colonel Rai had used up an infantry company. What was left of the first company he arrayed in a skirmish line in front of his base camp with orders to keep Pyramid's entrance under fire.

Rai next advanced his tank company codenamed Chariot Force. Fourteen Russian made Armata tanks, upgraded with the latest Israeli Trophy System. Jai fire was withering, knocking out several tanks as they approached. Part of one armored platoon closed to within 300 meters. Three tanks brought the tunnel entrance under fire and shattered the blast door, but when the tanks tried to push closer, two were destroyed by Jai lasers. Rai pulled back once again. After the failed armored assault, Rai consolidated his first two infantry companies with what remained of the armored company. They engaged Jai positions at long range, systematically bringing each under fire.

Rao listened in on the Chariot's radio net.

'Yes, I see the battery…two hundred meters…firing.'

'You missed, you missed Chariot-1'

'Firing again…'

'Hit…but the target is intact…'

'Impossible, that was a high explosive round.'

'I see the scorch marks. Battery is turning.'

'Yes I see it…I think it is targeting us…moving my pos…'

'Understood. Chariot-1…I am training my MGs on it now.'

'…This is Chariot-3. I am firing on target…'

'Direct hit, Chariot-3…'

The company commander chimed in, 'Chariot-Black. Does the entrance look clear? Can we force our way inside?'

'Uhhhh…Negative Chariot-Black,' replied Chariot-1. 'I see at least two other laser emplacements at least.'

'Anything else?'

'Yes. I am sure one of our missiles uncovered a rocket battery. But it has not fired yet.'

'Bring that battery under fire, Chariot-1.'

'Affirmative, sir.'

'We will advance again,' ordered Chariot-Black.

'We already tried that,' said Chariot-1. 'I lost half my tanks.'

'I will lead you in. All tanks will fire. Heavy weapons will lay down covering fire.'

'Yes, sir.'

'I will fire directly into the tunnel. C Company will come in behind the tanks. B and A companies, give me an update on your effectives.'

'This is Blue-1,' said A Company commander. 'I have fifty-six effectives.'

'Seventy three,' said B Company.

'Very well. A and B Companies will be ready to enter the tunnel once we have taken it.'

Both commanders acknowledged.

'We shall keep the tunnel under fire and advance on my word.'

The tanks took turns firing, each sending a depleted uranium shell down the tunnel to explode at the far end. Each explosion created a ball of fire which lit up the tunnel, revealing a floor littered with debris; twisted metal and chunks of rock blasted out of the walls.

When Rai was satisfied he said, 'Very well. Follow me.'

The ground before the tunnel came alive with Jai fire.

'Get that one…'

'Watch that laser…'

'We just lost Chariot-5…

'Blue-One is down…'

'Three Platoon just disappeared in that blast…'

'I am approaching the tunnel now,' said Chariot-1. 'Taking fire from above the entrance now. Inside 200 meters.'

'Hold it, Chariot-Black, I see the gun. Targeting. Fire! Fire!'

'It is still hitting me.'

'Firing again.'

'There!' Chariot-Black exclaimed. 'Drive, full throttle.'

'Sir.'

'Red-1, make sure infantry is behind me.'

'This is the XO, Red-1 is…'

'Hello! Hello! Damn it! I want infantry behind me now!'

'We are coming, Colonel.'

'I am approaching the tunnel. One hundred meters….holy…!' there was static. 'That was a big blast…that is it. I am inside their cone of fire. I am at the tunnel! Fire! Fire!'

Rao followed along as the infantry stormed the tunnel. Once the assault troops were inside the Jai had no chance, certainly not with an Armata tank firing at point blank range….

'Captain, you nodded off.'

Rao opened his eyes to see Commander Patel.

'How long?'

'Only a few minutes, sir.'

'What did I miss?'

'The Gurkhas have the entrance. The other assault battalion will begin landing soon.'

Rao yawned. 'Very well. I need rest.'

'Yes, sir.'

'You have the bridge, Commander. Two hours.'

'Yes, sir.'

Rao was tired but when he lay his head down he found sleep didn't come. Instead he was racked with fear that he was on the verge of becoming yet another Indian general officer to lose a battle after he had promised so much…

D-Day Minus 96

Rao nervously watched admiral Ganesan. She took a pair of glasses out of her breast pocket and read the folder Rao had handed her. Her eyes darted down the page, occasionally she stopped to underline something or make a note. She wore the dress blues of the United States Navy. Rows of medals adorned her chest, including a special medallion marking her participation in the Battle of Luna. Rao tried not to be impressed but failed. As he waited, Rao mentally reviewed his resume. *You are every bit the naval officer she is*, he said to himself.

After another uncomfortable minute, Ganesan took off her glasses and looked at Rao.

To Rao's surprise, she spoke in Hindi. 'Captain Rao, your plan for attacking Ceres meets with my complete approval.'

'Thank you, Admiral. I do have a question for you, though.'

'This side effort of yours, a reconnaissance of Jupiter's moons. Why?'

'You do not approve?'

'Oh no, Captain I do, absolutely I do. But why head to Jupiter yourself? Don't you feel you need to control the Ceres mission?'

'As you can see, I have already planned every detail. My subordinate is perfectly capable of carrying out the operation. She has my complete confidence.'

Ganesan nodded.

'Why go to Jupiter in your most powerful ship?'

'I plan to cruise to Jupiter, survey the system and strike Europa. But if there is trouble I want to be sure I can get out of it.'

'You mean if there is a fight, you want to be able to win it.'

'Yes, Admiral. If we get into a fight, I want to be sure we are able to fight our way out.'

William Stroock

INSS William Slim

Things had gone bad on Ceres. After Rai took the tunnel entrance, the Jai fired an earth penetrating missile up into the sky and brought it down upon the Gurkhas. The resulting impact annihilated the force at the entrance and collapsed the tunnel. Most of 1st Gurkha Battalion was gone. Now the task force was bombarding Pyramid in preparation for an attack by 2nd Gurkha Battalion.

The news from Mars was even worse. Ganesan was dead and the fleet scattered around Mars and its moons with several landing battalions trapped on the planet's surface.

'Alright, Captain,' Rao said to Chakravorti, 'given what we know about the drubbing taken by Task Force Mars, do you have any reason to fear the same for Task Force Ceres?'

'We have our own problems, Captain,' Chakravorti said referring to the stalemate on the surface, 'but we have been hammering Pyramid for two days and nothing has happened to us.'

'Any progress on a ground attack plan?'

'Yes. Colonel Rai wants to land his 2nd Battalion on the surface and retake the tunnel entrance and simply clear it out any way he can. He's asking for nukes.'

'Any other options?'

'I do not think so, Captain. Colonel Rai wants to land troops on top of Pyramid, but I think it will be a slaughter. I said no.'

'Use your discretion, Captain.'

Rao signed off and turned his attention to *William Slim*.

For more than a day *William Slim* had been slowing down. Now she was traveling at less than a gee and would soon slow to half a gee in preparation for assuming orbit around Europa. Jupiter loomed ahead. The great autumnal colored gas giant took up the forward view screen. The bridge crew looked on in awe, even Rao. It was hard not to. A milestone of sorts was being reached; the first manned mission to Jupiter. Rao considered making an announcement, but it had been many decades since anyone thought about space that way and most of the crew was too young to appreciate it.

Of course, Jupiter wasn't their actual target, Europa was. The Jai knew it; they had to.

'Sensors, anything?' Rao asked.

'No new contacts, no movement.'

Rao brought a sensor read out of Europa on his flat-screen. The Jai had placed a small orbital station above Europa's equator and a base on the pole itself. There were a few small stations along the equator, probably missile batteries.

The defenses looked challenging and for a moment, Rao wondered if they shouldn't just gather data and slingshot around Jupiter.

We need a success, he thought. Besides, taking the orbital station could yield prisoners. Jai prisoners were rare and of course, highly valued.

Rao zoomed in on the orbital station above Europa. It wasn't that big, just over a third of a mile long. To Rao's eye it looked like a modified carrier ship, built no doubt with materials mined from the asteroid belt. *Hmmmmm* he thought. *It could be done. It could provide an intelligence windfall.*

He flipped a switch activating the ships intercom. 'Captain Thapa to the bridge.'

Rao had seen Thapa's Gurkhas in rehearsals. They were trained for boarding and EVA actions, and were experts at zero G hand to hand combat. Most had studied tai kwon do with the South Korean Army. Rao had a job for them now.

'Captain Thapa reporting, Captain.'

Rao pointed to the flat-screen. 'That orbital station, Captain. Do you think you can take it?'

Thapa leaned into the console and peered at the read out. He stood up straight and said. 'Please, Captain, send it to my console. I will assemble my staff immediately and we will consider this problem.'

'Yes.'

'If you will excuse me.'

'Of course.'

Rao brought up a projection of Jupiter and its moons. They could drop off the Gurkhas, swing around Jupiter and then come back. Or they could simply stop before Europa.

Thapa called from the conference room. Behind him were the Gurkha officers and. 'Captain,' he said, 'we have been discussing the matter and we can do it.'

'Very good.'

'Would you come down to the briefing room?'

'On the way,' replied Rao. Rao stood. 'Commander Patel, you have the bridge.'

'Sir.'

Rao made his way down to the ship's small briefing room. All stood when he entered. 'Attention on deck.'

'Thank you,' said Rao. 'Very well, Captain Thapa what have you planned?'

The Captain walked over to the large flat-screen on the far wall.

'What we would like to do Captain Rao, is launch both Shuttle-1 and Shuttle-2, each with a full boarding compliment. Shuttle-1 will make for the main docking terminal here in the center of the station.'

Rao nodded.

'But this is just a feint. Shuttle-1 will engage whatever Jai defenses it encounters, in the meantime Shuttle-2 coming up behind Shuttle-1 will deploy parallel to the main dock, but on the other side of the station.'

'Is a docking bay there?'

'No, Captain. Shuttle-2 will hull the station. From there the 2nd Platoon will go EVA and board the station, fight its way to the dock, and secure it from the inside.'

'Why not simply storm the dock?'

'We believe a direct assault on the dock would be too obvious.'

'Your plan has my approval.'

'Then we shall prepare right away.'

Rao returned to the bridge and ordered helm to bring *William Slim* to a stop.

'We shall stay close to that orbital station. 20,000 kilometers.'

'Yes, sir.'

Commander Patel said, 'Captain, if I may?'

'Please.'

'Could we not leave the shuttles here, go around Jupiter and pick them up on the way back?'

'I had considered that commander, but no. I will not leave the assault troops on their own.'

Patel looked disappointed but said nothing.

'I am much more interested in Europa.'

'Yes, Captain.'

'Weapons.'

'Sir.'

'Begin firing solutions for targets on Europa.'

'Yes, Captain.'

Rao was following Mukherjee's firing plot when Lt. Peri said, 'Colonel Rai is getting ready to attack Pyramid again. Would you like to listen in?'

'Yes, on my flat-screen only please. The bridge will concentrate on the task at hand.'

Rao followed along closely. The 2nd Gurkha Battalion landed several kilometers away from Pyramid and approached the tunnel in two lines. Before the infantry, two tanks advanced each alternating fire into the tunnel, sending a stream of high explosive shells which flashed inside the tunnel upon impact.

'We are approaching the entrance cone of fire.'

'Still no activity.'

'Wait…there, enemy is firing.'

For another minute as the battalion pushed on, Rao heard a lot of cross-talk.

'Firing light. Ineffective.'

Rai must have destroyed most of their defenses, thought Rao.

'Advance elements inside the cone of fire.'

'Copy.'

'We are deploying lasers now. If the Jai fire another earth penetrator missile, we can intercept it.'

Rao nodded. *Good,* he thought.

The lead tanks stopped firing. Engineers cautiously approached the tunnel and surveyed. Rao viewed the image then beamed back. The tunnel was filled with wreckage, steel girders, concrete slabs, but with some work it looked passable.

'We will keep Pyramid under fire.'

'Yes, sir.'

'Engineers I want…'

Rao heard shouting, and the static. A few seconds later the signal returned but all Rao could make out was shouting and cross-talk. He heard the word 'gone' and then 'vapor cloud' and finally, 'Mine! They detonated a mine!'

'Damn it,' said Rao.

Almost immediately it was clear; the 2nd Gurkha Battalion had suffered debilitating casualties. One tank remained, and at least half the infantry were gone. While he listened, Rao examined the live feed of the entrance. The tunnel was now completely collapsed and the ground in front was churned over and heavily cratered, and no doubt incapable of supporting heavy equipment.

'It looks as if we will have to find some other way into Pyramid,' said Rao.

Peri interrupted, 'Sir, Captain Thapa says his force is ready to disembark.'

'Give him clearance.'

'Yes, sir.'

Rao sat back in his chair and watched the shuttles approach the orbital station. He didn't know what to expect.

Patel said, 'Do not worry, Captain. We see no obvious weapons blisters.'

'I know and that does not make sense.'

Lieutenant Commander Mukherjee said, 'They probably counted on defending the station with ships, or from Europa.'

'I agree, Captain,' said Patel. 'They never thought we would penetrate this far out into the system, especially with a battle raging on Mars as well.'

'Hmmmm,' said Rao.

'The Americans never thought the Japanese could strike Pearl Harbor.'

Maruvada said, 'Captain Chakavorti is calling.'

'Send her through to my flat-screen.'

Chakravorti's face appeared. 'Hello Captain,' said Rao. 'Please report.'

'As I am sure you know, Captain, the second assault on Pyramid has failed. We are regrouping and working on a new plan.'

'Is the tunnel even passable?'

'Not at this point, sir,' replied Chakravorti, 'but we would like to make another effort. This time by landing troops on top of Pyramid.'

'I thought you had dismissed that idea.'

'It is the only option left.'

'Go ahead and do it.'

'Yes, sir. We shall begin right away.'

'Alright and...'

'Excuse me, Captain,' said Commander Patel. 'The shuttles are making their approach.'

'I must go, now, Captain Chakravorti. Keep me informed.'

'Sir.'

Rao turned his attention back to Thapa and his boarding party. Shuttle-1 approached the main dock slowly and dramatically until it was a mere kilometer away. The operations officer aboard opened the EVA doors, releasing a dozen Gurkhas clad in body armor and propulsion packs. They were arrayed in a 'T' formation with the spine pointed toward the dock, and the cross prepared to lay down covering fire. Meanwhile Shuttle-2 accelerated past Shuttle-1 toward the other side of the station.

As Shuttle-2 passed directly over the station there was a flash and the radio net was filled with chatter.

'What was that?'

'We are hit?!'

'Damage?'

'Hit again!'

'Damage report?'

'I see it! Firing. Missile away!'

'Damage report, God damn it!'

On his screen Rao saw a flash and small explosion and then another on the station. The Gurkha's net filled with chatter and cross-talk as well.

'Someone is firing...'

'Return fire I...'

'They hit the sergeant!'

'Firing! Firing!'

Rao switched to a live stream from Shuttle-1's exterior fore camera and could see little winks of light as the EVA Gurkhas fired on the station.

Rao asked, 'Why are they firing lasers? Maybe the station really does lack heavy defenses.'

Mukherjee and Patel nodded.

Behind the Gurkhas, Shuttle-2 fired its laser several times, burning a breach in the station's hull. She followed this up with a missile and then more laser fire. This was followed by a flash and a brief burst of fire.

'That did it. Hull breached. Repeat hull breached. We are going in.'

'Copy.'

The EVA Gurkhas jetted toward the breach in column, and one after the other entered the orbital station.

'It appears as if we are in some sort of storage area.'

'Yes, I see crates, Jai markings.'

'Get the portal open.'

'We are, wait...' after a moment. 'Opened.'

'Throw a grenade through.'

Rao heard static as the grenade burst. Two Gurkhas pointed their rifles through the door, each aimed at opposite ends of the corridor and let loose a burst.

'Clear!'

'Clear!'

The rest of the Gurkhas filed into the corridor. They closed the door behind them to keep the corridor from being de-pressurized.

'We have atmosphere and gravity. And lights.'

'Copy. Helmets up.'

'Smells like Jai alright.'

'What do Jai smell like?'

'You know, kind of like sweat and...'

'Shut up.'

'Yes, sir.'

'Section A will secure this corridor. Section B will follow me to the next one. Section C will wait until we have cleared a path to the space dock.'

'Copy, heading now and I...'

'There's one!'

Rao heard the sound of rifle fire.

'And another!'

More rifle fire.

'Look out!'

There was an explosion and more fire.
'Keep covering…grenade! Grenade!'
'Got it.'
A grenade exploded.
'Go! Go! Go!'
'I got him!'
A quick burst of rifle fire.
'Where is Naryan!'
'I see his arm over….'
'Duck!'
Several bursts of rifle fire.
'I see the dock!'
'Grenade that corridor!'
'Everyone! Grenades!'
Rao heard a whole series of blasts followed by several rifle bursts.
'Anything?'
'I see Jai, all dead.'
'Section B take the airlock.'
'Affirmative.'

Minutes later the EVA leader radioed, 'Shuttle-1, Shuttle-1 we have secured the airlock.'

'Excellent Shuttle-2. We shall proceed to dock.'
'Any more Jai?'
'Not yet.'

On *William Slim's* bridge, Commander Patel said, 'It is not like them to leave stay behind forces.'

'Oh? The battle on Ceres would say differently,' Mukherjee replied.

'Yes but they are mounting an active, full-on defense. On the orbital station so far all the Gurkhas have found are a few hold outs.'

Mukherjee said, 'They are not suicidal in that way, Captain. Not in my experience.'

'No, they cannot afford to lose Jai. There are not enough of them here in our system.'

'Not enough to hold the station.'

'So why did the Jai leave them there if they did not intend to fight for the station?'

'I don't know, I wonder....'

Peri interrupted. 'Excuse me, Captain Chakravorti is beginning her assault.'

'Thank you, Lieutenant.'

Rao brought Task Force Ceres' tactical display onto his own flat-screen and tuned into its radio net. While *JFR Jacob* hammered Pyramid assault boats, Alpha, Beta and Gamma made their way down to the surface.

'No return fire?'

'Nothing yet I...oh there it is.'

'I see it, Jai laser upper left quadrant.'

'Are you hit?'

'It is nothing I can...there's another one.'

'*Jacob* redirect fire.'

'Yes, I have already fired a railgun volley.'

'Yes I see it.'

'Watching the impact area....boom...'

'Do we really need sound effects?'

'Yes, commander you are...'

'Fire again.'

'Approaching surface, cease fire, *Jacob*.'

'Copy. All batteries ceasefire. Ceasefire.'

'Coming up.'

'I see.'

'Alpha Boat down. Gurkhas out! Gurkhas out!'

Blue markers on the readout showed a quickly expanding circle of blue dots. Beta Boat came down a minute later with Gamma Boat coming down behind.

'What is that?'

'I do not see it, what?'

'That metal tube?'

'Laser?'

'It is too small…'

'Missile launch!'

'Fire! Fire on that position.'

'Second missile!'

'Watch it Gamma Boat!'

'Too late!'

'She's hit! She's coming in too hard!'

'Watch out!'

Gamma boat slammed into Pyramid and skid across the landing area and off the plateau.

'They took out Gamma!'

'Get that missile launcher and look for more.'

'I have two men on it now. Already destroyed.'

'Captain, I think we can get in through here.'

'Delta Boat down.'

'Get the heavy equipment unloaded. We'll bore our way in.'

Peri said, 'Shuttle-2 is docked, Captain.'

Rao raised Captain Thapa. 'May I have your report, please, Captain?'

'Certainly. We control the center of the station. No sign of any more Jai, but we shall have to check compartment by compartment.'

'Do you need more men, Captain?'

'I have twenty-three on board, Captain. That should be enough.'

'Very well.'

'And I hardly think some armed naval personnel will be able to fight alongside my Gurkhas.'

'Of course, Captain.' Now annoyed Rao said, 'Keep me updated. Out.'

Lt. Maruvada spoke. 'Captain?'

'Yes, lieutenant.'

'I have been examining our sensor records.'

'What for?'

'I was curious about the Jai orbital station. I thought they may have evacuated as we approached.'

'Would we not have seen that?'

'Yes, Captain. But their shuttles have a small sensor signature, and in all the commotion…'

'Ah I see. Have you found anything?'

'Yes, Captain. After we passed the midway point between Mars and Ceres I have found one shuttle signature. It departed the station about ten hours before we went into orbit.'

'Where did it go?'

'We lost the signal, but judging by its trajectory the shuttle went to the far side of Jupiter.'

'Hmmm…' Rao thought. 'I would think the shuttle would have made for Ganymede. We know the Jai have a base there.'

Peri interrupted, 'Captain, Captain Thapa calling.'

'Put him through to my flat-screen.'

Rao's flat-screen showed Captain Thapa. 'Captain, the station is clear.'

'Very good.'

'We are loading Shuttle-1 with captured equipment now.'

'Good.'

Behind Thapa, the sergeant said, 'Captain, we are ready.'

'I must go.'

After a few more minutes, Chakravorti called with an update.

'The Gurkhas have fought their way inside Pyramid.'

'How would you describe enemy resistance?'

'The Jai are contesting every corridor.'

'Do the Gurkhas have enough men to take Pyramid?'

'I do not know.'

'Very well. Patch me into Colonel Rai.'

Rai came on screen.

'Report, please.'

'Yes, Captain. We entered through an elevator shaft that seems to be the only way to the top of Pyramid. From there we had a fifty-meter drop to the top level of the base. We have cleared the first few levels of this facility. The Jai are fighting and retreating. They do not die in place but they make sure we have to pay to advance.'

'Understood,' said Rao. 'Casualties?'

'I have seven dead and nineteen wounded.'

'What about the Jai?'

'I do not have a count, but we have only found a few bodies.' Someone behind the leader tapped his shoulder and spoke. 'Excuse me, Captain. I am needed elsewhere.'

Rao listened in on the assault force's radio feed. For several minutes they were held up at a stairway which led down to the next level. The Gurkhas cleared the way with a flurry of grenades.

'Any bodies?'

'None that I see.'

'Again?'

'The Jai seem to know when we are attacking.'

'Wait a minute. They must have cameras here right?'

'Oh, God. Why did we not, think of that?'

'Well, start looking for them!'

For several minutes the Gurkhas tore the level apart, dismantling computers and smashing electronics with rifle butts. After several minutes they were satisfied that all potential cameras had been neutralized and began their assault on the third floor. Rao heard rifle bursts, grenades and almost unintelligible cross talk, but he was able to follow the direction and tone of the battle.

Ensign Peri said, 'Captain Thapa wants to know what you want to do with the station.'

'Put him on.'

'Captain Thapa here. Captain, your instructions?'

'What have you loaded?'

'The two prisoners obviously.'

'Can you tell me anything about them?'

'Neither is an officer. Other than that they are not talking, they seem quite stunned at the moment.'

'What else have you loaded?'

'All the computers we could dismantle.'

'Anything else?'

'The engineers are looking now, but I think we are done here.'

'Very well, get ready then.'

'Sir.'

Once the shuttles were loaded and had launched, *William Slim* destroyed the station with a volley from the A-Bomb caster. Lt. Mukherjee then dispatched the two facilities on Europa's surface with the railguns.

'Why not the caster?' Mukherjee asked.

'There is life down there, Captain. I'd like not to contaminate it.'

Rao nodded.

'Looks like they will have to find a new source of food, Captain.'

Patel said, 'Captain, may I make a suggestion?'

'Go ahead.'

'Why not proceed to Ganymede and engage the Jai base there?'

Rao looked skeptical.

'I have been working on the flight trajectory calculations, Captain and I've updated our intelligence on the Ganymede.'

'Send it to my flat-screen.'

Rao pressed a button bringing up a current map of Jupiter and her moons. 'With Ganymede on the far side of Jupiter…Hmmmm…'

Patel said, 'This would be an excellent opportunity to investigate. We could follow those ships that departed the orbital station.'

Rao said, 'Ensign Peri, get me Chakrovorty. I want a status update there before we do anything.'

'Yes, sir.'

Chakravorti's image came on Rao's flat-screen.

'Report, please.'

'Fighting is still quite heavy, Captain, but the Gurkhas have cleared another floor and are preparing to attack the next.'

'What kind of facilities have they encountered within?'

'Not anything important. Barracks, commissary, facilities like that.'

'Very well, keep pushing.'

'Yes, Captain.'

Rao signed off.

'Helm, plot course for Ganymede.'

'Already, have, Captain. We can fly out from here and intercept as she comes over from Jupiter's far side.'

'Very well.'

'Yes, Captain.'

'We will attack Ganymede and then slingshot around Jupiter. Get started on the calculations.'

As *William Slim* began the trek over to Ganymede, Maruvada pointed the ship's various sensor arrays at the moon, trying to augment what they already knew with last minute info. Details appeared on Rao's screen giving known stats. Rao read absentmindedly.

'One orbital station…looks like it's the same model as the station we just destroyed above Europa…a few small bases on the surface. What do you suppose these are here?' Rao pointed to several vehicles on the surface.

The bridge officers took a look at the real time images of Gannymede's surface.

'Let's see, sir. Vehicles…'

Ensign Peri said, 'That looks like a slag pile there.'

'Yes,' said Rao.

'We know Ganymede is high in iron ore content. They must be mining it.'

'Makes sense.'

'And that base there is a refinery.'

'Lt. Mukherjee, plan firing solutions.'

Rao was watching as Mukherji posted planned strike packages on his flat screen when Ensign Peri said, 'Captain Chakravorti for you, sir.'

Chakravorti came on screen.

'Resistance has stiffened considerably, Captain.'

'Where.'

'4th Level. The Gurkhas just attempted an assault and were bloodily repulsed.'

'It looks as if they finally threatened something important to the Jai.'

'It would seem so.'

Chakravorti said nothing for a few moments.

'Is there something else, Captain?'

'With all the casualties, Captain…'

'Yes?'

'I mean, it's just…how much can the Gurkhas take?'

'As many casualties as are needed.'

'But, Captain…'

Rao cut her off. 'The Gurkhas will press forward and take Pyramid. Do you think…?'

Behind Chakravorti a bridge officer interjected, 'Captain. I have lost contact with the Gurkhas.'

'Oh my God,' said someone else.

Chakravorti said, 'Excuse me, Captain.' He nodded.

Rao tapped into Task Force Ceres' net

'…happening. I do know…'

'No contact from the Gurkhas.'

'Look at that!'

'You don't think the Jai…'

'Yes, look at the way the plateau has collapsed.'

'They detonated a mine inside Pyramid.'

'Yes. You can see, it's still collapsing in on itself.'

Patel said, 'Captain, there really is not much more we can do on Ceres.'

Rao thought, 'Not right now.'

Rao stood.

'Time till Ganymede?'

Maruvada replied, 'One hour and thirty-seven minutes, Captain.'

Rao nodded. 'Very well. Commander Patel, you have the bridge.'

'Yes, sir.'

Rao visited with the Gurkhas, congratulated them and went over the attack. After that he got a bite to eat and then cat-napped in his quarters.

The destruction of the station above Ganymede and the facilities on the surface was anticlimactic. The Jai had never bothered to fortify Ganymede and Mukherjee was able to dispatch their bases with railgun and A-bomb barrages.

When they were finished Rao ordered Helm to make for the Jupiter gravpoint. Once more the gas giant filled the bridge's view screen.

'Hell of a view of Jupiter,' Patel said.

'Another milestone,' said Rao.

Lt. Maruvada sat engrossed in her screen as data from the sensor array scrolled across. Rao couldn't blame her for that.

Commander Patel said, 'Captain, what is that reading we are seeing on the radar?'

'Where?' Rao punched up the sensor reading on his flat screen.

'About eight million kilometers from here approaching Jupiter's south pole.'

'OK, I follow you.'

'Zooming in.'

Patel said, 'Captain…'

'Hold on.'

'Captain. That contact is big.'

Maruvada said, 'Captain, the computer says it's a Jai pole ship.'

'What?'

Rao looked at his flat-screen. 'This has to be some mistake.'

'I do not think so, Captain,' said Patel.

'Get a visual, zoom in close.'

'Sir.'

'I do not think this is a mistake, Captain,' said Patel.

Rao stared at the screen, clearly showing a Jai pole ship. The computer said it was exactly like the one destroyed over Antarctica and on the Moon.

'Is it running away from us?' ask Rao.

Maruvada said, 'Yes, Captain. On a course that will take it to Jupiter's South Pole.'

'Why are they running?'

Patel offered, 'Probably trying to conceal their existence to us.'

'This makes sense.'

'They failed,' said Mukherjee.

Patel said, 'Captain, if that thing is like the other two pole ships…'

'Then they have 64 carrier ships,' finished Rao.

Maruvada asked, 'Did they build it here?'

Patel said. 'I doubt it. It must have come from their home system.'

'Approaching the grav-point, Captain.'

'Captain,' began Patel, 'Let's engage that pole ship.'

Rao looked askance at Patel.

'Seriously, Captain.'

'Are you daft? One cruiser against a pole-ship, not to mention dozens of carrier ships.'

'They will never be able to launch them all. If we pursue now we can overwhelm them before they are ready.'

'No.'

'What if we just made a fly by, to assess their defenses?'

'No.'

'Captain just give me a few minutes to come up with…'

'Enough!'

The bridge was awkwardly silent for a few moments.

'Sir.'

'Lt. Maruvada, make sure you gather all the data on that new contact that you can.'

'Yes, sir.'

'We are entering the grav-point.'

'Execute gravity assist….'

William Slim swung around to the other side of Jupiter. She was doing more than 6 gees giving her a travel time of just over one day back to Ceres.

When they were clear of the system Rao said. 'Very well.' He activated the intercom. 'This is the captain. We have just over a day back to Ceres. Secure from battle stations. Crew will go to 50-50 status.'

Rao switched off.

'Commander Patel, you have the bridge.'

'Yes, sir.'

For about half an hour Rao jotted down notes and wrote out his thoughts on the operations around Jupiter. When he was finished, Rao took off his shoes and lay on his bunk, tired and a little down. When he awoke Rao felt only a foreboding. After washing up he went back to the bridge and relieved Patel. Only a few stations were crewed and not by regular personnel.

'I thought the bridge crew needed rest,' said Patel.

Rao nodded. 'Oh, Commander. I jotted down some notes and left them on my desk. Pick them up, would you? I'd like you to write the report on our foray to Jupiter.'

'Yes, sir.'

Patel left the bridge in a bit of a huff.

'Carry on,' Rao said to the half dozen young officers present.

These were the understudies. A few paged through technical manuals. Others read books. Mukherjee was doing sketches of the Jupiter battle. Out of curiosity Rao walked over and stood over the man's shoulder. He drew a sketch of the Jai pole ship on its way to Jupiter's south pole. In the background was a great, ghostly Shiva getting ready to strike.

'Why so macabre?"

'Sorry, Captain.'

'Not at all, carry on.'

'Yes sir...' he looked at his image of Shiva. 'It's just that...'

'Yes?'

'Well, after seeing that massive ship it seems like there's no point to our mission.'

'I don't understand.'

'We have to fight another one of those things, sir. Maybe not now, but sooner or later.'

'Hmm...,' said Rao. 'The rest of you feel this way?' he asked.

The crew there remained silent.

'Come on,' Rao demanded.

The sensor technician said, 'I might not have stated it in that manner, but yes, sir.'

Added the helmsman. 'To put it in military terms, morale is low.'

'You all agree?'

Nods.

'And the rest of the crew as well?'

'Absolutely.'

He looked about at the young faces. 'Thank you.' He turned to Lt. Commander Mukherjee. 'You have the bridge.'

Rao returned to his quarters and summoned Commander Patel. *I need to get this crew's attention*, he thought. *I did not know I could be this Machiavellian. It is almost a shame.*

'How is the report coming along?'

'I am almost through with the write up, sir...'

'Excellent. I'll put you to work on the general report as well.'

'Yes...sir'

'Something wrong, Commander?'

Patel remained quiet.

'Speak freely.'

'I did not take this assignment to write your reports.'

Rao looked his XO over before saying, 'You have been grumbling for this entire mission.'

'Sir, I...'

'You have and I am tired of it.'

'Yes, sir.'

'Until such time as I feel you are ready, you are relieved as executive officer of *William Slim*. Immediately.'

'Sir, I...'

'Say nothing. Dismissed.'

'Sir.'

Rao picked up his intercom. 'Lt. Commander Mukherjee to the Captain's cabin.'

When Mukherjee arrived Rao said, 'Effective immediately, you are *William Slim's* executive officer.'

'Yes...yes, sir,' said Mukherjee. 'May I ask?...'

'No,' said Rao. 'I wanted to inform you before I made the announcement.'

'Yes, sir.'

'Who do you recommend to take your place as weapons officer?'

'Ensign Bagchee.'

'The rail-gunner?'

'Yes, she has my complete confidence.'

'Very well, it is done,' said Rao. 'Proceed to the bridge immediately.'

'Yes, sir.'

Rao switched on the intercom. 'This is the captain. Effective immediately, Lt. Commander Mukherjee is the executive officer of this ship. That is all.'

Rao lay back down and got a couple more hours of sleep. When he awoke he finally felt rested and more himself. After grabbing a quick meal down at the officer's galley, he walked the ship, stopping here and there to speak with the crew. He was met by men and women's long faces and heard more than one pessimistic remark. He returned to the bridge. The crew there all looked away when he entered. Rao laughed to himself, they were probably all afraid he'd relieve them next.

'Report, Lt. Commander Mukherjee.'

'We are eleven hours from Ceres.'

'What news from the rest of the task force?'

'Captain Chakravorti forwarded a report an hour ago. It is on your flat-screen for inspection.'

'And?'

'No new developments there, Captain. The fleet is keeping Pyramid under observation and bombarding suspected weapons points.'

'And Mars?'

'No good news, Captain.'

Rao sat in the Captain's chair and gave the latest dispatches from Task Force Mars a look over. 'I see. At least they have troops on the surface now.'

'Yes, sir.'

'Looks as if we are all on hold, I suppose,' Rao said, more to himself. 'Where is Commander Patel?'

'In her quarters I believe, sir.'

He said bluntly, 'That is fine.'

Rao picked up the intercom. 'This is the Captain,' he began. 'I've spoken with most of you and I do not like what I have seen and heard. Let me be clear. This ship has just made history. We traveled to Jupiter, smashed the Jai on Europa and then did the same on Ganymede. This ship has done a great service not only for India but to all humanity. Remember that. We have written our names in the annals of naval history. I am proud. Now, I know you are all wondering about that Jai ship we spotted. I won't lie, it's a pole ship, just like the ones that did so much damage to Earth.' He paused for a moment. 'So what?' he said. 'You heard me, so what? Twenty years ago the Americans destroyed one such ship over Antarctica. They did with F-18 fighters and Stealth and B-1 Bombers. Did they have space ships? No. Did they have lasers, railguns, Shiva class missiles? No. No they did not. What do those Jai think they are going to do with an old ship? Why I feel sorry for them. In a few years, we will go back with our American friends and kick their asses!'

Rao heard a faint cheer. On the bridge, a few crewmen pounded their consoles in affirmation.

'Now, I want everyone to get a good meal and get some rest because....' He looked at the time to transit clock, 'in ten hours and forty-three minutes we're going to take that base on Ceres. Good work, crew. That is all.'

Mukherjee was smiling.

'Get some rest. Lt. Commander. I have the bridge.'

'Yes, sir.'

Rao spent the next several hours making edits and adding details to Commander Patel's report, there was little else to do. When he was finished he turned back to the Bhagavad Gita.

Three hours out of Ceres, Captain Thapa asked to see him in the Gurkhas' wardroom.

The Gurkhas were sitting, and chatting amongst themselves, eating freeze-dried packets of beans and lentils. Empty and half-empty Styrofoam cups of tea were on the table and in armrests. All stood when Rao entered.

'Sit, please,' Rao said.

Thapa said, 'We would like to discuss an idea with you, Captain.'

'Very well.'

On the large flat-screen was a technical schematic of Pyramid. The large hangar was highlighted.

'What is this idea?' Rao asked as he squinted at the schematic.

'Well, Captain, it is very simple,' said Thapa. 'We would like to fly the shuttles right into Pyramid's hangar bay.'

'You would?'

'Yes. I do not see why we cannot take the bays and fight our way through the rest of Pyramid.'

'With seventy Gurkhas.'

Thapa said, 'Fifty-three, actually sir. And we are hoping to be reinforced by what is left of Colonel Rai's force.'

'What makes you think you can even get in?'

'We are hoping *William Slim* can blast the doors.'

'Well...' Rao thought. 'I should think we can.'

'As long as *William Slim* can do that, the pilots can shuttle us into the bay.'

Rao shook his head. 'This seems suicidal to me. We have already hit Pyramid three times.'

'Three times isn't enough. We have to hit it again.'

'No.'

'Captain, the Mars attack is foundering.'

'I know.'

'Do we really want to return to Earth having failed to fulfill our mission?'

Rao thought about that for a moment.

Thapa said, 'Captain, we are Gurkhas. We expect to risk our lives and we expect victory.'

'Assuming we can open a path for you, what makes you think the Jai won't blast your shuttles as they approach the hangar bay?'

Thapa said, 'The shuttles have missile racks and lasers mounted forward. We'll go in behind a hail of fire.'

'And what do you do once inside?'

'We fight.'

'You are going to push deep inside a facility you do not know?'

Thapa offered. 'We have drones. We will send them forward to map the facility.'

Rao thought for a moment. Thapa was right, no one wanted to see another setback. Besides, what was the point of having Gurkhas if you weren't going to let them fight?

'Alright.'

Thapa said, 'We will get to work right way.'

Well, it's something, Rao thought.

As *William Slim* approached Ceres, Rao called Chakravorty and updated her on the plan.

'Any activity within Pyramid?' Rao asked.

'Negative, Captain. They are holed up within.'

'They have not even fired back?'

'Negative, sir.'

'Very well. We are approaching. ETA until the attack…' he looked at the clock, 'Forty-seven minutes. *William Slim* out.'

What are the Jai playing at? Rao wondered.

As *William Slim* moved into attack position Rao issued orders.

Mukherjee asked, 'Captain, what about Commander Patel?'

'You have my complete confidence, Lt. Commander.'

'Yes, Captain. But I just thought she would like to participate.'

'That will be all, Lt. Commander Mukherjee.'

Let her rot in her quarters, Rao thought.

There was nothing else to do until the attack began, Rao sat quietly in the captain's chair. He shook his head as he contemplated the Gurkhas impossible bravery. *Three assaults on Pyramid and they want to go back… remarkable.*

Peri said, 'Captain, the attack force is departing.'

'Thank you, Lieutenant.'

Rao listened in.

'Shuttle-1 clear.'

'Shuttle-2 clear.'

'ETA to target in eleven minutes.'

'Ensign Bagchee.'

'Sir.'

'You may execute your firing solution.'

'Yes, sir.' Bagchee turned to her bevy of weapons technicians, 'Caster, three fingers, variable spreads.

'Yes, sir.'

'Railguns, when those A-Bomb fingers are clear, fire on the ship bay. Alternate volleys.

'Yes, sir.'

Rao watched a live feed of Pyramid and followed along as a series of blue fireballs exploded in a line toward the bay doors.

'No countermeasures,' Mukherjee noted.

'First railgun volley approaching.'

Rao saw an explosion on the bay doors, then another and another.

'Railguns, keep up the rate of fire.'

'Yes, Lieutenant.'

Peri said, 'Sir, look there it goes.'

Rao looked and saw a great explosion emanating from Pyramid. Even as fire engulfed the bay, the railgun fire continued, adding to the conflagration.

'Very good, Ensign Bagchee, cease fire.'

'Railguns, cease fire.'

'Sir.'

Mukherjee zoomed the forward mounted camera in on the target. 'Let's see what we have here…'

'I see it,' said Rao. 'The bay doors are gone.'

The railguns had sheared off one of the doors, and opened a massive gash in the other and knocked it off the hinge. It hung suspended in space, sticking out to port.

Rao called the shuttles. 'Captain Thapa do you see?'

'Copy, that *William Slim*, we see it. Will accelerate now.'

'Good luck.'

'We shall work over Pyramid to cover your approach.'

'Copy.'

'Ensign Bagchee…'

'Already working out firing solutions, Captain.'

Aboard Shuttle-1 Captain Thapa sat in the shotgun seat on the flight deck. Through the cockpit, he could already see the target and the left side door hanging off its hinge. He tried to peer inside the bay itself, but couldn't make anything out at that distance.

'Two minutes,' said the pilot.

There was a flash of light above the entrance.

'Laser,' said the co-pilot.

'Engage it.'

'Roger.'

The copilot pressed a button activating a small joystick and bringing a crosshairs up on the canopy. As the Jai laser fired again, he lined up the target and fired the shuttle's own forward mounted laser.

'I think I got it.'

There was another flash and this time Shuttle-1 shook, rattling Thapa in his seat.

'You missed.'

'Firing again.'

This time there was a small explosion on the target.

'Got it.'

There was another flash.

'Commander....' The pilot said, annoyed that another laser was firing.

'I'm engaging now.'

The pilot said, 'Missile launch.'

'Uh oh...deploying countermeasures.'

'I think...'

The shuttle shook and slammed Thapa against his harness. He winced in pain as the straps dug into his shoulders.

'We're hit!'

'Missile's away.'

'Damage!'

'We have lost the port wing....engines are out!'

'ETA, 34 seconds.'

'Can we make it?'

'I don't...target destroyed!'

Thapa saw the bay looming large almost filling the entire canopy. There was a flash and a banging sound and suddenly the flight deck was filling with smoke.

'Can you see?'

'We are…entering the bay. In the bay!'

Thapa picked his helmet up from between his feet and secured it on his EVA suit collar.

'Hold on!'

'Brace for…'

Shuttle-1 slammed into the deck of the launch bay, bounced up, and then slammed down again. Thapa saw a whirling tapestry as the shuttle spun on the deck and then slammed into a Jai workshop.

Thapa unhooked his harness and walked back to the flight bay. He felt the curious, heavier pull of Jai gravity. The Gurkhas were un-strapping themselves and checking equipment and loading rifles. When he was satisfied that the platoon was ready, Thapa looked over at the shuttle load master and nodded. He opened the cabin door to the ship bay.

'Follow me!'

Aboard *William Slim*, Rao listened as the Gurkhas stormed the bay, advancing by squads through wrecked workshops, cranes and computer terminals.

'It looks like there is no one in here.'

'They must have evacuated when they saw our assault developing.'

'I think so.'

'Bay secured.'

'That just leaves the exit door.'

'Missile team! Missile Team! Blast that door open.'

'Sir!'

'A Section… stand ready! B Section to cover!'

'Ready.'

'Fire!'

A burst of static.

'It's down!'

'A Section get your machine guns forward.'

Two men ran forward to the blasted entrance door and set up an MG. They fired one second bursts down the corridor.

'Clear.'

'What do you see?'

'Just a long corridor. Ranging it, fifty-four meters.'

'Send a drone down.'

'Copy.'

One of the Gurkhas opened a case and took out a small survey drone. He walked it over to the entryway, flipped a switch and tossed it down the corridor. The drone flew inside and then disappeared around the corner. Back in the bay, another technician collected data gathered by the drone, quickly creating a map of the interior. It flew unmolested for nearly two minutes before the drone tech lost contact.

'We must have found the Jai, said the tech.'

Thapa contemplated the partial map. Before them was a rectangular shaped facility divided into eighths. Video footage showed what looked like quarters and commissary facilities.

'These must be for ship crews,' said Singh 'Beyond that must be the long underground facility we know lies beneath Pyramid. Once we clear it out, we shall go into the bunker.'

Aboard *William Slim*, Rao was pleased. *And if I bring back Zetroc Nanreh…*

'A Section,' Thapa ordered. 'You will clear this front area. B Section will prepare to assault the tunnel.

Mukherjee said, 'Captain, what if the Jai detonate another bomb?'

'I had considered that, Lt. Commander. But I believe that they would have done so already if that was their plan.'

Mukherjee nodded.

'And besides, we have sacrificed too much to turn back now.'

Thapa said, 'Captain, we are ready to go in.'

'Very well. Go ahead. I will be listening,' said Rao.

Ensign Peri said, 'We have audio only, Captain.'

'It will have to do.'

At first they tried a missile, but the blast doors absorbed most of the impact.

'Whatever is behind there is important enough to protect with a steel door that can take a direct hit from a missile.'

'Try explosives.'

'Two charges?'

'Do not be timid. Put a kilo on that door.'

The sapper protested. 'But, sir that will demolish this room.'

'So be it.'

'Yes, sir.'

The sapper attached several charges to the door and said. 'Sir, everybody needs to clear on out back to the bay before I set this off.'

'You heard him!' Thapa shouted. 'Everyone out!'

The sapper was the last into the bay.

'When you are ready,' said Thapa.

'Brace yourself.'

The sapper closed his eyes and triggered the explosives. They heard the blast, then felt it reverberate through to the bay.

'That ought to do it,' said the sapper.

No one else got the reference.

Thapa ordered, 'B Section, forward.'

'We shall send a drone through first.'

Thapa nodded.

The drone entered the tunnel, flew toward the far end and returned without incident.

The techs knelt by their computer, analyzing the data and then shared it with Thapa.

'It seems as if it's a single large room. Look at its footage, Captain; a lot of equipment.'

'Yes,' Singh said. 'Tables, computers.'

'This room is well illuminated.'

'Like a lab.'

'That is because this is a lab.'

'What the hell is all this?'

'Quiet.'

'No, look, Captain. Those big beakers.'
Rao heard someone tapping glass.
'Whatever is inside them is not moving.'
'They look like…oh God…'
'What is wrong?'
'That is a human baby…'
'No it isn't, it has the head of a Jai.'
'Well, which is it?'
'I'm going to be sick.'
'There must be half a dozen of these things in here.'
'They are being preserved. They are dead.'
'What is this over here?'
'They have this body in a sterile operating theatre.'
'It is human.'
'Yes, a fetus.'
'How old?'
'Perhaps six months.'
'That is a Jai head.'
'Where is Vikrum?'
'He is over there, vomiting.'
'What about…?'
'What?'
'These are alive, in these incubators.'
'No way!'
'Yes, look.'
'Alright, I see. I do not understand what we are looking at.'
'That is a human body with a Jai head, look.'
'How?'
'I do not know. But there are two incubating fetuses in here and they are alive. There's the umbilical, and they are moving, see?'
'What are they doing?'
'Who?'
'The Jai? What are they trying to do?'

'Never mind about that. What do *we* do now?'

'Captain, look over here.'

'What is it?'

'This looks like some kind of cryogenic storage container.'

'What is in it?'

'Can anyone read Jai?'

'A little…this word says….egg…'

'You don't think?'

'I do. That word there is the Jai word for human.'

'Good God.'

'Is it possible?'

'Why would they label this otherwise? They have human prisoners…'

'Not here on Ceres.'

'Well, somewhere.'

Rao picked up his receiver and called Thapa, 'This is Rao.'

'Yes, sir.'

'Get that area secured and don't touch anything. I will send someone down there to take charge of that…lab.'

'Yes, sir.'

'Beam me back photographs of those things.'

'Yes, Captain,' said Thapa. 'They are human, sir. Or, human bodies with Jai heads. Holy…'

'I know.'

'They…'

'Keep looking through the station.'

'Affirmative.'

Rao signed off and stood. 'Lt. Commander Mukherjee, you have the bridge.'

'Sir.'

Rao went down to Commander Patel's quarters but when he knocked on the bulkhead there was no answer. He called out to her but still no response. When he opened the door anyway, the room was empty. By not being in her quarters Patel was violating orders, but Rao was confused rather than angry.

He tried the officer's wardroom. Not finding Patel there, he picked up the phone.

'This is Captain Rao. Commander Patel to the officer's wardroom.'

Still nothing.

The receiver buzzed. 'Captain.'

It was Mukherjee, 'Uh, Captain, please come to the bridge. We have found Commander Patel.'

Mukherjee had sent the latest images from the Gurkhas to Rao's flat-screen.

'What is this?' Rao asked.

The flat-screen showed a charred human body, one of the Gurkhas identified her by her body armor.

'That is Commander Patel, sir.'

'What?'

'It looks like she snuck aboard the Gurkha shuttle. She was killed early on.'

'I don't understand.'

'She was pretty upset, when you relieved her, Commodore. I suppose this was redemption.'

Rao flopped down in the captain's chair. He shook his head. 'By getting herself killed in a fire fight?'

Mukherjee shrugged. 'I do not understand either, Captain. She was an intense woman, and she took after Admiral Ganesan.'

'She is dead now also.'

Rao sat dejectedly in his chair. 'Start making preparations to pick up the Gurkhas.'

'Yes, Captain.'

'We shall destroy the Ceres base and get out of here. We don't have the firepower to withstand an attack from that Pole Ship.'

Rao scrolled through the lab photographs of human fetuses with Jai heads. 'Just…'

'Horrifying?'

'To say the least.'

Rao looked at the photographs again. 'Why?'

'Why, what, sir?'

'Why create these genetic horrors when a new pole ship arrived from home?'

Rao shook his head.

'What do we do now, sir? What do we do?'

Connecticut

Cosgrove always hated hospitals. For a while, Cosgrove had tried to stay away, partly because he didn't want to bring germs home to the new baby, and partly because he suspected he might one day check in for the same reason. Melody was making him go though.

Gingerly he walked into Rodden's hospital room.

There he was, lying elevated on a bed, asleep.

Like Cosgrove, Rodden had been an active, vigorous, robust man. The cancer was eating away at him. He was emaciated, his complexion very pale, face gaunt and skin almost hanging off his cheeks. Rodden had no hair, revealing a red scar going across his head; a shrapnel wound suffered earlier in the war.

Cosgrove cleared his throat. Rodden snapped awake. Instantly he fixated on Cosgrove, his eyes narrowed. They were hateful.

'I thought we agreed we'd never visit each other like this.'

'I didn't really want to.'

'Who put you up to it?'

'Melody.'

'C'mon, man,' Rodden said, for a moment slipping into the lingo of his youth. 'She can't suck it that good.'

Cosgrove laughed. 'Well, it's right that I came, isn't it?'

'You wanted to see me like this?'

'No,' Cosgrove said. 'But suddenly I'm glad I'm here.'

'Alright, come on and sit.'

Cosgrove took a seat next to his friend's bed.

'But let's get one thing straight.'

'Ok.'

'This is it. You ain't coming here every day to watch while I waste away as the goddamn fucking nurses, none of whom are cute, by the way, change my colostomy bag. I am not putting on a happy-cancer-patient-face. Not even for you.'

'Deal.'

They shook on it. Rodden's grip was clammy, but still firm.

'They say how long?'

'You are a macabre bastard, aren't you?'

'Big events happening. I bet no one told you.'

'No one bothered, no.'

Rodden shook his head. He had maintained his swinging bachelor status throughout. Now there was no one to visit him. Cosgrove found one more reason to give thanks for Melody's little 'accident'.

'Well?' Rodden insisted.

'Sorry...the Indian Navy really slammed the Jai.'

'Well, that's descriptive.'

'They took Ceres alright and sent a recon mission out to Jupiter.'

'Jupiter, crap,' Rodden managed.

'They slagged Europa and Gannymede before finding the other Jai Pole Ship.'

'It's already here? Holy shit.'

'Yeah...'

'What about Mars?'

'Still fighting.'

'You're not telling me something.'

'Afraid it's a major fuck up at this point.'

'Ugh...'

'Sorry I...what's that smell? ...Oh!' realized the new father who knew all too well what human shit smelled like.

'That's it,' said Rodden. 'Get out! Get out! Nurse!' Rodden furiously pressed the nurse's call button. Cosgrove excused himself while the nurse changed his friend. When the nurse was finished he walked back in and sat down.

'You're back.'

'Yes, thank you.'

'I want you to leave.'

For the first time Cosgrove saw the sadness in his friend's eyes. 'Ok, I'm leaving.' He stood up and extended his hand. 'Good bye, Tony.'

'Good bye Peter.'

Cosgrove leaned forward. 'I want you to know something.'

Rodden coughed. 'Ok.'

'Melody and me, we named our baby boy Anthony Rodden Cosgrove.'

With his free hand, Cosgrove cupped the back of his friend's head and kissed his forehead. 'Good bye, friend.'

Cosgrove walked out and hoped he had gotten far enough down the corridor so Rodden couldn't hear his sobs.

Made in the USA
Lexington, KY
13 August 2016